Belize
Navidad

KAREN HULENE BARTELL

𝓟
Pen-L Publishing
Fayetteville, AR
Pen-L.com

To my traveling companion through life, Peter Bartell.
To the sweet beach dog that befriended me on Ambergris Caye.

Prologue

Carole Kennedy craned her neck to see out the commuter plane's cockpit window, marveling at the cerulean and indigo waters below. Their gradient blues indicated their depths like an immense mood ring. The warm, shallow waters nearest the shore shimmered a pale aquamarine in the sunlight. As the depths increased, the temperatures decreased, and the hues intensified, becoming azure, then sapphire, until at the reef, where the waters dropped off two hundred feet, the colors deepened into a cool, cobalt blue. Vibrant with life, these tropical waters captivated her. Their capricious whitecaps seemed to wave at her, inviting her to join their warm freedom and escape from the icicle constructs of her Manhattan public relations world.

But she had a deadline and, with a sigh, she returned to the rewrites on her laptop. The only way she could talk her managing editor into giving her Thanksgiving week off was to telecommute. No matter that her entire future hinged on these few days. The deadline was this afternoon, and her editor was adamant. Finish the rewrites by COB today or cancel the flight to Belize. Working for Campbell and Glenrock, New York's most prestigious PR firm, presented its own challenges. Editing forty pages on a laptop with a failing battery while experiencing air turbulence on the plane was only one of them.

Seated in the narrow copilot seat, Carole caught a reflection of herself in the window. Her mouth was set in a determined moue, her lips curling at the corners like a cat's. Her heart-shaped face with its pointed chin and intelligent, green eyes fringed with long, dark lashes gave her face an arresting appeal. Shaking her dark mane to brush a stray hair from her face, she focused on her notebook's screen.

The ad copy was for a new client. If she could edit it by the end of the day, she had a chance of nailing the account. It could mean a promotion. Pre-Christmas was the busiest season, the worst time to take off. She resented being out of the office, missing any opportunities that might present themselves.

Still, the thought of seeing Nick McKuen brought a lilting smile to her lips. She pressed her knees together, an involuntary reflex to the butterflies she felt in the pit of her stomach, the longing for him a tangible ache. It had been three lonely months since he had visited her in Manhattan.

Closing her eyes, she visualized the last time she had seen him. Particularly poignant, it was the night Nick had returned to Belize. They both had known it could be their last time together. They had agreed that their relationship could not drift aimlessly as it had for the past two years. They would either marry or break up, and they would give themselves three months to decide.

It had been twilight, the last rays of sunlight filtering through the wooden shutters of her East Side, brownstone walkup. She could see his haunting eyes, as cerulean blue as the sea, staring intently at her from his angular, deeply-tanned face. His long, sun-streaked, blond hair tickled her cheek as he bent to kiss her goodbye. She tucked an errant strand behind his ear while he kissed the hollow of her neck. Harbored by the velvet warmth of his lips, she felt anchored, moored for a timeless moment in his arms.

After he left for the airport, she felt adrift, flotsam on the sea of life. It was this connection that had compelled her to meet Nick in Belize. Even if it were the last time, she had to see him once more.

Responding to a deeper urgency, she had come to force the issue—either marry or break up, so she could get on with her life.

Carol returned to her computer with resolve. The sooner she finished the editing, the sooner she could turn her attention to Nick, but the blue beauty of the sea below distracted her. It waved its independence like a vast blue flag, tantalizing and taunting her in a love/hate relationship. It was impossible to view its grandeur without thinking of Nick. The two merged as indivisibly as the blue hues. The sea was his office. It was his mistress, her competition. Nick was a dive master with a start-up dive shop. Insisting that his burgeoning business in Belize needed his constant supervision for at least the next two years, he was adamant. He couldn't leave.

The problem was, she couldn't leave New York, either. There *was* nowhere else for a struggling PR rep. To leave in a year or two might be a different story. Perhaps by then she could start her own firm elsewhere after having put in her time in a large corporation, paid her dues, made her contacts. Or maybe she could finally write that novel she had been secretly plotting, but for now those ideas were out of the question.

To leave New York at this point in her career would be to give up any hope of success in her chosen field. He wanted his right to pursue his business. She wanted her right to pursue her craft. *I love Belize, the sea. I love him. But I have just as much right to succeed as he does.*

Why didn't he come to New York for a year, and then they could return to Belize and his business? That was her reason for making the trip, to deliver an ultimatum: choose between his business and her. She mentally rehearsed her speech for the ninetieth time—

For two years, we've been trekking between New York and Belize, taking turns with the airfare and the long-distance phone bills, re-affirming our love every three months, and then refusing to move to the other's environment. It's a few weeks before Christmas, and I want to settle this issue before New Year's. Let's either marry, with one of us moving to the other's territory, or call off this long-distance relationship. I have to get on with my life.

Chapter One

Once Carole saw the white sand beaches and palm-tree lined airport as the plane touched down in San Pedro, her resolve faltered. The island's breezy openness contrasted sharply with her confining office cubicle and cramped apartment in New York. She breathed in the fragrance of the frangipani and the brisk ocean air as she kissed Nick. In his arms, she realized life without him would be unimaginable. Their lives were inextricably intertwined.

"I've missed you," he said, holding her tightly between kisses, not letting go for a moment. Still clasping her hand, he picked up her suitcase with his free hand. Her laptop case slung across her shoulder, she picked up her carry-on, and they walked to his converted golf cart—San Pedro's main form of transportation.

As Nick drove her to his oceanfront condo, she noticed the new construction along the town's main roads. It was obvious that the sleepy fishing community was fast becoming a tourist mecca.

"It's a boomtown," she said, surprised at the rapid growth in the six months since she had last visited.

He smiled a boyish, dimpled grin. "Ambergris Caye is becoming the next Cancun. It's got the best reef outside of Australia's Barrier Reef, and it's only a couple hours from Houston." His expression took on a sly nuance. "You can see why I want to capitalize on it. A year from now may be too late."

Her joy dimmed as she recognized that his response was actually the opening remark in their ongoing debate. In answer, Carole reminded him of her own responsibilities. "Don't let me forget to email my edits back to the office. The deadline is four o'clock Belizean time."

He frowned but did not counter her rebuttal as they stepped onto his condo's veranda. The coral and crimson bougainvillea veiled the second-story balcony from the beach, isolating them. As the palm trees whispered their welcome in the gentle November breeze, Carole and Nick lost themselves in each other, oblivious of time or space.

"I've missed you," he murmured between kisses, but words were unnecessary. That he had missed her was evident, and Carole's misgivings dissolved in the genuine warmth of his love.

He led her to an umbrellaed garden table with a bottle of wine and a bowl of fruit, hidden from view by palm fronds and clouds of ruby bougainvillea, white frangipani, and blue-green sea grapes. Dappled with sunlight and shade, they toasted each other in the play of light. The heat from the November sun warmed the overhanging frangipani blossoms, and the tight white blooms unfurled, releasing their scent, adding another level of enjoyment, and heightening the pleasure of the moment. Being with Nick again, reconnecting, Carole relaxed, feeling the tension wash away like waves washing away footprints in the sand.

Then the jarring, incessant trill of his cell phone interrupted their conversation. Carole murmured, "Let it ring."

Nick agreed, but his body tensed, and he became distracted, his focus obviously elsewhere. When the phone rang again a moment later, she did not try to dissuade him from answering it. Instead, she sat back in the cushioned seat, listening to the business tones of his deep voice.

Covering the mouthpiece, Nick whispered, "It's Miguel, my assistant. Several clients flew in from Houston unexpectedly, and suddenly we're swamped with business. They want to go to Shark Ray Alley. Developers and legal eagles want to test their machismo by diving with nurse sharks and sting rays."

"Can't Miguel handle it?"

He shook his head. "There's a second group—with my *best* client—insisting we move up tomorrow's scheduled dive to this afternoon." He planted a quick kiss on her forehead. "Sorry, love. I didn't anticipate this, but I can't say no to these groups."

The old grudge resurfaced. *Nothing's changed.* She kept silent so she wouldn't say too much. Despite her attempt at self-control, her tight, white lips and narrowed eyes gave her away.

Nick saw the storm clouds gathering and tried to placate her. "Look, this will only take a few hours. We'll have all evening, and we'll have all day tomorrow, maybe take in a tour of Altun Ha." Hand poised over the mouthpiece, he smiled winningly, waiting for her approval.

Despite the initial disappointment, Carole returned a grin. Nick knew the workings of her mind only too well. The Preclassic Mayan ruins at Altun Ha were something she had wanted to see for years. In fact, she had an idea for a novel set in the ancient ruins.

Relenting, she drew in a long breath. "All right, but I'm counting on spending *a lot* of time with you this evening."

He smiled at her as he ended the phone conversation. "Give me a minute to change, and I'll drop you off at the hotel on my way to the dock."

Five minutes later, Nick reappeared on the veranda in a pair of shorts and sandals. Carole compared his wardrobe to her own. Wearing a business suit, stockings, and heels, she was dressed for New York's cool weather and cold business climate. *Got to admit, the island's informality appeals to me.*

That evening, she and Nick walked hand-in-hand to the end of the pier. The first rays of moonlight illuminated their path, while the blinking, twinkling stars shone overhead. Nick explained that a water taxi would pick them up and deliver them to the restaurant at the far southern end of the island.

"Why don't we take your golf cart?" she asked, barely suppressing the grin.

His smile surfaced in his voice as he leaned against a bulkhead. "Why do you have that silly smirk on your face every time you talk about my golf cart?"

"I never knew anyone whose only vehicle was a golf cart." Her raw-silk dress billowed in the balmy breeze, and her dark hair blew gently about her shoulders.

Nick put his arms around her slim waist, playfully pulling her to him. "Until a few years ago, carts were the only motorized transportation on the island, although now there are a few cars and pickups."

"And boats—which reminds me. How did your dive go today?"

Warming to his element, Nick enthusiastically plunged into a description. "We went to the Blue Hole. Diving conditions were perfect. Visibility was two hundred feet after we broke through the thermocline."

"The thermo-what?" she asked, leaning into him as she fell under his spell.

"The thermocline is a layer of water that separates areas of different temperatures. Because of the depth, the temperature gradient is abrupt. Once you dip below it, the cold water increases visibility substantially." His blue eyes grew wider as he related the experience. "It was unbelievable! The divers were experienced, so we went deep."

"How deep?" Carole turned her attention to his story.

"About a hundred and fifty feet straight down sheer limestone cliffs. You should learn to dive, Carole. Get certified. It's another world down there— serene, blue, beautiful. It'd open up new vistas for you!"

She shrugged. "I've seen the Blue Hole."

"When?"

"This morning, from the plane. We flew right over it. With the reef surrounding it, it looked like a gigantic eye in the Caribbean—a cobalt-blue pupil in a turquoise iris."

His lip lifted in a sour smile. "Your perspective is off. Viewing it from two hundred feet above in a fly-by isn't experiencing it from the inside out."

"It's a giant sinkhole, isn't it?" she asked, trying to engage him in another line of conversation. "If most of the sea life occurs in the shallow waters around its rim, I could experience that by snorkeling."

"Yes," he agreed. "You'd see coral heads and purple seafans, but you wouldn't see the stalactite formations. They don't start until a hundred and ten feet down."

"I've seen stalactites before." She jerked her chin. "I've been in caves."

"You've seen them, but you haven't experienced them. You haven't swum beneath their monstrous formations. You haven't seen the surface's eerie blue light above them and marveled that these stalactites were once on dry land. You haven't played hide-and-seek with hammerhead sharks among their limestone columns."

"I'm perfectly happy snorkeling, seeing the colorful schools of fish near the surface. You even said yourself that's where most life exists, in the shallow waters."

His eyes locked with hers. "Don't you see? You're just skimming the proverbial surface. You have to dive deeper to fully appreciate it." His tone became serious. "That can be said about life, too."

"I don't need to scuba dive to enjoy life." She purposely sidestepped his analogy.

"If you'd ever stay longer than a few days, I'd teach you how to dive. It might change your perspective about life, about Belize, even about us. Why don't you stay another week?"

This time, the sound of the water taxi's motor came to her rescue. "Is that our ride?" she asked, relieved to avoid his question.

The stars shone overhead like twinkling white lights on a Christmas tree. From the deck, it seemed as if Nick and she were alone at sea, enjoying the night in total privacy. The boat's captain was silent, either lost in his own thoughts or discreet. Except for the muffled sound of the engine and the water lapping against the ship's hull, all was quiet. Carole sighed, at peace for the first time since she had arrived.

As they approached the southern tip of the island, she caught her breath. "Nick, look at the palm trees!" The trunks of gracefully arching palm trees were wrapped with thousands upon thousands of miniature white lights. The entire shoreline of the restaurant was lit up with an elegant grandeur that enhanced the setting's natural beauty. Because the trees grew along the bay's edge, the water doubled the effect of the lights, mirroring their wavy reflection.

"Do you like it?" Nick's eyes danced as the tiny lights' reflection played over them. "I thought you'd enjoy the restaurant's subtropical ambiance."

"I love it!"

Strains of a mariachi band wafted across the water. As they approached, they could see couples dining at small tables beneath the palm trees. Candles in hurricane lamps flickered from each tabletop. An infectious peal of laughter crossed the water, and in response, they shared a grin.

The water taxi pulled alongside the t-shaped pier. Nick climbed out and then held out his hand to steady Carole's high step up to the quay. His grip was warm and reassuring. In the twilight of the velvety dark night and the twinkling lights, she felt the underlying strength of his grasp. For the second time that night, she felt secure.

A waiter met them at the end of the pier and escorted them to a table beneath the stars. Two impressive palms listed overhead, their trunks wound round and round with strings of tiny lights. The tiny table boasted fresh linen and a candle that glimmered flirtatiously in its hurricane glass.

"Try the pina coladas," Nick said. "They make them with fresh coconut cream." Nick also ordered conch ceviche.

"Isn't ceviche made from raw fish?" she asked, turning up her nose. "And do you mean conch, as in the conch seashell?"

He laughed, correcting her pronunciation. "You sound like a tourist. It's not pronounced conch with a *ch* sound. The locals pronounce it *conk*, with a *k* sound—to rhyme with *honk*. But to answer your questions—yes, the ceviche is 'cooked' in limejuice, and you're right, it's made from the meat of the familiar conch shell. It's delicious! Try it."

The waiter quickly returned with two pina coladas, ceviche appetizers, tiny seafood forks, and crackers. Carole nibbled the skewered fresh pineapple garnish from the tall glass and lifted the drink in a toast.

"To a great evening," she whispered over the sound of water lapping at the shore.

"To us," he said, lightly clinking his glass against hers. Then he heaped a fork full of the ceviche on a cracker and offered it to her. "Try it."

She checked its contents skeptically in the candlelight—finely chopped red chili peppers, onion, cucumber, and white bits of conch with tiny green leaves. She breathed in its aroma, smiling in recognition—cilantro. She bit into the morsel daintily, wanting only to sample its taste. Then her face lit up with delight.

"Nick, this is delicious!"

"You have to try things before you decide whether or not you like them. Don't pre-judge."

She grimaced at his rebuke and popped the rest of the cracker into her mouth, chewing with her eyes closed, relishing its zesty taste.

"Enjoy it while you can," he warned. "Conch season is ending."

"What's in season?"

"Lobster."

"Then let's order lobster. 'Tis the season, ho-ho-ho." She gave a poor imitation of Santa before breaking into a giggle and motioning to the waiter.

Sporting a smile as white as their starched tablecloth, the waiter recommended a whole lobster. "Butterflied, flame-broiled to perfection, and served with a garlic-basil sauce. But the only way to really enjoy it is with Belize's own Beliken beer."

They laughed and finished their pina coladas just as their waiter reappeared with a frosty mug of microbrewed beer.

After the waiter set the mug in front of Carole, she asked, "Where's his?"

"I thought the gentleman didn't want any."

Nick declined with a wave to the waiter. "None for me, thanks." Then he turned to Carole. "One's my limit before a dive. I shouldn't have had that, but tonight's a special night." He flashed Carole a warm but tentative smile.

"What do you mean, 'before a dive'?" She waited, consciously controlling her jaw from clenching. Suspicious, but refusing to jump to conclusions.

His eyes shifted, but finally met hers. "I wasn't going to tell you this until after dinner. I didn't want to ruin the eve—"

"Tell me what?" she interrupted, poised for the inevitable.

He sighed. "An important night-diving gig came up."

She rolled her eyes, knowing what was next. "So let me guess—we have to cut the evening short, so you can accommodate one more client . . . tonight . . . our first night together, right?"

"Carole, it came up unexpectedly. My best customer is paying very handsomely for a private dive." His eyes crinkled at the corners, pleading with hers.

She looked past him, refusing to meet his eyes, focusing instead on the starry skies. "When you walked out this afternoon, you promised we'd have all evening."

"I couldn't refuse. This client comes into town once, sometimes twice, a month. I can't say *no* to him."

"But you can to me?"

When her eyes met his, he looked away. Gone was the softness of her lips. Her jaw was angular and stiff, her lips white and tight.

"I feel cheated. I've been waiting to see you for three, long, *lonely* months."

Gesturing with his hands, he tried to explain. "Words are inadequate." Sighing, he tried again. "Carole, I want to be with you, but starting out in a business is so risky. I can't afford to offend any customers."

"Yet you'll risk our relationship for a buck, is that it? Let's see if I have this right. It's all right to ignore me *twice* on our first day together in three months, but you're concerned that you *might* offend a customer." When he couldn't answer, she stared hard at him, her eyes piercing his. "Is this how you feel?"

Eyes still averted, he mumbled, "I'm really sorry." Then he raised his head, his eyes searching hers. "But that's the way this business is. Dive shops come and go in a season. If I can build up a solid clientele over the next year," he raised his eyebrows, calculating the time more realistically, "a year *and a half,* the business will take care of itself. Trust me. This is just temporary, just until the dive shop gets on its feet."

"Excuse me," said the waiter, interrupting their conversation. He began clearing the glasses and silverware, making room for the dishes. "Your lobster," he said, ceremoniously removing the cover from the sizzling shellfish.

The aroma would have stopped conversation even without the waiter's flourish. The fragrances of cilantro, basil, lime, butter, garlic, and serrano peppers filled the air. Suddenly, Carole realized she had not eaten all day. She was famished.

They called a tacit truce and dug into their meal with relish, the seafood helping to restore Carole's good spirits. They ate in silence, welcoming the strains of the mariachi band as it wandered from table to table.

When the band approached their table, it began playing *Feliz Navidad.* After tipping them, Nick attempted a light touch, singing *'Belize' Navidad.* Instead of cheering her, it depressed her. Even in the moonlight, Nick could see the grim set of her mouth.

When the band moved to the next table, she sat upright, her spine her only support as she struggled with her emotions. Suddenly it became clear, and she decided to voice her ultimatum. "Nick, although I'd meant to work up to this and not spring it on you our first night together . . . ."

"Here it comes," he muttered. He touched his napkin to his lips, folded it, and set it on the empty platter, a sign that dinner and the truce were over.

"I can't spend a year or two twiddling my toes on a beach, waiting for you. I have to get on with my life. You're going to have to choose between your business and me." Nick paled, stunned, despite knowing the inevitable moment would arrive.

He made his case again. "In eighteen months . . . two years tops . . . the business will be able to maintain itself without my constant supervision, but, in the meantime, I have to be there day and night. I don't have a choice in the matter."

"Oh, yes, you do." She felt almost as if she were dealing with a PR client. This was a negotiation, and she was all business. "I'm giving you that choice right now."

He swallowed hard, moistening his dry lips before starting. "Look, why don't you move to Belize for that year or two, and then, after that, I promise we can move anywhere you choose—even Manhattan."

She knew how New York was anathema to his love of the sea and island life, and she softened. Leaning across the table, she reached for his hand and reminded him why that was impossible for the fortieth, fiftieth time in their relationship.

"Nick, there *is* nowhere else for a struggling PR rep. New York is the only place."

"So we can go back, together, *after* I make of go of the dive shop."
"We've been over this before. This next year or two are critical for my career, too. If we went back now, stayed until I put in my time with a large corporation, paid my dues, and made my contacts, it would be a different story. We could return to Belize, and you could start your business then. Maybe I could start my own firm here. With Internet access, I could have my own web site. Or maybe I could finally write that novel I've been noting in my journal. But for now those ideas are out of the question."

"You've mentioned the web. You can be connected to New York instantaneously," he offered.

"It isn't the same thing as being on Madison Avenue, getting established. For me to leave New York at this point in my career would be to give up any hope of success."

He took a different tact. "Who says you have to work? I can take care of us on my income."

Carole snickered. Then she gave him an alternate choice. "What do you want? An individual with a career, a soul, a creative life of her own? Or do you want a camp follower, an apron-clad 'little woman' venting her frustrated creativity in the kitchen?"

"I'm not trying to limit you, Carole. I only want us to be together."

She saw he was sincere, but only partly honest. "*And* you want the green light to pursue your business, right?"

"And pursue my business." He nodded his agreement.

"Well, I want the right to pursue my business, too. I love Belize. I love *you*, but I have a duty to myself to be the best I can be at what I do." She felt like shaking him. "Nick, don't you get it? I have as much right to success as you. Why don't you come to New York for a year, and then we can return to Belize and your business?"

Carole saw the set of his mouth, listened without hearing to his repetitious reasons why he couldn't leave Belize, and was crestfallen. She had looked forward to this trip for three months, doing without small pleasures to afford it, turning down dates with attractive men. She had spent too many lonely Saturday nights. All to be with the man she loved.

This time would be different, she had told herself. *This* time they would settle their lifestyle differences once and for all. She had forced the issue, knowing the risk, and she had lost.

"What a lousy start to the Christmas season," she muttered. As the mariachi band began playing *Feliz Navidad* softly in the background, she added sarcastically, "Belize *Navidad*."

"Let's—" Nick stopped mid-sentence as three men approached.

"Nick, what an unexpected surprise," said the man leading the trio. Then he noticed Carole. "I see you have company. Sorry, don't want to impose."

Masking her disappointment, Carole smiled politely at the new arrivals. She noticed a certain air of authority about the tall man in front. Wearing khaki pants and a navy jacket, he personified island success.

"Carole Kennedy, I'd like you to meet Damon Eastwood."

"A pleasure," said Damon, extending his right hand.

"How do you do," Carole murmured, annoyed at the interruption. As she shook hands, she noticed a gold Rolex peeking from his jacket's sleeve. When she tried to break loose, Damon hung on, smiling at her, watching her.

"What brings you to Belize, Ms. Kennedy?"

Trying to extricate her hand, she said grimly, "Pleasure."

"Taking a break from business, then," he said, still holding onto her. "What is your business?"

None of yours. The nerve of this guy. With a tug, she broke loose from his grip. "Public relations."

"Really? Do you have an office here? A branch?"

"I'm not here on business," she reminded him. *Isn't anyone listening to me? Not here on business, not here on pleasure. What am I doing here?* Frustration mounting, she took a deep breath.

"This is fortunate," he said, pulling up a chair, uninvited. "Nick, you don't mind, do you?" He glanced at Nick, not expecting an answer, and then addressed the other men. "Marty, Joe, would you mind grabbing us a table? I'll be along in five minutes."

Carole was used to working with assertive clients, but this wasn't a business meeting. The evening had been a fiasco. The visit was a disaster. Her relationship with Nick was ending, and she wanted nothing except to get back to her room and lick her wounds.

Jaw set, lips pressed firmly together, Carole said pointedly, "We were just leaving."

"Then I'll make it fast—four minutes." A smile played at Damon's lips. "I can see you're a woman who speaks her mind."

With a strained smile, she muffled an exasperated sigh.

"I need a documentary video to show prospective investors how Eastwood Enterprises is helping the ecology as well as the economy of Belize. Interested?"

"As I mentioned—"

"A week's work for five K."

She lifted her left eyebrow, intrigued by his generous offer.

"I'm desperate," he said. "The videographer's schedule moved up, and I need a copywriter—starting yesterday. You'd be doing me a service if you could write the preliminary copy."

Jaw slack, she took a deep breath. "I'd have to—"

"You'd have to think it over, of course." He took a business card from his wallet and scribbled on it. "This is my cell." Standing up, he handed her his card. "Sleep on it. If you're interested, call me in the morning. We can discuss it over breakfast." Then he turned to Nick. "We should be back from the dive by eight, shouldn't we?"

Lifting her eyebrows in surprise, Carole silently questioned Nick.

He nodded. "Damon's the client I told you about."

The water taxi met them at the end of the pier. Though the night was still starry and clear, Carole focused inwardly, ignoring the sky's grandeur. Despite the balmy temperature, she wrapped her light shawl around her shoulders, creating yet another barrier, ever so subtle, between Nick and herself. Apparently, even the captain sensed the chilled relationship, and he started up an animated conversation with Nick. Absorbed in her thoughts, she welcomed the solitude.

Though she wanted to discuss Damon's business offer, she didn't feel like sharing anything with Nick—neither her thoughts nor her life. Marriage seemed more distant than the three thousand miles to Manhattan. They spoke in polite monosyllables during the short walk to her hotel. Their shoulders brushed against each other, but neither tried to hold the other's hand.

"Better make it an early night," he said. "Have to get the diving gear set up for the trip." Taking his cell phone from his belt, he handed it to her. "Your cell won't work in Belize. Use this while you're here."

She opened her mouth to tell him how disappointed she was about the evening, how saddened she was about this turn of events, but all that came out was, "Thanks."

"Looks like we'll have to postpone our tour to Altun Ha for another day, but we'll do something tomorrow. I'll call you in the morning."

Silent, she nodded. At the door, he bent his head to kiss her, but she offered only her cheek and a frosty half-smile.

"Night," she said, splaying her fingers in a wave. She needed to be alone.

She found a book online about ancient Mayan civilizations and read herself to sleep, the light still on when she woke the next morning.

Chapter Two

When she opened her eyes, it took a moment to remember where she was. Then she recalled their argument, and disappointment grabbed her like a rip tide. The angst in the pit of her stomach felt like swallowed seawater.

How could I come all this way just to argue with him?

She hated the thought of breaking up with Nick, yet he infuriated her. Why was he so intractable? Then her inner ear heard a question. *Why are you so stubborn?* She chuckled to herself.

We're two of a kind. Who said opposites attract? We're exactly alike except that he likes the sea, and I like the city.

So now what? Since we can't agree on where to live, do we break up and move on? A fish and a bird can fall in love, but where will they build their nest?

She tried to still her thoughts long enough for an answer. *Do I have to pursue my career in New York? Or is this just a case of neither of us wanting to give in?*

She sighed. It's too early to think. Then her eyes fell on Damon's business card. Eastwood Enterprises, Ltd., Houston, Texas.

She debated calling the cell number listed. *I'm on vacation, and it's the Thanksgiving season. I want to spend this time with Nick. That is, when he's not off diving.*

Then she remembered the five-thousand-dollar fee. *It would more than pay for this trip. Plus, it would keep my mind busy while Nick's working.*

Nothing ventured, nothing gained. Card in hand, Carole dialed the number. On the third ring, a man's voice answered.

"Mr. Eastwood? This is Carole Kennedy."

"Glad to hear from you, Carole, and please call me Damon." The smile came through his voice.

"I'd like to hear more about your project."

"Excellent—let's meet for breakfast at the Azure Grill, not far from where Nick tells me you're staying. It's right on the beach. Say at nine o'clock?"

What do I wear to a business meeting on the beach? It disturbed her that Nick had not called, but she had little time to worry between showering, dressing, and locating the grill, all within twenty minutes.

The moment she walked onto the beach, the sea breeze gently tousled her shoulder-length, chestnut-brown hair. She held out her arms to better feel the wind billow her sundress. She looked up at the perfect blue sky and breathed in the fresh sea air. *Heaven.*

Peeking from behind a palm tree, a native girl smiled and gave Carole a shy wave. She waved back, chuckling to herself when the girl's shy smile turned into a wide grin. Nearby, a young dog seemed to be watching her, its head cocked to the side. It looked friendly, and Carole was tempted to stop to pet it, but she was in a hurry to get to the meeting. A brisk, five-minute walk on the sand brought her to Damon's table.

"Good morning," he said, his eyes running the length of her body, taking in her slim silhouette as the breeze pressed her dress against her legs. "You look positively radiant in the morning light." He stood up, and pulled out her chair. "Belize agrees with you."

"It's gorgeous here. I can see why so many businesses establish themselves on Ambergris Caye."

"You get right to the point, don't you?" he observed. "I like that."

"Coffee?" asked the waiter, overturning her cup and pouring before she answered.

"Sure." She exchanged a smile with Damon, noting his graying blond hair, figuring him to be in his early forties.

"Do you like *huevos rancheros?* They have the best on the Caye." At her nod, Damon turned to the waiter. "Make that two."

"So please tell me more about your venture," she said.

"I'm developing two properties into spa resorts—a cove here and a small island just off Tulum. Are you familiar with that site?"

"Ironically, I was just reading about it last night. It's a pre-Columbian Mayan city on the Mexican Riviera, isn't it?"

He nodded approvingly, his lips pursed. "And you were on the mark when you referred to these properties as being on the Mexican Riviera. It's a hotspot of tourist activity."

"How would I fit into your plans?" she asked.

"Always direct." He chuckled. "I need a person with copywriting skills to put together a script for the video Mario's filming today." His eyes bore into hers. "Are you game?"

She tilted her head and smiled. "Possibly. What's the deadline?"

"Yesterday," he deadpanned. "Seriously, the sooner you can script it, the sooner we can get it to market. As I mentioned, a week's work for five grand, but . . . ." His eyes appraised her. "If you can finish this by Tuesday evening, I'll sweeten it with another grand."

"Tuesday evening," she repeated, her eyes widening. He nodded. "Why the rush?"

"The sooner to market, the sooner the return, and Wednesday morning is a stockholders meeting in Houston."

"Tuesday . . . that's a tall order." She took a deep breath, weighing the time/work ratio. "How long is the video?"

"It hasn't been shot yet, but I'm figuring fifteen to twenty minutes." When she didn't respond, he added, "That's six thousand bucks for a few days' work . . . . Are you in?"

She thought of Nick. The whole purpose of her trip had been to spend time with him. *Okay, to convince him to come back to Manhattan with her. But he's been busy since I got here.* She looked at Damon, doing her best not to scowl. *And he's the reason.*

"Incidentally," Damon continued, "if this goes well and you have any plans to stay on in Belize, Eastman Enterprises could keep you busy indefinitely with PR collateral and copy."

Grinning, she held up her hand, waving off the idea. "No, I'm here on a . . . " she hesitated momentarily, catching herself before she said mission. ". . . vacation," she finished, adding, "I'm ready to turn in my briefcase for my bikini."

Raising his eyebrow, he grinned crookedly. "Who said you can't mix business with pleasure?"

She assessed him. *Was that a double entendre or simply an observation?*

As if in answer, he said, "Belize has a jumping economy. Hop on early and get your share."

He makes sense. "All right," she said with a nod. "I'm your 'gal Tuesday.'"

The waiter set down plates of steaming *huevos rancheros* and home-made corn tortillas.

"Perfect, I'll fly us to Tulum after breakfast." To her surprised look, he added, "Might as well get started while Mario's filming."

After breakfast, they stopped by her hotel for her laptop, and a cab took them to San Pedro's airport. A half hour later, they were in the air, flying low over the azure waters, atolls, and mangrove islets.

"This is your first time seeing Tulum?" he asked over the hum of the engines.

Seated next to Damon in the cockpit, she nodded.

"Look down there." He pointed to ruins atop a bluff overlooking the sea as he swooped down in a flyby.

Carole gasped when they lost altitude so quickly and didn't begin breathing until he leveled off. "Gorgeous." She managed a stiff smile as she said a silent prayer.

A Lincoln was waiting for them at the airport, complete with driver. A woman sat beside him in the passenger seat. Holding the door for Carole, Damon introduced them.

"Carole, this is Dante," he said, gesturing first to the driver and then to the passenger, "and this is Gabriela, our student intern." As the three exchanged greetings, Damon said, "Dante's your go-to man for whatever you need."

"Chief cook and bottle washer, at your service," he said with a comical flourish.

Carole sensed she'd made the right decision in taking this contract.

"Gabriela's a wizard at unearthing little-known facts and local lore. If she doesn't already know it, she can research any background material you need."

"Just sit me in front of the web, and I'll dig up whatever you want." Gabriela winked. "I'm an archaeology major." Her dark eyes crinkled in a smile, and Carole returned the smile, liking her immediately.

"Is Mario shooting footage yet?" asked Damon.

Dante nodded. "He started on the beach at dawn—before any tourists destroyed his long shots."

"Did it work?" asked Damon.

"Not a single footprint in the sand." Dante chuckled. "He's filming by the *Castillo* now."

Gabriela turned toward the back seat, facing Carole. "Are you familiar with Tulum's history?"

"Only vaguely."

"It was one of the last Mayan cities built between the thirteenth and fifteenth centuries," said the student. "Tulum was a walled city on three sides, with the Caribbean fronting it on the fourth. In fact, the word *tulum* means wall or fence."

"It was one the Mayans' best fortified sites," said Dante. "Their surrounding wall was sixteen feet high and twenty-six feet thick."

Carole gave a low whistle.

"Try scaling that if you were an invader," said Dante with a laugh.

"Why was it so heavily fortified?"

"It was an important port and trading hub, controlling both the sea and land routes." Gabriela pointed to the ruins on top of the bluff. "*El Castillo*, the castle, was one of three watchtowers, as well as a kind of lighthouse."

"Lighthouse," said Carole. "I didn't know the Mayans had them."

Gabriela nodded. "A barrier reef surrounds this site with only a narrow passage through it to the cove. Trading canoes could not see their way at night and would crash on the reef, so they built two windows high on the castle's wall facing the sea. After dark, they'd light fire pits inside the castle, and the windows' light would act as a beacon. When ancient mariners saw light coming through *both* windows, they knew to turn."

"And if they missed their turn?"

She grimaced. "Turning too soon if they saw only one light or turning too late after they had passed the brightest point of both lights would have meant wrecking on the coral."

"That was an incredible feat of engineering," said Carole. "I mean, to build the castle with openings placed exactly at those coordinates."

"Tell her about the descending god," said Damon, addressing Gabriela and then turning toward Carole. "Besides ecology, I'd like the video to reflect the area's mythology."

"In addition to being a valuable commercial center, Tulum was a pilgrimage destination," said Gabriela. "The diving or descending god was an important Mayan deity. You can still see its image in the Temple of the Frescoes' facade and its bas-relief figure in the Temple of the Diving God."

"Diving god," repeated Carole, imagining the marketing possibilities. "That might appeal to the sun worshippers."

Nodding, Damon raised his eyebrow. "That's a good angle."

"It's actually closer to sky-diving, like this." Gabriela demonstrated, as she bent her elbows and clasped her hands in front of her. "The image represents a winged god, its arms down and feet up as if descending from the sky."

"Descending god," mused Carole. "It almost has Christian overtones."

"Interesting that you mention it. Several groups, including the Mormons, believe that Christ visited Tulum."

"Really? Why?"

"Tulum's original Mayan name was *Zama*, which means City of Dawn. According to the translated record of the Mormon Prophet Joseph Smith, Christ visited the Americas after His resurrection, where Smith identified the ancient city of Zion as being called *Zara*, although local tour guides corrupt that to *Zama*."

"Possibly Smith had read of Tulum . . . . " Carole's words hung in the air as she tried to rationalize.

Gabriela shook her head. "Tulum wasn't discovered until seven years after Smith's translations. Incidentally, based on his records, some members of the Church of the Latter-day Saints believe Christ was born on April sixth."

"What's that date got to do with anything?" asked Carole.

"I'm glad you asked." Gabriela smiled mischievously. "The Temple of the Descending God was aligned with both Venus and the sun. Since the image faces west, the setting sun highlights it. On the winter solstice, light comes through a tiny east window, lighting the image just below its clasped hands. Also on that day, but at sunrise the morning light aligns with the cornerstone of the Palace. However, during the summer solstice, the morning light from it aligns with the House of Columns, more evidence of the Mayans' engineering abilities."

"But its connection with April sixth?" pressed Damon.

"Venus rises directly over the temple's door on April sixth. Its light streams through that opening on that day only, so it's known as the birthday of the descending god."

"Forget about December twenty-fifth," Dante joked. "Maybe we should wait 'til April sixth to celebrate Christmas."

"How interesting," said Carole, turning toward Damon. "The mystical aspect could be another marketing campaign to explore. Then facing Gabriela, she asked, "Is there any other evidence to support the idea that Christ visited Tulum?"

With a bell-like laugh, Gabriela said, "So you're a skeptic, but ready to cash in on others' beliefs."

"Cash in? Not exactly," said Carole, running her fingers through her thick hair, thinking it through. "But capitalize on? Absolutely."

"A woman after my own heart," said Damon, an admiring glint in his eyes. "It all boils down to business."

In a meeting of the minds, their eyes met, and they shared a conspiratorial smile.

"If you like commerce," said Gabriela with a lilting laugh, "you'll have to include the Mayan god *Ek Chuah.*"

"Why's that?" asked Carole.

"He's the god of commerce and warfare."

"What an intriguing combination," said Carole.

"And did I mention chocolate? He's the god of commerce, warfare, and chocolate."

Carole grinned. "Now that's definitely a god to include!"

"But you'd asked if there was other evidence that Christ walked here. Actually, there is," said Gabriela, "and not just in Tulum, but throughout the Yucatan. Time and again, the descending god is portrayed in ancient, Mayan stonework."

"Aren't stone carvings subjective?" asked Damon, clearly not impressed, his mouth twisting in a skeptical half-smile.

"It's true. The carvings are open to interpretation, but there's an interesting connection," said Gabriela. "According to the Bible, there were two disciples who were brothers, James and John. The Book of Mormon mentions two disciples—brothers—who accompanied Christ to Tulum. Some claim to have found evidence that these three visited not only

Tulum, but also the ancient Yucatan cities of Uxmal, Chichen Itza, Itzamal, and Dzibilchaltun."

"Anything else?"

"Besides the teachings of the LDS, there's another spiritual movement that's popularized the idea—New Age Mayanism." With a sigh, Gabriela rolled her eyes. "The 2012 Mayan Calendar craze was an extension of that."

"I take it, that's not one of your beliefs," said Carole, grinning.

"In my opinion, some people took it too far and made a cult of it, but, at its core, there are several parallels between New Age Mayanism and Christianity."

"Like what?" Carole asked.

"When we get to the *Castillo*, you'll see for yourself, but above the three windows are three niches. Two of them contain figurines, and the third is empty. The central niche contains the descending god, which some associate with Christ. According to some interpretations, the niche on the right contains Hunab Ku, which translates as 'only god.' Certain sects associate Hunab Ku with the Christian Heavenly Father, but few anthropologists accept that."

"Why is the third niche empty?" Carole asked.

"Good question. Some explain that as depicting the Holy Spirit, which is invisible, so no figurine."

"So according to that interpretation, the three niches would signify the Triune God." Carole nodded, letting the idea settle into her mind. "Again, weak links but possibly with enough substance to connect it to Christianity."

"As you mentioned, carvings are open to interpretation." Gabriela turned toward Damon and grinned. "The Mormons believe the three panels signify something similar to that analysis but discount any association of Hunab Ku with God the Father."

"Anything else?" asked Damon.

"I'll point them out on our tour of Tulum, but there are several other stone works that raise questions." Counting them off on her fingers, Gabriela said, "There's the figure of a woman kneeling before a god, holding what some interpret as an infant descending god. There's a fresco that others believe is the 'laying on of hands,' a baptismal cistern, a tomb shaped like a cross, and stone portrayals that others say represent scenes from the Garden of Eden."

"Doesn't sound as if there's any definitive evidence," said Carole, pressing her lips together, wondering how she could work that into her script.

"No, but Tulum's become a Mecca," said Gabriela. "Groups tour it every day looking for self-enlightenment, New Age spiritualism, LDS links, yoga retreats, or temazcal ceremonies."

"Yoga?" asked Carole, her eyes narrowing skeptically. "What does yoga have to do with Tulum?"

"The Mayan name for Quetzalcoatl, the feathered serpent, is Kukulcan," said Gabriela. "Kukulcan can also be translated as meaning the sacred coccyx serpent—*Ku* for sacred, *kul* for coccyx, and *can* for serpent. Yoga Upanishads describe Kundalini as a sleeping serpent waiting at the base of the spine to be awakened. Some claim Kukulcan and Kundalini are closely related."

"That's enough proof for me," said Damon. "Definitely include the otherworldly side in the video."

"There is a strong spiritual feeling about Tulum," said Gabriela, "whether or not there's proof of any Christian or chakra connections."

"See for yourself," said Dante, parking the car.

As she opened the door, Carole breathed in the sea-scented air. She stepped onto the brilliant, white sand, feeling its grit as her sandals sank into it. Gulls and pelicans flew overhead, calling to each other in a cloudless, blue sky, and in front of her loomed the majestic *Castillo* perched on a bluff overlooking the azure Caribbean Sea.

A sigh escaped. "I can see why people flock here." She breathed in deeply. "Tulum has a certain aura about it, as if it's steeped in ancient, sacred traditions."

"Exactly," said Gabriela. "You have to experience its mystique to understand it."

"And that's what I want your writing to bring out," said Damon. "Make prospective investors experience that sensation from the video. Let them *feel* your words, not hear them. Make your written depiction an invitation they can't ignore."

Carole breathed in deeply again—this time, not so much the intoxicating air as a silent prayer that she could deliver . . . and in less than a week. *It's a tall order.*

As if sensing her reservations, Damon added, "Originally, I'd wanted this to be a full-blown PR campaign, but, since you're here for such a short time, I suggest we start with a quick week's worth of video scripting." He paused, watching her closely. "Of course, if that goes well, and should you decide to prolong your visit, I can see that week turning into a full-time position, with either a salary or retainer."

Shaking her head, Carole opened her mouth to respond. "I—"

"Food for thought," he interrupted, wearing a beguiling grin. Then he peered down the path toward the *Castillo*. "Here comes Mario." As the man approached, Damon made the introductions. "Carole, meet Mario, our videographer. Mario, this is our new copy writer, Carole Kennedy."

"Nice to meet you," he said, switching his folded tripod to his left hand and extending his right. He sported an oversized backpack bulging at the seams with a telephoto lens peeking out of one of its compartments. "Let me know what you want in close-ups."

"Will do, but I'm just getting my bearings this morning." Carole turned to the intern with a smile. "So far, from what Gabriela's been telling me, we'll need both long shots and close-ups of the Temple of the Frescoes' facade and the bas-relief figure in the Temple of the Diving God to start with. Oh, and can you get a night shot of the Castillo's two windows from the sea." She turned to Damon. "Wouldn't a night sequence of approaching Tulum from the Caribbean and reenacting mariners having to rely on the light from the *Castillo's* two windows make a dramatic entrance scenario?"

Damon nodded thoughtfully. "Possibly."

"It might just set the tone for introducing the mystical side of Tulum."

Damon turned toward Gabriela. "Ready to start the walking tour?"

"Sure, let's begin at the Temple of the Frescoes," said Gabriela, leading them along a paved path beneath overhanging white frangipani and sea grapes.

Carole breathed in the frangipani fragrance. Then gently drawing a cluster of sea grapes toward her, she examined their fiery flowers. "So delicate, yet so vibrant." She made a mental note to use the flamboyant flowers in some of Mario's framing shots.

"Unfortunately, the Temple's roped off," said Gabriela, "so this is as close as we can get, but you can see the descending god's image in its façade."

"Look at that," said Carole, pointing. "You can still see the pigments from the paint."

"It was typical for the artists to manifest their deities' powers in color. These faded remnants are all that remain of the bright paints used for the gods and cardinal directions." Gabriela shook her head. "Originally, the bland limestone buildings that you see before you were covered in vivid shades of red, green, blue, yellow, and black."

Carole looked at the faint pigments on the descending god, trying to imagine what Tulum had looked like in its heyday. She thought for a moment, and then turned to Damon.

"What if we include artistic recreations of the buildings in the video? Show the buildings as they appear now, and then superimpose mattes over them, giving the viewers the illusion of being present in ancient Tulum."

"That's a good idea." Nodding thoughtfully, he said, "I like it."

"Think we could find a graphic artist here?"

"If not here, certainly in Houston." Damon grinned. "It's less than two hours' flight time." He turned to Gabriela. "After the tour, can you do an online search, make a few calls, and set up an interview or two? I want to move on this tomorrow."

Carole stared at him, wondering why he had hired her cold when he had all these resources at his fingertips. She waited until after the tour had ended and Gabriela had left them to begin her search for a graphic artist.

As she and Damon descended the immense, wooden staircase to the beach, Carole turned to him. "Why did you hire me without references or without any knowledge of my ability to deliver when you have employees connected to computers, and you're only two hours from Houston?"

A sea breeze blew his sandy-gray hair into his eyes. "You definitely don't have problems speaking your mind." Finger-combing his hair back, he said, "I'm a good judge of character. Have to be in my line of business."

"You still haven't answered my question." The breeze whipped at her hair and billowed her sundress.

"My instincts told me you could get the job done . . . and there is that little matter of a deadline. Call it fate. I needed a copywriter, and you were here."

"Actually, there," she said. "Belize, not Tulum."

When they reached the beach, Carole kicked off her sandals and dug her toes into the sparkling, white sand. "Oh, that feels marvelous." She took a deep breath, inhaling the salt air.

Sandals in hand, they walked to the edge of the water, letting the surf lap against their bare feet. Carole waded out to her ankles, feeling the tide's tug as the waves flowed and receded. Laughing, she called over the surf, "It tickles."

"Good, include that sensation in your copy."

She looked up at the *Castillo* and noted the windows that had acted as beacons. Beneath one opening, an agave grew from a crevice in the limestone wall, while an iguana stood sentinel on the rooftop.

"What a magical place."

"That's the feeling I want you to impart in the video," he said. "Document how Eastwood Enterprises is helping the ecology, but also enchant prospective investors with the Yucatan's charm."

She breathed in deeply as she clasped her hands under her chin. "That's a tall order, especially in seventy-two hours." Then she smiled. "But it's doable. I'll need to get together with Mario tomorrow to give him a list of shots and let him know the angles I'm after, literally." She turned toward him. "I'll also need to know what Eastwood Enterprises is doing to help the ecology. Is there something you can show me that Mario can capture on film?"

"Basically, just emphasize that Eastwood Enterprises uses sustainable design and eco-friendly principles to preserve the natural beauty and local culture of Belize."

"That's a good introductory blurb." She frowned thoughtfully. "But can you give me any tangible examples, some demo we could film for your prospective investors?"

"Like what?"

Pressing her lips together, she scratched her head as she racked her brain for similar situations. She smiled as one came to mind. "For instance, I helped with a PR project for ecological sustainment in Puerto Rico. We showed scenes of students learning about protecting the sea. It was a great photo op because the children created construction-paper seahorses and squid. Film with kids and color—it sells every time."

"Good idea. I'll have Gabriela organize a training at a local school." He looked at her expectantly. "Anything else?"

"Don't you have any current programs or standard operating procedures?" Perplexed by his lack of policy, she cocked her head and squinted.

He worked his jaw. "Eastwood Enterprises is contributing to Belize's economy by providing jobs and hiring Belizean nationals at every level of employment whenever possible. That increases the tax base, funding the infrastructure."

Grimacing, Carole rubbed the back of her neck. This wasn't what she had expected to hear. She tried once more. "What about your construction methods? Is Eastwood Enterprises a green builder?"

"Of course."

"Good. Now we're getting somewhere." She smiled. "Give me an example we can script and film."

He gave her a reassuring smile. "We leave a small footprint."

"Okay, how?"

"Since we haven't begun construction yet, it's difficult to film any of these efforts, but Eastwood Enterprises reduces its overall impact on the environment through efficient use of energy, resources, and water. It complies with environmental legislation, as well as internationally accepted best practices for sustainable tourism and supports the conservation and protection of the environment, historical sites, cultural assets, and natural attractions of Belize."

"Again, that's good introductory copy," she said, "but what specifically are you doing to improve the current situation?"

"We're establishing the Coral Propagation Corps, where students from the future Aquatic Biology School will conduct research on coral transplantation."

"This is exactly the kind of story we need," she said, her eyes widening. "Can you fill me in?"

He nodded. "To help heal the coral reefs and create sustainable fisheries, the students will research how broken fragments of coral can be collected and brought to a coral nursery to rehabilitate for several months." He held up his hand and made a fist. "Then, when the fragments are about this size, they'll be reattached to stony corals to jump start the reef."

"And what's the name of this university?"

"Eastwood Enterprises is committed to helping support the proposed Aquatic Biology School."

She raised her left eyebrow. "Proposed—"

"Plans are being finalized." His no-nonsense tone barred further questioning.

She pressed her lips together and took a deep breath. "Well, that'll have to do for this documentary." Giving him a tight, professional smile, she asked, "How soon can Gabriela organize the children's training?"

"Tomorrow—"

Nick's ringing cell phone interrupted their conversation, startling her. Setting her sandals on the sand, she reached into her shoulder bag for the cell. "Excuse me." She stepped away to answer. "This is Carole."

"Good morning," said Nick.

Her heart skipped a beat. With the morning's meetings, flight, and tour, she hadn't had time to think about Nick or their misunderstanding. All she heard was the voice of the person she loved. That grounded her, putting the morning, the video project, and even the visit into perspective. *Everything will work out . . . somehow.*

"Good morning," she said brightly.

"Wondered if you'd like to go snorkeling."

She looked out over the Caribbean, its azure and cerulean blues inviting her to do more than just wade. Then she remembered her contract with Eastwood Enterprises.

"Would I ever . . . ."

"But . . . ."

"You know me too well, but . . . ." She gave a chuckle. "I'm in Tulum."

"Tulum? What are you doing there?"

She heard the concern in his voice. "Remember the PR project Damon asked me to do? Long story short, I'm under contract until COB Tuesday. Think we could postpone our snorkeling 'til Wednesday morning?"

"I thought you came to Belize to see me?"

Though she heard his injured tone, she reacted to the thinly veiled accusation. "I thought so, too, but ever since I arrived you've been running off on dives, leaving me to my own devices."

"Well, I'm free this morning. I thought—"

"Carole," called Damon. "Gabriela's trying to set up the training for tomorrow morning. She wants to know if that'll fit into your schedule."

"Tell her yes," she called, nodding.

"Who was that?" Nick asked.

"Damon."

"What's he—"

"Look, I'm on the clock. I really do have to go . . . but I'd love to see you Wednesday morning," she said. "Think that could be arranged?"

Smiling, Nick said, "Yeah, I think that can be arranged."

"I'm glad," she murmured, suddenly regretting having accepted the contract.

"I'll pack a lunch. I know an out-of-the-way island with a private cove where we can . . . get reacquainted." His smile lit up his voice.

"Sounds wonderful! It's a date! Of course, I hope to see you before then, too." She clicked off the phone, subdued the smile she felt playing at the corners of her lips, and, summoning her most professional tones, turned toward Damon. "Sorry for the interruption."

"Not a problem." Damon picked up her sandals and handed them to her. "You know, I like your ideas . . . the environmental educational shots, the historic matte overlays . . . so much so, in fact, that I'm seriously considering postponing the stockholders meeting in Houston 'til Thursday. That would give us another day to finalize the video."

That would also delay my date with Nick and end any chance of a bonus. Pursing her lips, she took a deep breath, gathering her wits for entering verbal battle.

"Of course," he said slowly, as if reading her thoughts, "the bonus deadline would be extended to Wednesday." Arms folded, head cocked to one side, grinning arrogantly, his eyes glinted in the sun, narrowing to slits as they tracked her. "In fact, let's up the ante. Include the historic artwork in the script and work in the environmental classroom footage by Wednesday, and I'll sweeten the deal to seven K for four days' work." He held out his hand. "Deal?"

His body language forced a second look. *What kind of game is he playing?* Carole tried to read his eyes as she weighed the pros and cons. *Pay for the trip* and *turn a profit—but what about Nick?* She sucked in her breath, remembering their date. *Although he did leave me lonely my first day here . . . twice . . . and for another of Damon's projects.* As that settled in her brain, she pursed her lips and grunted. *What's good for the goose . . . .*

Carole looked at his extended hand, gave him a smile, and shook hands. "Deal . . . with the caveat that this is our final delivery schedule."

His smile pinched and his eyes glittering coldly in the bright sunlight, he squeezed her hand tightly. "Concur."

"You'll have your script by Wednesday, including the artwork and classroom footage—that is, providing Gabriela can locate a school or youth group." She met his eyes and raised her eyebrow. "You have my word on it, but that will conclude our contract. That's the day I turn in my briefcase for my bikini. Are we clear?"

"Crystal." She caught his amused grin before he bobbed his head in a subtle nod, apparently trying to hide his expression.

Inhaling deeply, Carole deliberately chose to ignore it. It was only another four days' work, and she'd never see the man again. The credo that had sustained her for the past few years flit through her mind—*it's business.* With the exception of her relationship with Nick, that pretty much summed up her life—*it's business.* It took the burden off her conscience.

Forcing her most amiable, professional smile, Carole said, "Maybe it's time we headed back. I need to start putting words to paper if we want this video scripted by Wednesday."

"No better time than the present."

On the way back to the wooden staircase, they met a little boy throwing food to the iguanas.

"What's that you're feeding them," Carole asked, pausing, watching him.

"Sea grapes," he said. "They love them."

"Did you pick them from here?" She gestured to the clusters of fruit on a nearby tree. He nodded, and she picked a handful of pale-green fruit.

"Here, baby," she said, bending down to the iguanas' level, holding out a grape in front of her and inviting the iguana take the food from her hand.

"Careful, they have sharp teeth."

She nodded, heeding the boy's warning, and tossed the grape toward the spiny dragon. It approached cautiously, not taking its eyes from its target, its long toes slowly edging toward her.

Carole immediately respected the scaly opportunist. Wild, yet obviously tolerant of people, the iguana braved a giant twelve, fourteen times its size to get what it wanted.

There's a lesson to be learned from this lizard. Carole looked at Damon and reaffirmed her reason for visiting Belize. She'd make the most of this opportunity, complete the contract, and accept her bonus, but she wouldn't lose sight of her target—Nick. *Money talks—but it doesn't kiss you good night.*

"What?" Lost in thought, Carole had not heard the boy.

"They're called spiny-tailed iguanas because of the ridges on their tails," he repeated.

She looked at the miniature dinosaur's swollen tail and then turned back toward the boy. "You seem to know a lot about these iguanas. Where did you learn it?"

The little boy shrugged. "Cub Scouts."

Getting an idea, she glanced at Damon and then turned back to the boy. "Do you have a phone number for your group's leader?"

Chapter Three

Carole stocked up on coffee and filters for the hotel's coffee maker and stayed up until 3:30 AM writing copy. Up again at 5:30, she tracked down online environmental educational materials suitable for Cub Scouts and put together a presentation.

At 8:25, she was showered, dressed, and hustling toward the beachfront restaurant to meet Damon. Again, the friendly puppy cocked its head as it watched her. Carole slowed down when she saw it, tempted again to pet the young dog. It wagged its tail, as if inviting her to approach, but she did not want to be late for the meeting and hurried on. By 8:30, she was impatiently waiting at the Azure Grill to show Damon the printouts of the telescript and Cub Scout training.

When he arrived, a steaming pot of coffee was waiting at the table.

"Good, I'm glad you're early. I've got so much to show you," Carole said, her words coming out faster than intended. *Guess the caffeine's kicking in.*

Over fresh slices of papaya, honeydew, cantaloupe, and strawberries, Carole pointed out the copy she had written for each location. She accounted for the long shots from the Caribbean as the viewers approached Tulum from the sea to the *Castillo* to the close-ups of the descending god and Ctenosaur iguanas.

Then, talking as much with her hands as her mouth, Carole depicted how the overlaid mattes would work for the historical pieces. They would bring the ruins to life by showing stucco-covered stonework and vivid colors, the freshly-built edifices contrasting against the crumbling remnants seen today.

"What about the educational piece?" Damon asked.

Carol smiled proudly, lifting folders of handouts from her briefcase. "I found plenty of educational material online," she said, citing the various universities and governmental entities that had made them available to educators.

"Did Gabriela get in touch with the Boy Scout leader?" he asked.

"No, but I did. Gabriela is stocking up on reams of colorful construction paper, crayons, and blunt-tip scissors." She flashed him a confident smile. "Don't worry. This is going to work out fine. I have experience working with children's groups."

"What about an instructor?" asked Damon. "Were you able to get in touch with anyone?"

Carole dropped her smile momentarily. "Gabriela was trying to locate a Spanish-speaking instructor the last time we talked."

"When was that?"

"It was ten o'clock last night when she said she had a lead."

Grimacing, Damon scratched his ear. "This is all being thrown together so fast. I hope we're not overextending ourselves within this time frame."

"I agree." Carole nodded, deeply inhaling the sea air. "It's a tight schedule, but I had a few ideas last night that should pull it all together."

"Where are we shooting it?"

She flashed him a mischievous smile. "Right here."

He looked around him. "At this outdoor café?"

Shaking her head, she laughed. "No, but on this beach. We weren't able to convince the Mexican authorities to let us close off Tulum's beach while we filmed. Instead, we contracted here on Ambergris Caye to shoot on an out-of-the-way strip of shore a mile from here."

"I'm still not clear on this," he said, his concern reflected in the deepening lines of his forehead. "Weren't you able to get a classroom?"

"Not on this short notice." She finished her cup of coffee and poured another. "What children did you get?"

She flashed him a self-satisfied smile. "A group of Belizean Boy Scouts."

He shook his head as if to clear it and picked up his menu. "Tell me about it over breakfast."

Smiling, she folded the menu, took it from him, and set it back down. "There isn't time. We're meeting the crew at nine o'clock." Stuffing the handouts back into her briefcase, she stood up. "C'mon, I'll tell you on the way."

As they walked to the street and caught a cab, Carole told him the timetable.

"The Boy Scouts and leaders are meeting us on location. We had t-shirts printed for them, reading 'Belizean Boy Scouts' on the front and 'Eastwood Enterprises, Ltd.' on the back." She winked. "After all, you said you wanted a documentary video to show prospective investors how Eastwood Enterprises is helping the ecology, as well as the economy, of Belize."

Nodding his head slowly, he looked at her, appraising her. "You're good."

"But that's not all," she said, grinning. "After the educational portion this morning, where Mario will get all the shots and angles he needs for many videos to come, we're supplying gloves and garbage bags for the boys. They'll put theory into practice by cleaning up the environment . . . and Mario will be there to video every piece of trash they remove." Thinking out loud, she added, "Maybe we can fast-forward that into a kind of time-lapse, showing the before, during, and after shots of the beach." She turned toward him. "I think it'll be effective."

"If that doesn't convince investors Eastwood Enterprises means business, I don't know what will." He raised his eyebrow and gave her a *See?* look. "You're worth every penny."

They paid the cab driver and walked to the beach. Gabriela and Dante were already there, handing out breakfast tacos and cartons of fruit juice to the twenty boys and their leaders.

"Get 'em while they're hot," Dante called, wearing his perennial grin while brandishing foil-wrapped tacos.

Turning to Carole, Damon said, "You think of everything, don't you?"

She winked. "Hey, Dante, Gabriela, thanks for getting here early and setting up." She surveyed the folding tables and chairs set up under the palm trees, already crammed with little boys happily munching tacos. "Is Mario here?"

Gabriela nodded, pointing toward a rocky outcrop on the beach. "He's scouting out the best location for the garbage pick-up, the area that will show the most results the fastest."

"Were you able to get the scissors, crayons, and construction paper?" Carole asked. Gabriela nodded. Pointing, Dante said, "It's all there in those boxes under the tables."

"What about the Spanish-speaking instructor?"

Gabriela grimaced. "Sorry, that's the one thing that fell through the cracks."

"What happened?" asked Carole, biting her lip, trying not to show her aggravation.

"I left message after message with the instructor's husband who assured me that the woman would not only show up, but call to confirm. So far, she's a no-show."

Carole stifled a sigh. "Maybe it's a good thing we couldn't film in Tulum. At least English is the national language of Belize, so Spanish translation isn't crucial."

"Maybe," said Damon, "but who can we get to be the instructor?"

All eyes turned toward Carole.

Taking a deep breath, she grimaced. "I'm the one that read the teachers' syllabus. As a last resort, I can share what I read." She rolled her eyes. "Mario will just have to shoot around me—show the boys listening and not me teaching."

"Here," said Dante, handing her a taco and a steaming cup of coffee. "You'll need sustenance."

She laughed, regaining her sense of humor. "We can call this the *Teach on the Beach Outreach* series."

Chuckling, Damon looked at Gabriela and Dante. "You know, it has a certain ring to it."

As if in echo, Carole's phone rang. 'Excuse me." She walked a few feet away to answer.

"Good morning," said Nick.

"Oh, am I glad to hear your voice," she said, meaning it.

"Meet me for breakfast, and you can hear a lot more of it," he joked, his smile coming through the phone.

"Wish I could, but I'm on set."

"On set? Where?"

"Here, on Ambergris Caye."

"What?"

"Hey, Nick," she said slowly as an idea began gelling. "Why not join us? In fact, I believe I even have a soap box for your environmental platform."

"What are you talking about?"

"I'll explain more when you get here, but how would you like to talk to a group of Boy Scouts about your two pet peeves?"

He sighed. "I don't know—"

"Hey, I'll reimburse you for your time with all the breakfast tacos you can eat."

"Maybe you could repay me by going parasailing with me this afternoon?"

She winced. "We'll be shooting all day, but," her scowl softened into a smile as the idea took hold, "how about dinner tonight?"

"You drive a hard bargain." He chuckled. "Tell me where you are, and I'll meet you in a few minutes."

"Nick . . . ." Hesitating, she recalled how he'd deserted her twice for business, but now she saw how quickly he'd come to her aid when she needed him. "Thanks."

"Glad to help."

"Really appreciate it. I . . . ." Inwardly groaning, she paused, unsure if this were the right time, uncertain of his response.

"Yeah . . . ?"

"Nick . . . ." She turned toward the surf to be sure no one could overhear. "Love you." Before he could respond, she hung up.

A half hour later, Nick pulled up on the beach in a silver sea kayak. The effect was dazzling as the morning sun glinted off the water and kayak. Squinting against the reflection, Carole grinned as he approached. *His vehicle may not be a white horse, but he's my shining knight.* While the crew and boys looked on, she gave Nick a chaste, self-conscious kiss.

"Glad you could help us out," she said, squeezing his hand, wishing she could say more. Turning toward the crew, she put on a professional smile as she made the introductions. "Everybody, this is Nick McKuen. You already know Damon and Dante," she said, as they shook hands. "This is Gabriela, our intern, and Mario, who'll be filming your talk." She walked him toward the scouts, now clad in their red t-shirts. "Boys, this is Mr. McKuen, a certified diver, marine expert, and ex-SEAL."

The boys' eyes lit up in admiration, and they shyly murmured their hellos.

"Hi, guys," he said with a wave and an easy smile.

"Boys, if you'll take your seats, Mr. McKuen will tell you all about lions and tigers and bears, oh, my!" When they gave her a blank stare, not recognizing the connection, she grinned and tried again. "Mr. McKuen will talk to you about lionfish and tiger prawns, and why they're bad for the reef. Please sit down and give Mr. McKuen a big hand." She applauded as a cue for the boys and nodded to Nick and Mario, signaling they were on.

"How many of you have ever seen a lionfish?" Nick asked as Mario began taping.

Half the boys raised their hands.

"They're beautiful, but they're very dangerous. If you see them in the water, keep away from them. Their spines are poisonous, and their sting can kill." He met the eyes of the boys, addressing each individually as he spoke. "Are lionfish native to Belize?"

Half the boys nodded and said yes. The other half shook their heads, saying no.

"No, lionfish are native to the Indian Ocean and parts of the Pacific. They don't belong in the Caribbean. They're invasive." He paused. "What does invasive mean?"

He pointed to the first boy to raise his hand.

"They invaded the water . . . like pirates."

Nick glanced at Carole. "That's right. Like pirates, lionfish have taken over the sea and are killing the native fish of Belize." His eyes roved from scout to scout, searching for an answer. "Why is that bad?"

He pointed to another boy raising his hand.

"They're harming the native fish."

"Exactly, they're endangering small local fish called social wrasses. They eat so many of these fish that they may become extinct. The lionfish are upsetting the natural balance between predator and prey." Again he peered from face to face. "Who can tell us the difference between predator and prey? You," he said, pointing.

"The predator eats the prey."

Nodding, Nick chuckled. "That's a good definition. Lionfish have no natural enemies to eat them, so they keep multiplying. As their numbers grow, they eat more of the local fish."

Nick called on a boy raising his hand.

"Don't all fish eat other fish?"

"Yes," Nick agreed with a nod, "but lionfish are top predators. They eat up all the young snapper and grouper, along with algae-eating parrotfish.

Those are the fish that normally keep reefs healthy. Between 2004 and 2008, lionfish increased by up to 700 percent in some areas, and their numbers are still increasing. Some coral reefs now have 1,000 lionfish per acre. That's bad news for the reefs and bad news for people."

"Why are they bad for people?"

"They're very poisonous," said Nick. "They—"

"Oh, oh, I know," said a boy waving his hand wildly. "I know! I know!"

Chuckling, Nick pointed at him. "Okay, what can you tell us about them?"

"They can kill you." He turned toward the scouts. "A girl died from a lionfish sting a month or two ago." Hands at his throat, he demonstrated choking to death, finally falling to his knees on the sand, and then flopping over lifelessly on his back.

Nick swallowed a smile. "Although their venom can be deadly, death is rare, but the sting is painful." Nick called on another boy with his hand raised.

"How did the lionfish get here?"

"That's a good question. No one knows for sure, but probably lionfish escaped from their aquarium into the sea during a hurricane. Here's another question. Without natural predators to control their numbers and keep a balance in nature, what could happen?"

Most of the boys shrugged their shoulders, but the 'dead' one revived enough to wave his hand. "I know, I know!" Nick nodded, and the boy said, "Instead of all different kinds of fish, there'd be just lionfish."

"Exactly. There'd be no diversity. The same thing is happening with tiger prawns," said Nick. "What are prawns?"

"A kind of shrimp."

"Right, they're a large species of shrimp. Like the lionfish, they're invasive. Originally from Australia and Southeast Asia, they were accidentally released into the Atlantic. Now they've spread to the Caribbean."

"Are they eating all the fish, too?" asked a scout.

Nick smiled as he shook his head. "No. In fact, several kinds of fish eat them, which helps control their numbers. The problem with tiger prawns is they spread viruses that kill native shrimp, oysters, and crabs. So whether they eat the native fish and shellfish or spread diseases that kill them, lionfish and tiger prawns harm the coral reefs around Belize. They upset the natural balance." His eyes traveled from boy to boy as he asked, "Who can tell us the only way to get rid of these lions and tigers?"

"I know, I know," said one scout, grinning. "You eat them!"

Nick laughed. "Good answer . . . and they're both delicious." He caught Carole's eye before he turned back to the boys. "I believe Miss Kennedy has something planned next for you, but thank you for being a wonderful audience!"

Applauding, Carole told the boys, "Please thank Mr. McKuen for joining us and telling us all about the lions and tigers of Belize."

Nick gave her a warm smile and then addressed the scout leaders. "Let me know if your troop would be interested in snorkeling some Saturday. I'd be happy to volunteer my services."

With whoops and hollers, the boys enthusiastically convinced the leaders to take him up on his offer.

Grinning, Carole saw Nick in a new light. Seeing him from the scouts' perspective, she could not take her eyes from him. Then she felt eyes watching her and turned quickly.

Several feet behind the sandy beach, she thought she saw movement in the shadows of the trees. *Was that a face peering out?* Then the foreground came into view, and she caught Damon staring intently. A cold shudder passed over her, rousing her from her reverie.

She took the stack of papers from her briefcase and held up her hand, getting the boys' attention. "Thanks again for joining us, Mr. McKuen." She gave Nick a private wink and then turned her attention to the scouts. "Now you know about the lions and tigers of Belize, but who can tell me about the turtles? How many kinds of sea turtles does Belize have?"

"A hundred?" asked a boy.

"Not quite," she said with a smile. "There are three common kinds of sea turtles and two more that you might see. The Hawksbill, Green, and Loggerhead Sea Turtles are the most common, but once in a while you might spot a Leatherback or Olive Ridley." She motioned to Gabriela. "Could you hold up these pictures while I describe the turtles?"

Gabriela took the papers from her and held up the first picture.

"The Hawksbill turtle used to be harvested for its shell or carapace. Called tortoiseshell, they were used make glasses and jewelry from its shell. Now there's a ban on tortoiseshell. What's a ban?"

A boy raised his hand, and Carole called on him.

"It's people who play music."

"That's a band," said Carole, emphasizing the 'd.' "A ban means something is stopped or is not allowed. It's not legal to harvest or own tortoiseshell anymore."

Gabriela held up another picture.

"Green turtles can weigh up to five hundred pounds. Could you lift that?"

"No," the boys said as they shook their heads.

"Green turtles are vegetarians. What do you suppose those turtles eat?" The scouts shrugged.

"Turtle grass," Carole said with a grin. She told them about the other turtle species and divided the boys into five groups, naming each after a different species. Next, she gave each group the picture of its namesake turtle, along with paper plates and crayons. "Color the paper plate to match your turtle's shell." Then she handed them printouts containing outlines of the turtle's head and flippers. "When you finish coloring, cut out the turtle's head and flippers. Then tape them to the paper plate to create a turtle."

Carole and Gabriela helped the boys with their projects while Mario taped the footage. When the scouts finished creating their paper-plate turtles, Carole continued the lesson.

"Sea turtle numbers are dwindling. They—"

"Why?" asked a boy with glasses. His magnified eyes had a perpetual surprised look.

"Sea turtles can't breathe underwater. They have to surface to breathe. When they get caught in shrimp trawls and gill nets, they can't surface, so they drown. Another big reason sea turtles are decreasing in numbers is development along the coast."

Squinting, another boy asked, "What do you mean?"

Carole turned toward him and, from the corner of her eye, saw a girl hiding in the trees' shadows. As the girl grinned and waved, Carole recognized her from the first morning. She smiled and winked back before answering the question.

"Building on the beaches ruins turtles' nesting habitat. They have nowhere to lay their eggs. Development also causes other problems for turtles' survival, like dredging and waste disposal—"

"Why?" asked the scout, pushing up his glasses with an index finger.

"Because both dredging and sewage destroy their food supply," she said.

"What's dredging?" asked another scout.

"Dredging is—"

Damon interrupted, calling Carole over. "I think we have enough 'classroom' footage. Didn't you say you were going to lead the scouts in a beach cleanup?"

She jerked her chin, her jaw working. "Yeah," she said slowly, skeptical of his motives.

"Why don't you wrap up this portion?"

"The lesson's only got a few minutes left." She rubbed her chin, trying to read him. *Is he bored or trying to change the focus?* She said, "I can end it sooner . . . if that's what you want."

"It is." His mouth settling into a tight, grim line, he forced a smile while his eyes bored into hers.

"All right." She pursed her lips as she turned away from him. *You're the boss.* "Dante, can you hand each scout a pair of canvas gloves and a garbage bag?" Then she returned to the boys. "What we're going to do next, guys, is help the sea turtles and all the other marine creatures by cleaning up this beach. We're going to pick up all the papers, cans, bottles, and other trash we see." She held up a twenty-dollar bill. "Whoever fills his garbage bag first gets this twenty-dollar bill." She looked at them. "Has everyone got their gloves and a garbage bag?"

A chorus of exuberant 'yeses' greeted her.

"Okay, on your mark. Get set. Go!"

Twenty boys scrambled in all directions.

Chuckling, Carole called to Mario. "Are you getting this on film?"

His eyes peering through the camera's viewfinder, he answered without looking at her. "Yup."

"Great, I want you to capture the whole process. We can fast-forward that into a sped-up time-lapse, showing the before, during, and after shots of the beach in a kind of Benny Hill montage."

Mario nodded. "'Kay."

Again, she felt eyes watching her. Carole looked for the girl, but she had disappeared. This time, she noticed Nick leaning against a palm tree. Arms crossed, he grinned as he studied her. Fixing her eyes on his, she returned his grin and sauntered toward him.

"What?"

"Just watching you in action." He unfolded his arms and placed his hands on her shoulders. "You're really good at what you do."

"And why should that come as a surprise?" She chuckled, tickled by his touch, glad to be sharing their easy banter. Their relationship had seemed so strained since she landed in Belize. *This is more like it.*

"Carole, what's planned after this shot?" asked Damon, standing beside her, their elbows nearly touching.

She flinched as she half-turned toward him, and Nick's left hand fell from her shoulder. She had not seen him approach.

"After we finish shooting here," she said, gathering her thoughts, she switched mental gears. "We'll need to pack up the site—"

"Dante and Gabriela can do that," Damon said. "I was thinking you, Mario, and I could get the footage you'd mentioned for the sea approach to Tulum. I'll navigate while you direct Mario's shots."

Though she stifled a sigh, her chest heaved. "Sure," she said with a noncommittal shrug, unintentionally shaking Nick's remaining hand from her shoulders.

"Ready to roll?" asked Damon.

Carole narrowed her eyes, thinking it sounded more like a command than a question. A sharp retort came to mind, but she thought better of it and used logic instead.

"What about the beach cleanup and twenty-dollar prize? Don't you want to tape at least until the winner's declared?" When Damon didn't answer immediately, she added, "For a Benny Hill montage, we need to film the cleanup in its entirety."

"Look, I'd better get off the set," said Nick, looking pointedly first at Damon and then at Carole, "so you can get back to work." He winked at her. "See you at seven."

Grabbing his hand, she gave it a friendly squeeze. "Really appreciate your stopping by and speaking to the boys, Nick." Her heartfelt smile and raised eyebrows silently thanked him for sensing the friction and bowing out gracefully.

"Yeah, thanks," said Damon, extending his hand, holding it midair until Nick let go Carole's hand and shook his. "Look, I've got some clients coming in this week. Can you squeeze in a couple more dives?"

"Just let me know the dates. If I can, I will, but you already know that." Nick gave him a steady smile, nothing confrontational and nothing deferential.

With a wry grin, Carole recognized it as the same bland mask she used in transactions. *It's business—nothing more, nothing less.*

After Nick's departure, Damon visibly relaxed. He rooted the boys on and didn't bring up the idea of leaving until after a wiry scout shouted his bag was full. When Carole took out the twenty-dollar bill, Damon shook his head.

"This is on Eastwood Enterprises." He handed the boy a bill.

The beaming scout did a double-take. "Fifty dollars! Thanks, mister!"

Damon called the scout leader over, thanked him, shook his hand, and gave him another fifty. "Take the boys out for pizza. They earned it." He spotted the videographer shooting final scenes. "Mario, how much longer?"

"Five minutes," he shouted back.

"Gabriela, call us a cab, would you?" As she pulled out her cell, he turned to Dante. "Can you and Gabriela clean up here while we shoot more footage at Tulum?"

"Can do, boss, Belize it or not." His eyes twinkling mischievously, Dante shot Carole a shrewd grin. *So that's how he handles Damon. He humors him.*

Forty minutes later, they were in the air. Damon piloted while Carole sat in the passenger seat and Mario rode in the back. A few minutes after takeoff, Damon tipped his right wing, saying, "See that beach? That's where Eastwood Enterprises will be building."

"Do you want an aerial shot of it?" she asked.

He shook his head. "Not yet, not until the first phase is complete." He glanced at her, raising his eyebrows, his expression direct. "There's a lot of PR work we need done over the next year or two. If you change your mind about relocating to Belize, Eastwood Enterprises could give you as much business as you could handle."

She smiled at him blandly, but she read more than a business offer in his expression. She took her eyes from his, turning her head to look at the island. "With a jungle interior and sandy beach surrounding it, it looks like a paradise."

"There's a natural cove on the west side," he said, pointing. "There's even a small cave on the north side where the seawater washes through. You can walk or swim through it."

Carole grinned. "That sounds like fun. Who wouldn't want to live there?"

Again, Damon's eyes bored into hers. "That could be arranged."

She glanced at him quickly to see if she'd heard what she thought. She had. Carole ignored Damon's innuendo, staring instead at the sea as he flew over the blue hole. Suddenly, she spotted a boat with a fly bridge.

"Isn't that Nick's boat?" she asked, perking up as she recognized his 38-foot dive boat.

Damon tipped his wing and buzzed it as the people onboard looked up, shielding their eyes from the sun, and waved.

Carole did not have time to analyze it, but she had never felt farther away from Nick than at that moment, not even when she was in Manhattan. She watched his boat get smaller and smaller as they dashed towards Tulum.

Chapter Four

Carole finished showering, slipped into a silky, aqua dress, and topped off the outfit with the iridescent pearls Nick had given her for her birthday. She peeked at her watch—7:02. Hoping she had enough time before Nick arrived, she quickly applied a touch of mascara and lip gloss.

Her eyes took in the room. Her briefcase was dumped upside down on the bed, its contents spilled out on the bedspread from when she'd searched for her thumb drive. Everything was where she'd left it. *Is there time to tidy up before he gets here?*

After organizing its contents, she tucked the briefcase behind the desk and looked at her watch—7:12. *Where is he?* She checked his phone. No messages, no missed calls. She called his landline and went straight to voice mail.

"It's me. Just wondering where you are. You did say you'd pick me up at seven, didn't you?" She paused, scratching her head. "Hope you hadn't said to meet you somewhere."

At seven-thirty, Carole kicked off her sandals. Exhausted from having been up most of the previous evening, she decided to skip dinner and turn in early. As she took off her pearls, a knock sounded at the door.

"It's me," said Nick's voice.

She rolled her eyes. Pearls still in hand, she put them on again, hooked their clasp, slipped back into her shoes, and answered the door.

"What happened?"

From behind his back, Nick produced a bouquet. Wearing a smile that showed off his dimple, he asked, "Peace offering?" He pointed to each flower as he named it. "Purple Vanda orchids, ginger, heliconia, plumeria, and . . . ." He paused, squinting, biting his lower lip, trying to remember. Finally, he said, "And some other native flowers that I forget."

"Thank you," she said, admiring them, inhaling their sweetness. She took her time, debating whether she was annoyed or relieved to see him. Finally, she tipped up her eyes to watch his response. "How come you're late?"

"Our friend, Damon, called just as I was walking out the door. You heard him this morning. He has prospective investors coming to town and wants to schedule multiple dives. Sorry, but I couldn't get him off the phone." He smiled crookedly. "If it's any consolation, I turned down his request for a last-minute dive tonight."

"Hmmm . . . think I'm seeing a connection here. That man bears watching." Giving him a smile, she added, "A hug might make up for the delay."

He clasped her to him so close, she could feel his chest rise and fall with his breathing. In his arms, all seemed right with the world, no matter the time, no matter Damon's scheme. She reached up to kiss his cheek.

"Are you still up for dinner?" he asked.

She nodded. Then breaking away gently, she held up the bouquet. "Just let me put these in water."

They walked along the beach, the moon lighting their way.

"This is the place," said Nick, leading her into a restaurant lit by flaming torches. "Remember my talk this morning about lions and tigers?"

She squeezed his arm playfully. "How could I forget?"

"While on a dive this afternoon, I speared both. This place grills, bakes, fries, sautés, or boils lionfish, tiger prawns, and anything else you catch to perfection. Hope you enjoy it." His eye caught hers, and they shared a smile.

"Incidentally, thanks again for helping me out this morning with your talk. You captured the boys' imagination."

"Anytime, you know I'd do anything for you."

She turned toward him, eyebrow raised. "Anything?" she asked pointedly.

He groaned. "Let's hold another truce at least through dinner?"

She chuckled. "You silver-tongued devil, you."

A waiter seated them at a table overlooking the beach. The glass-topped rattan table was graced by Vanda orchids and a ruby-red candle holder with a flickering candle.

"Would you like to see a wine list?"

"Sure." Handing Carole the list, Nick turned toward her with a crooked smile. "No night dives to interfere."

"How does pinot grigio sound?" She looked at him coquettishly.

"Perfect." Nick smiled. "Now the hard part—how do you want your lion and tigers prepared?"

"I don't know." She cocked her head to the side, apprehensive about her upcoming culinary adventures. "What do lionfish taste like?"

"It's hard to describe," he said. "Some say it tastes like chicken, but I think it's more a cross between sea bass and lobster. I like it sautéed in butter with a drizzle of fresh lime juice." He winked his encouragement.

Taking a deep breath, she reached a decision. "Make that for two."

The waiter wrote down their order.

"What about the tiger prawns?" asked Nick. "How would you like those?"

She turned to the waiter. "What's the house specialty?"

"Coconut Prawns," he said with a grin.

"Sounds delicious," she said, nodding.

"An excellent choice. And you, sir?"

"The same."

Within moments, the waiter returned with a lightly chilled bottle of pinot grigio, an ice bucket, and two slender-bowled glasses. He uncorked the bottle, poured, and discreetly retreated, leaving them to their privacy.

Nick lifted his glass. "To us."

Carole raised her eyes to meet his and lightly touched glasses, a tinkling, crystal ring resounding. "To us," she echoed.

After dinner, they took a moonlit stroll along the beach, listening to the surf lap gently against the shoreline. The stars shimmered overhead in the clear, evening air. A breeze lifted the fine, white sand, and it drifted, reminding Carole of snow in the Adirondacks.

"What would you like to do for Thanksgiving?" he asked.

"The good news is that as of Wednesday night, I'll be finished with my contract," she said. "Hopefully, by Wednesday afternoon. Then I'll be free to snorkel and windsurf with you to your heart's content. I can't wait for vacation to start!"

"Then why wait?" asked Nick. "You have to snorkel at least once while you're here."

"It's not that I don't want to," she said, looking up from his sleek torso to his moonlit face. "I just don't know if I can squeeze it in before this contract ends."

"You're supposed to be on vacation," he said, wearing a crooked grin. "At least you were the last time I heard. Ambergris Caye sits on the largest barrier reef system in the western hemisphere. It runs the whole length of Belize and offers the best snorkeling in the Caribbean—maybe in the world. Besides, Hol Chan's only a fifteen-minute ride away."

She watched his twinkling eyes and couldn't resist smiling back. "A fifteen-minute ride, you say?" Pretending to think it over, she paused, working her jaw. Then she tilted her head sideways and asked, "What's Hol Chan?"

"It's a huge reserve that means break in the reef. The best snorkeling's at the Cut, a natural channel through the reef that starts in just three feet of water." He put his arms around her waist. "Fifteen minutes travel time each way, an hour or two splashing around the reef, looking at brightly colored corals and big shoals of snappers, huge grouper fish, and maybe even an elegant eagle ray swimming through the channel."

"It's tempting." She looked up into his eyes, fully knowing she was flirting, and enjoying it.

"We might even see tarpon, green moray eels, sea turtles, and nurse sharks if we're lucky." He nuzzled her neck, tickling her, making the hairs rise on the back of her neck. "What do you say?"

"I'd love to," she groaned, "but I have to go to work in the morning."

"If we leave at seven," he whispered, "we'll be back by nine—in plenty of time to get to work."

His breath tickled her ear, making her squirm. "Well, as long as we're back by nine."

Tuesday morning, she met Nick at the pier. After she boarded, he untied the ropes and lithely jumped aboard just as the boat shoved off.

"I picked up some seafood burritos," she said, handing one to him. "They're still warm."

They ate standing up, the breeze whipping their hair as they watched the sun rise over the sea, turning the water into molten gold. Flying fish danced alongside the boat, escorting them to the reef.

After a short ride, he tied up on a mooring buoy. "To avoid any anchor damage," he said, motioning to the surrounding area. "This whole seven-and-a half-square-mile reserve is protected."

After they put on their fins, masks, and snorkels, Nick tossed a snack into the crystal-blue water. Immediately, huge schools of fish gathered about the boat. With a practiced, backward summersault, he dove off the side of the boat, momentarily scattering the fish into silvery waves of color. Carole took a different approach. Facing the sea, she climbed down the ladder backwards on her heels, her long fins pointing outward into the water. She eased into the water, barely making a ripple, enjoying the fishes' company.

As she floated on the water, face down, looking at the underwater world through her mask, she saw brightly colored corals. Snappers and groupers watched them while clown fish capered about them. Nick caught her hand, and together they snorkeled off to explore the reef.

Schools of electric blue fish swam in front of and around them, their metallic blue colors vibrant in the shallow, sunlit sea.

"Blue chromis," he said through his snorkel. Though her ears were partially underwater and his words were muffled, she heard and acknowledged him with a nod.

Pointing to her right, he indicated a diamond-patterned fish capped with sawtooth fins. "Harlequin bass," he said. She watched the masked bass comically dart among the coral and then peer at them like a swimming jester.

One of the coral heads caught her attention, and she pointed. "What's that?" she asked, careful not to swallow a mouthful of salt water as she spoke into her snorkel. "Stars?"

"Blushing star coral," he said, nodding.

Hand-in-hand, they paddled in for a closer inspection. She stared at the coral's repeated star pattern, each star sporting twelve points instead of five. "Beautiful."

As they snorkeled over deeper water, iridescent green fish with intense yellow spots on their pectoral fins swam beneath them. "They look like they're covered with feathers, not scales," she said, pointing.

"Male stoplight parrotfish," he said. Then pointing to red-finned fish, he added, "Female stoplight parrotfish."

"Look!" Amazed, she watched as the scales of the red-bellied females rapidly changed from red to white.

Then she spotted what looked like a star crawling on the sandy bottom.

Letting go of her hand, Nick said, "Be right back." Taking a deep breath, he dove down to the bottom and slowly brought a live starfish to the surface, its tentacles moving across his hand. "Baby starfish."

"I love sea stars!" She touched it tentatively and then pulled back.

"Hold your palm up." Gently placing his hand beside hers, the baby crawled onto her palm.

"It tickles." She handed it back to Nick.

Taking another deep breath, he dove back to the ocean floor with the starfish, returned, and reached for Carole's hand. Together, they gently kicked, letting their fins glide them through the water as he pointed out the flat, skeletal sea fans and bushy gorgonians. Peering through their masks into the crystal water, they floated past multihued sponges, sea anemones, feathery orange crinoids, and branching staghorn coral.

As they floated above the reefs and canyons, yellowtail snapper, Atlantic spadefish, schools of silver-blue bar jacks, blimp-shaped triggerfish with bright white lines running along their dorsal and anal fins, and dusky, blue-polka-dotted, gray angelfish patrolled the waters below them.

It seemed they had barely gotten into the water before Nick tapped his waterproof watch. "Time to go."

Though the warm water buoyed her up, Carole felt her spirits droop. She sighed. "Wednesday, let's do this again."

Chapter Five

True to his word, Nick got her back by eight-thirty. By nine, she had showered, dressed, and found the San Pedro storefront that Damon used as local headquarters. Dante met her at the door and gave her a quick tour.

"This is Damon's office when he's in town," he said, pointing to the larger of the two offices. She peeked in the door to see sumptuous rattan furniture and built-in, dark teak bookshelves. He led the way across the hall, ushering her into the smaller office. "This is where you'll have your desk—that is, if you don't mind sharing space with Gabby." He grinned while the women greeted each other. The phone rang in the front office. "Un-Belizable," he said, raising his eyebrows with a comical flourish as he rushed out to answer it.

"Gabriela, what's Dante's job title?" Carole asked, chuckling at his antics.

"Please, call me Gabby," she said with a grin. "All my friends do."

"Okay, Gabby." She smiled back, feeling at ease with her new office mate. "Dante does a little of everything—staffs the front desk, greets people, answers phones, chauffeurs Damon—but what's his actual job?"

"Dante has his real estate license, so I think, technically, he's the agent for Damon's properties, but you have it right. Dante's everyone's go-to man. Whatever you need, he finds it Whatever you need done, he does it—or he knows who'll do it and arranges to have it done for you."

"He sounds like a good person to know," Carole said, admiring the man's low-key professionalism yet entertaining style.

"He's Damon's right-hand man. Has been with him for years." Gabby stood up and patted the desk beside hers. "This is where you'll be sitting. Feel free to use your laptop, or use a thumb drive in this PC. It's got most, if not all, the software you'll need, but if you need anything installed, Dante or I'll get it for you."

"Thanks, Gabby, but I'm only going to be using this desk today and tomorrow. Then I'm on vacation through the Thanksgiving weekend and back to Manhattan Monday." She smiled. "Appreciate your help, but I might as well just use my laptop while I'm here."

"Oh . . . hmmm . . . . " Gabby's voice trailed off. Wearing a confused expression, she scratched her ear as she studied Carole.

"You look surprised."

"I was under the impression you were staying on here. I could have sworn Damon said you'd be working with us."

"That's true," said Carole, "I'll be for these next few days, but I've only signed a short contract with Damon. Then it's back to my job in New York."

"That's too bad. I was looking forward to having an office mate."

Carole smiled, wishing her Manhattan office were as congenial. "Well, you will—for today and tomorrow, anyway." Then she remembered the tight timeline. "By any chance, have you gotten the mattes back from the graphic artist?"

"Yes," Gabby said, returning to her seat. "He sent proofs this morning. Let me forward them to you."

"Great, thanks." Carole breathed a sigh of relief. As pleasant as the surroundings were, she was anxious to complete her contract on time, collect her bonus, and spend her remaining time with Nick. *After all, that's my reason for coming to Belize.*

Carole set up her laptop and viewed the mattes. "I think these will work just fine," she said to Gabby. "Do you like them?"

"They seem to follow the architectural and geographical elements of Tulum," said Gabby, nodding. "From an archaeological perspective, they look realistic."

"Now all we have to do is have Mario film the sites from these angles. Then blend the two scenes, superimposing them, to make it appear to the viewer as if he's traveling back in time, seeing Tulum's ruins when they were new buildings." Grimacing, Carole looked at her watch. "Which reminds me, is Mario scheduled to film today?"

"Yes, he should be shooting footage in Tulum as we speak."

Carole chewed her lip, wondering aloud. "How am I going to coordinate with him if he's in Tulum, and I'm here?"

"Got it covered," said Gabby, beaming. "Damon should be in any minute. He normally checks his mail and has his morning meeting. Then he's planning to fly you over."

"Great." Carole's eyes opened wide, impressed at Gabby's administrative skills. "You're quite the coordinator."

"I've always been the organizer." She grinned, nodding. "Even as a kid, I was the one who arranged the family get-togethers and planned the events. Which reminds me . . . ." She paused dramatically.

Half skeptical, half amused, Carole bit. "Yes?"

"What are you and Nick doing for Thanksgiving?"

"Not sure." Carole shrugged. "He brought it up last night, but we never made a decision."

"Then it's settled," said Gabby with a pert nod. "You're coming to dinner at my place."

Shaking her head, Carole said, "I'd have to check—"

"I won't take no for an answer. Besides, have you ever had a traditional Belizean Thanksgiving dinner?"

Carole grinned. "No, can't say that I have."

"Then you're in for a treat." Beaming, Gabby's eyes lit up. "From an anthropological point of view, it's all very interesting. Thanksgiving's an American holiday, right?"

Carole nodded.

"Ex-pats and vacationing Americans brought the idea with them, but Belizeans accepted the tradition with open arms." She chuckled. "Let me put it this way. The menu's eclectic."

"What can we bring?"

"Your appetites," laughed Gabby. "I'll email you directions and expect you at noon Thursday."

"Okay," said Carole, appreciating Gaby's warm hospitality. Suddenly, she felt the holiday spirit. *Hadn't expected this.* With a delighted laugh, she said, "I'm looking forward to it!"

"Giggling like a bunch of schoolgirls," said Damon, wearing an amused smirk.

The two women immediately sobered. Neither had heard him come in. Realizing how unprofessional they must have looked, Carole said, "Always believe in maintaining office morale." She turned to Gabby with her back to Damon. Using well-modulated tones, she said, "Thank you for scheduling the shoot with Mario this morning." Then, with a wink and a gleeful grin, she whispered, "And for the invite!"

Playing along, Gabby kept a straight face as she nodded cordially. "No problem."

Carole regained her bland smile and turned back to Damon. "I understand you're piloting us to Tulum. When do you want to leave?"

"As soon as you pack your laptop."

Carole closed its top and slid it into its carrying case. "Ready when you are."

Twenty minutes later, they were in the air. Carole looked at the foliage below them. Although the jungle was green, there were so many trees in bloom and colorful birds perching in them that from above, it looked like the trees were turning color.

"With all the red, orange, and yellow flowers and feathers, it reminds me of fall," she said. She thought of Gabby's invitation with a smile. Suddenly, she was in the mood for autumn, Thanksgiving, and the holiday season.

Damon looked at the foliage. "Hadn't noticed it, but it is beautiful." He turned toward her. "You seem to like it here. Do you?"

Cocking her head to the side, she inhaled as she thought about it. She looked out again at the colorful foliage and then at the colors of the sea merging, azure to sapphire to cobalt blue. She thought of Nick and their enjoyable morning together. "Yes, I suppose I do."

He rubbed his nose, his hand only half covering his smirk. "Have you ever thought of staying on here?"

She recalled previous conversations with Nick. "I'd given it some thought, but my job demands that I work in Manhattan."

"Not necessarily." He left his words hanging in the air as he put the plane on auto pilot. Then he turned toward her. "I called Campbell and Glenrock last night."

At the name of her public relations office, Carole's ears perked. She sat up straight, wondering how he had learned its name and why he would have called.

"Really."

"From our earlier dialogue, I suspected you were determined to return to New York, so I took the next logical step. I contracted with Campbell and Glenrock for your services."

Pursing her lips, she made a mental note to call her manager. She needed more than his word to confirm the deal. *And how will that affect our present contract? Damon doesn't inspire trust.* She eyed him skeptically, trying to understand his motives.

As if he reading her thoughts, he said, "That contract begins the day after our initial contract ends." The lines around his eyes creased in a calculating smile. "Don't worry. Deliver on time, and you'll still get your bonus."

"Why are you going to all this trouble?" Raising her eyebrows, she said, "You could hire any number of PR people from Houston. Why go out of your way for me?"

He shrugged. "Simple—I only surround myself with the best. Gabriela's the best at what she does. Dante's the best at what he does. Same goes for Nick, and the same goes for you. Since you weren't willing to work directly for me, I had to find a workaround."

With a scoffing laugh, she crossed her arms over her chest and shook her head. "Got to hand it to you, when you want something, you find a way." She suddenly recalled Gabby's remark about working together. "Who else knows about this arrangement with Campbell and Glenrock?"

"I mentioned to Gabriela that you might be joining us."

She nodded. "What about Nick?"

"What about him?" The lines around his eyes lost their smile.

"I take it you haven't told him." She chuckled to herself, wondering how this would affect their relationship.

Life's strange. Now that I'm on assignment in Belize, will Nick assume I'll stay? Will he think I planned it? Will it enable us to get married? Do I want to live in Belize? Of course, as long as I have a job . . . .

"What?" From his blank stare, she realized that Damon had asked a question.

"How do you feel about it?" he repeated.

Raising her eyebrows, she opened her mouth to speak, but with so many thoughts coursing through her mind, nothing came out. She cleared her throat and tried again.

"It's a bit overwhelming. It changes every facet of my life." The adventure of it appealed to her, and the move would open up opportunities she had not considered. It was the suddenness she resented. "I just wish you'd asked me first, given me time to think about it."

"If you have any misgivings, you can always turn down the assignment." Then he grinned and asked pointedly, "You're a free agent, aren't you?"

She did a double-take at his innuendo. "Not really. How long is this contract? And where would I stay? What about my sublet in New York, my belongings, my life?"

"Let's start with the first, shall we? The contract is for however long you want it to be. It can continue indefinitely or terminate with two weeks' notice on either side."

She nodded. "That sounds reasonable, but what about my apartment in Manhattan? And, if I stay here, where would I live? In the same hotel?"

"Eastwood Enterprises will take care of the living expenses, both here and in New York. Consider it *per diem*."

She thought of her cramped quarters. "The hotel room's one thing for a week or two, but it's quite another for any length of time."

He waved off the question as if it were a gnat. "Eastwood Enterprises owns several furnished condos for entertaining prospective investors. I'll have Dante arrange one of those for you."

She breathed in deeply, letting her mind absorb the details. "Logistically, this might just work."

"Of course, it will," he said confidently. A slow smile crept across his face, almost a sneer.

But what about Nick? How will this affect us?

Carole and Mario reviewed the matte proofs together, choosing the ones best suited for Tulum. To be certain the visual effects would align with the video, Mario shot more scenes of the main buildings from various angles. Once they were satisfied, they previewed it for Damon.

"All that remains are the voiceovers and final editing," said Carole. "There'll be a continual voiceover throughout the video interspersed with cutaway shots that relate to the script. For instance, when the actor describes what Tulum's Citadel looked like when it was new, the clip cuts to shots of the mattes."

"Basically before and after shots," said Damon, nodding.

"Exactly," said Carole. "It'll give the viewer the impression of being here both in the twenty-first and thirteenth centuries."

"Besides footage of the bas-relief figure of the descending god, do we have any other video to reflect Tulum's mythology?" asked Damon.

"Moving from mattes to mats," said Carole, chuckling, "this morning, we're taping a Kundalini yoga class on the beach. Then this afternoon, we're taping bowl meditations, energy healings, and Mayan clay massages."

"Mayan clay massages?" Damon scratched his chin. "What's that?"

"Calling it the Mayan Clay 'Goddess Therapy.' They say mud baths and massages with local clay and honey detoxify the body, reduce wrinkles, regenerate tissue, and even balance your electromagnetic energy field."

"And people pay good money for this?"

"Spas are cropping up all over Tulum, claiming Mayan mud has special healing properties," she said. "Because the clay contains copper, chromium, magnesium, silicon, and zinc, they claim it's therapeutic. Add sun, surf, and self-reflection to that and . . . . Well, here, let me read you what the brochure says. 'Explore your inner goddess. Tap into your deepest potentials. Release your hopes, dreams, and desires in this healing, empowering experience.'"

"Amazing . . . . " Damon's sarcastic tone relayed his thoughts.

She snickered at his sarcasm and matched his irony. "If that appeals to you, here's something I think you'll love. The latest beach therapy is called nesting."

"What?"

"Nesting—you know, like hatching sea turtles. You immerse yourself in powdery Tulum sand, all except for your neck and head. Supposedly," she said, again reading from the brochure, "this sand cocoon lets you feel the pulse of the earth as you participate in an affirmation meditation. At its end, you break free and race into the sea, flushing off your impurities and renewing your spirit."

"And how does this tie in with Tulum's mythology?" asked Damon, rolling his eyes.

"As Gabriela told us, the translation of Kukulcan as the 'sacred coccyx serpent' relates to yoga. Then she found an association between spas and Ix Chel, the Mayan goddess of sacred femininity. Ix Chel was once worshipped here in Tulum, and many consider Tulum to be a 'portal of energy.' Apparently, yoga, spas, and basically anything that enhances the well-being of women thrives here in Ix Chel's shadow."

Chapter Six

The cab dropped Carole off in front of her hotel just as the sun was setting. Bushed after a day of shooting and the commute back to Ambergris Caye, she gazed out to the ocean, watching the last iridescent rays of the sun turn to fuchsia, deep amethyst, and finally charcoal gray as the sun dipped below the horizon. Dusk was her favorite time on the beach. She inhaled the salt air—renewed, reinvigorated—and called Nick.

"Hey, I'm back from Tulum."

"How'd it go?" he asked.

She paused, debating whether to tell him on the phone or in person. "Interesting . . . ."

"Sounds intriguing."

"You could definitely say that. Actually, a lot's happened, and I'd like to get your feedback."

"Okay, are you hungry?"

"Starved."

"Why don't you tell me about it over dinner? Pick you up in a half hour?"

They shared cioppino for two with a loaf of crusty Italian bread for dipping and washed it down with Beliken beer.

Nick listened attentively throughout Carole's summary of Damon's ploy. When she finished, he asked, "What do you plan to do?"

Carole rubbed her forehead, stalling, trying not to appear overly anxious, but she wanted him to speak first. *How can I keep any emotional distance when my future hinges on his response?* She licked her lips and took a deep breath.

"Isn't this the crux of what we've been argu . . . discussing for the past two years? Isn't this what you've wanted? I'm just . . . ." She sighed with a groan. "I don't want you to think I'm giving up my dream and giving in to you."

Oh, that's keeping my cool. Shaking her head, she rolled her eyes, frustrated with herself.

With a sympathetic smile, Nick reached across the table and took her hand in his. "Maybe today's events will simplify matters, put the 'truce' in trousseau."

Her jaw dropped. "Are you saying what I think you are? No, scratch that. Forget I said anything." She waved off the thought with her free hand, trying to appear casual, and then leaned across the table, eye to eye, nose to nose with Nick. "Tell me, what *are* you saying?"

Gently tugging at her hand, he started slowly. "Hey, you're not the only one having trouble expressing yourself tonight."

She laughed nervously.

"This isn't any easier for me than it is for you, but here goes." He took a deep breath and looked into her eyes. "Carole Kennedy, would you—"

"This must be my lucky night."

Stunned to hear Damon's booming voice inches from her ears, Carole flinched.

"Imagine running into two of my favorite people," he said, looking from her to Nick. "Don't tell me. You're celebrating Carole's good fortune." He clapped Nick on the shoulder. "Don't let me interrupt. Y'all have a great evening. See you in the morning, Carole."

Leading two clients, Damon continued on to their table. Carole stared after him, blinking, wondering where he'd come from. He turned back suddenly and caught her watching. His lip curling, his smile looked more like a sneer.

She broke eye contact and turned to Nick. "Let's get out of here. With all these people, suddenly, I . . . ."

He nodded, motioning for the waiter. "The mood's broken." Then he leaned toward her and kissed her nose. "Let's see if we can't fix it with only the moon looking on."

As soon as they left the restaurant they were engulfed in a cool, moist, sea breeze. She heard the whoosh of the palm fronds billowing in the breeze and breathed deeply, inhaling the salt air. With the stars twinkling overhead like tiny Christmas lights, Carole felt the two of them were cocooned in a glimmering fairyland. She reached for his hand, wanting to share their solitude.

Silently, they walked along the beach, listening to the gentle lapping of the waves. Nick pulled her hand around his waist as he put his around hers. Side by side, keeping stride with each other, they strolled toward her hotel.

Finally, Carole turned to him, watching his expression in the moonlight. "What were you about to say to me in the restaurant?"

They slowed their stride until they came to a stop, and Nick turned toward her and embraced her. With one arm around her waist, he put his other around her shoulders.

Lost in the magic of the moment, Carole wrapped her arms around his back, stared up into his eyes, and held her breath.

"Carole, I've been giving this a lot of thought for the past two years, especially these past few days. Now that your job's located here, would you—"

The shrill blasts of Nick's cell phone ringing in her handbag shattered the stillness, reeling her back to reality.

With a frustrated groan, she pulled away from him and began fumbling in her bag for the phone. Finally, her hands connected with it and she pressed a button, silencing the din.

Turning back toward Nick, she mumbled, "Sorry, I didn't think anyone would call me on your cell except you."

She winced as she heard Damon's voice boom from her purse.

"Nick?" questioned the voice, and then louder, "Nick, we seem to have a bad connection. Are you there?"

Her lips pressed together in a grim line, and she debated whether to hang up or hand the phone to Nick. "I meant to turn off the ringer," she whispered. "I must have pressed the speaker button."

Shoulders sagging, Nick held out his hand.

She grimaced and sighed as she handed him the phone. *The moment's gone anyway.*

"Yeah," he growled into the receiver.

"Nick, glad I got hold of you tonight. Got some great news for you. My two associates are interested in a series of dives, starting first thing in the morning. What's your schedule looking like?"

Nick took the conversation off speakerphone and turned away as he worked out the dives' details

Carole stepped away, partly to allow him privacy and partly to hide her disappointment. "The long arm of Damon," she muttered to herself. Dejected, she kicked at the sand. "Can't escape his reach even here. What is it with this guy?"

A high-pitched bark startled her, and she jumped.

Barely visible in the starlight, she saw a small dog sitting under a palm tree, watching her. She took a step toward it, recognizing it as the one she had passed on the beach. "Why, you're not much bigger than a puppy."

It cocked its head and wagged its tail.

She took another step closer. The dog padded toward her on the sand and rolled over on its back, whimpering.

Smiling despite Damon's bad timing, she couldn't resist. She knelt down and started rubbing the young dog's belly. "What a good girl."

"What do you have here?' Nick asked, kneeling beside her.

"Look what just walked over and plopped at my feet." Her chuckle turned into a groan. "With no collar." She looked around the deserted beach. "And no visible owner." She looked into Nick's eyes. "Now what do we do?"

Nick stared at her blankly for a moment. "Are you asking me about the dog or about us?"

"Yes."

"I'm not sure if it's the alignment of the stars—"

"Or Damon's meddling," she interjected, grimacing.

He frowned. "Tonight just doesn't seem to be the right time for us to make any plans."

She studied his face. "You mean because of the interruptions?"

He groaned. "You're not going to like this."

She sucked in her breath, anticipating bad news. "Yes . . . ."

"Damon wants me to take his guests on a night dive."

"What?" Her explosion startled the dog, making her cower. "Sorry, girl," she said, scratching her ears. Then she turned to Nick. "How could you do this?" She stared at him, not believing her ears. "This is the third time since I got here that you're leaving me alone."

"Carole, be fair. If you hadn't answered the phone, I wouldn't have connected with Damon."

She squirmed, knowing it was the truth, yet she was miffed that the evening was ending on a sour note.

"Plus," he said, putting his arm around her shoulders, "this way, I can spend Thanksgiving with you. That was the deal I made with Damon."

"Really?" She put her arms around him and kissed him. "Maybe we can try this again then."

He kissed her back. "Sounds like a plan."

"Almost forgot in the excitement," she said. "Gabby invited—"

"Who?"

"Gabriela. You remember, Damon's assistant. You met her at the beach cleanup."

"Oh, the intern."

Carole nodded. "She invited us to Thanksgiving dinner at noon Thursday." Smiling, she squeezed closer to him. "That would still leave us the evening to ourselves."

"What do you say we continue this then?" Nick started to kiss her, but the dog objected with a high-pitched, puppy bark. "Hey, you," he said, grinning, "no more rivals. I want her all to myself."

The dog playfully growled as she tugged at their clothing.

"I think she's trying to tell us something," said Carole, laughing, still holding onto Nick with one arm and petting the dog with the other.

"What are you going to do with this big puppy?" he asked.

"I'll sneak her into the hotel tonight and put up signs with her picture tomorrow, asking if anyone's lost a dog."

"What'll you do if no one claims her?"

With a determined nod, she made a decision. "Dante will just have to speed up my move into the condo."

"Job, condo, dog," said Nick, grinning. "You've been busy gathering bones today, haven't you?"

Pursing her lips, she surveyed him shrewdly. "Apparently, not *doggedly* enough."

Chuckling, he winced. "That's bad."

Chapter Seven

Wednesday morning, the puppy woke her at dawn, whimpering to go out. Carole pulled on a t-shirt, a pair of jeans, and sandals. She grabbed the phone and keys and carried the puppy outside. Once on the beach, the puppy romped and played, chasing the white foam as each wave lapped against the shore. As the sun rose, they watched the sky light up into a translucent powder blue that contrasted against the aquamarine of the sea. They beachcombed, finding flat, white sea dollars, interesting bits of driftwood, and ridged, speckled clam shells.

"Wouldn't these be great for crafting?" she asked the puppy.

The dog cocked her ears attentively and then barked.

At the sound of childish laughter, Carole's own ears perked. She looked around the empty beach and finally spotted a young girl sitting on a log. Several feet behind the sandy portion, she was almost hidden in the shadows of the trees.

"What's so funny?" Carole called, smiling, recognizing her.

"You are," said the girl, standing up, brushing off her jeans, and walking toward her. "You talk to dogs."

Carole chuckled. "You're right. That *is* funny."

The dusky, woolly-haired girl held out her hand to pet the puppy. "Is this your dog?"

"No, I found her on the beach last night. Do you know her?"

The girl shook her head, the tips of her cornrow braids bouncing. "Uh-unh, there are a lot of dogs here that belong to everybody, nobody." She looked up at Carole. "If you like her, keep her."

"If I can't find her owner, I will." Carole nodded, surprised by the girl's apparent offhand attitude.

"What's her name?"

"I haven't thought of one. What do you think would be a good name for her?"

Just then, the peal of church bells rang through the island, and the girl's eyes lit up mischievously.

"Belle," she said, grinning.

Carole laughed. "A perfect name! Now I'll have to get her a collar with a bell on it so she can 'jingle all the way.'"

"That's a good name, too," said the girl in an innocent attempt at diplomacy.

"What is?"

"Jingles," she said, sitting on the sand and pulling the dog on her lap.

Carole smiled at them, thinking their pose would make a good portrait. "I like your idea better. Belle, it is." Taking out the smartphone, she set down the shells and turned on the camera app. "This will make a cute picture for the 'Found Dog' poster.

The girl looked down at the dog. "If people see me holding the dog, won't they be less likely to claim her?"

"Good thinking," Carole said, impressed with the girl's reasoning. "Tell you what. I'll crop you out of the picture I use for the poster. Say 'Belize.' Belle, look up." She whistled until Belle raised her ears and cocked her head. Then she clicked several shots. "At least one of these ought to make a good close-up."

"She's a great dog," said the girl, petting her. "I hope nobody claims her and you keep her."

"To be honest," said Carole with a wink, "I hope so, too."

Looking at the clam shells, the girl asked, "Do you like shells, Miss?"

"Carole," she said warmly. "Please call me Carole. What's your name?"

"Estrella," said the girl, looking up at her with chocolate-brown eyes. "Do you like shells, Carole?"

"I do, and I thought these would be terrific for crafting."

The girl's eyes lit up. "These would make great Christmas ornaments."

Carole picked up the shells and arranged them in her hand. "If we drilled little holes in them, we could hang them from Christmas trees."

"I know where we can find cowrie and starsnail shells," said Estrella. "There's a cove not far from here."

"I'd really like to go," said Carole, looking at the time on the smartphone, "but I've got to get ready for work. Don't you have to go to school?"

"Not yet." Then her face brightened. "Tomorrow, I'll show you the cove. Be sure to bring a bag for the shells."

"Okay," said Carole, glad for the company. She looked around the area, recognizing the location from the beach cleanup. "Want to meet here?"

The girl nodded. "See you just past sunrise." She put the dog down, stood up, and waved as she retreated toward the trees. "Bye, Belle. Bye, Carole."

Carole waved, but Estrella had disappeared into the trees' shadows before she could say goodbye.

On the walk back to the hotel, Carol tried calling her managing editor again at Campbell and Glenrock. This time, her cell got reception, and she got through.

"Simon, what's going on?"

"That's what I wanted to ask you," he said. "You've certainly made an impression on Eastwood Enterprises. You sly fox, why didn't you tell me you were scouting out new clients?"

"I wasn't. This all came about unexpectedly." She paused. "I just want to be sure this deal is legitimate, and that C&G is onboard with my abrupt move to Belize."

"We ran a Dun & Bradstreet credit report on Eastwood Enterprises. Their D&B rating is 4A, and, as far as we're concerned here at C&G, take the money and run."

She inhaled deeply, glad for the good news. "Thanks for putting my concerns to rest, Simon."

" . . . Just a minute."

She heard muffled voices as Simon held his hand over the receiver.

"Carole, are you still there?"

"Yeah."

"Look, I have to run, but C&G wants you to know how pleased we are with the way you've brought in this new client. Expect a little holiday bonus for your chutzpah."

"Music to my ears, Simon. You have a very happy Thanksgiving, too!"

"Keep up the good work. Talk with you after the holiday."

Carole fed the puppy, showered, and walked into work by nine.

She waved hello to Dante, who was talking on the phone, and said, "Can't beat this commute." Gabby nodded and smiled. Within ten minutes, she had downloaded the pictures, cropped the best close-up of Belle, and printed out twenty-five posters.

"What's this?" asked Gabby, picking up a poster.

"I found a dog on the beach last night." She grinned sheepishly. "I'm hoping no one comes forward, but I have to make an attempt to find her owner."

"Cute dog," said Dante, walking in.

"Do you recognize it?" asked Carole.

"Nope. It looks like fifty others, but cute."

"There are so many stray dogs here," said Gabby, shaking her head, "and not enough homes. This is one lucky pup—and a cutie."

"I'm smitten," said Carole, grinning. "But I have to go through the motions of locating an owner. Would anyone mind if I put up a poster in the front window?"

"Sounds like you're joining us," said Dante. "Hope you know what you're in for."

Carole shot Dante a sharp glance, but then saw he was joking. She chortled. "I'm just swapping one island for another, Ambergris for Manhattan."

"No other differences, right?" mugged Dante, his eyes twinkling.

"It isn't all big city lights, but Belize has a charm of its own." Poster in hand, the dog's picture reminded her of the need to relocate. "Did Damon speak to you about a condo?"

He nodded. "How 'bout we look at it Friday morning?"

"Perfect."

Gabby's computer chimed.

"Hey, guys. Just got the link from the post-production company." She grinned. "Anyone want to see how the video turned out?"

"Let me finish taping up the poster," said Carole, hurrying. "Ready."

The three gathered around Gabby's screen as she clicked the link.

Carole felt butterflies in her stomach. Now that all these plans had been set in motion, what if the video stank, and Damon decided he didn't need her services, after all. *Then I'll just have a paid, two-week vacation. Relax.* She took a deep breath and crossed her fingers. *How did I get so caught up in this venture so quickly? This isn't like me.*

The video opened with sweeping shots of the Caribbean as its viewers glided over its aquamarine waters, wing to wing with crying seagulls. They swept down toward the citadel until they saw sunlight gleaming through its two windows and then turned, gliding just over the waves. The voice-over began with a woman explaining this was the Mayans' ancient lighthouse used to guide mariners through the dangerous coral reefs. The sun lit up the coral just below the water so the viewers could see the path for themselves.

So far, so good. Carole tentatively congratulated herself.

The videography seamlessly led from the beach up to Tulum, capturing the majesty of its architecture. The voice-over talked of the ancient pantheon of gods worshipped at the City of Dawn and how sun worshippers today paid homage.

Using the mattes, the video brought the city to life, depicting the descending god's image in its colorful glory. Then it cut to snippets of a guided LDS tour, bowl meditation, energy healing, Mayan clay massage, and Kundalini yoga class, incorporating the unique energy and spirituality of Tulum.

'Goddess Therapy' was what the well-modulated voice-over called it, mentioning how the translation of *Kukulcan* as the 'sacred coccyx serpent' related to yoga. The voice-over concluded the segment by tying it all in with *Ix Chel*, the Mayan goddess of sacred femininity.

As the video cut to scenes of the Boy Scouts listening to Nick's environmental talk and making the paper-plate turtles, the voice-over discussed the corporate ethics and values behind Eastwood Enterprises, focusing on its active environmental stewardship. It then showed the boys' sped-up beach cleanup and ended with long shots of the pristine island, home of the proposed resort.

"Wow," said Dante, "where do I sign up?" He laughed. "If that doesn't bring in prospective investors, I don't know what will."

Carole grinned. Seeing the finished product reaffirmed her ability to translate marketing concepts into motivating visuals. "Gabby, your research was invaluable. The mysticism, the link to the old gods, is what nailed it." Then her mind moved onto logistics. "Everyone filmed in that video has signed a release, right?"

Gabby nodded as she patted a manila folder on her desk.

"The Boy Scouts, their leaders, the yoga class, everyone interviewed at the spa?" Carole asked. Her eyes narrowed as she mentally rewound the video, seeing every person filmed or interviewed in her mind's eye. Nibbling on her upper lip, she wanted to be sure nothing and no one fell between the cracks. "The last thing we need is for someone to sue us for using their photo without permission." Her mind kept returning to the beach cleanup. *What am I missing?* "What about Nick? Has he signed a waiver?"

Gabby looked through her stack of papers and sheepishly turned to her. "Nope." Then she laughed. "No worries, we'll waylay him tomorrow at Thanksgiving dinner." She turned to Dante. "You're coming, aren't you?"

"I'll try, but Damon might have other plans for me." He snapped his mouth shut with a crooked smile. The phone rang in the front office. "I don't Belize it," he said as he rushed out to answer it. A moment later he returned. "That was the boss," he said, turning toward Carole. "He wants you to know that he saw the video, likes it, and is showing it in Houston this morning. He also said to give you this since he can't be here in person." Dante handed her an envelope.

"Thanks." Curiosity getting the better of her, Carole opened it. Inside were her bonus check and a letter, outlining her next project. "Looks like I've got my marching orders," she said with a crooked smile. "Damon wants us to begin shooting another video on the development site, showing a sped-up time-lapse of the property's development and construction."

Dante grinned. "As long as we have some time today, why don't I show you that condo? Maybe we can get you moved in before Thanksgiving."

Carole looked at Gabby. "Is there anything you need me for here?" she asked.

"I need a dinner guest tomorrow who's settled in and relaxed. Go! Enjoy! I'll see you and Nick tomorrow at noon."

Dante drove Carole to the condo in a converted golf cart.

"Okay," said Carole, grinning, "I know this is San Pedro's main form of transportation, but it still seems strange to ride highways in this contraption."

Dante stopped by one of Eastwood Enterprises' condos. He unlocked the door closest to the road and led her inside the first-floor condo.

Carole took it all in. The floors throughout the condo were Saltillo tile. The living room was paneled with angled boxcar siding. Carole thought it gave the place a cozy den feeling. Rattan and glass-topped living room and dining room furniture, along with a comfy sofa, promised comfortable and low-maintenance living. She immediately felt at home. The completely furnished kitchenette was more than adequate. Louvered shutters provided privacy for the bedroom, and the netting over the king-sized bed made the condo feel tropical.

But it was the portico that charmed her. The semi-enclosed porch in the back, entering onto the beach, caught her eye. Coral and crimson bougainvillea veiled it from the other condos, while palm fronds and clouds of ruby bougainvillea, white frangipani, and blue-green sea grapes secluded it from the beach. With its low fence enclosing the area beyond, Carole knew this was the place for her and Belle.

"It's perfect," said Carole, "especially the portico." She breathed deeply, inhaling the flower-scented, salt air as she looked around. "I can't believe it."

Dante winked. "*Belize* it. I thought you'd like this one. Incidentally, housecleaning comes by twice a week." He grinned. "When can you move in?"

Carole looked up expectantly. "You mean, it's available now? Today?"

He nodded. "Yup."

Instead of an idea, moving from her little hotel room to this charming condo was suddenly an imminent reality. *What a perfect place to spend the holidays.* She grinned, delighted at the prospect. Chuckling, she said, "All I have is Belle and two suitcases to pack. It'll take about ten minutes."

"Then let's hop to it! Here," said Dante, tossing her the keys. "These are yours now."

An hour later, Belle and Carole's belongings were ensconced in the condo. As they pulled up to work in the converted golf cart, Dante turned off the ignition and handed her the keys.

Carole squinted. "What are these for?"

"Your condo's a good twenty-minute walk from here," he said. "Damon wants you to have the use of this while you're at the condo, courtesy of Eastwood Enterprises."

She raised her eyebrows in surprise. "That's a nice perk. Thanks. I wasn't expecting anything like this."

He gave her a lopsided grin. "Eastwood Enterprises has a fleet of 'em for visiting investors. Might as well put this one good use."

Carole called Nick with the good news. "Hey, I moved. I'm probably a fifteen minute walk from your place. Can you come over tonight to see the new place?"

He groaned. "Nothing I'd like better, but I'm still taking Damon's associates on sunset and evening dives."

She stifled a sigh, not wanting him to hear her disappointment. "I thought your series of dives with his associates had ended."

"They had, but this is another round of investors with another round of dives."

This is getting to be a habit. She hesitated, debating whether to shrug off her disappointment or confront Nick. The pregnant pause grew into an awkward moment.

As if sensing her quandary, he added, "I can come by tomorrow morning. Say . . . nine? That'll give us plenty of time to inspect your condo and still get to Gabby's by noon."

"You talked me into it." She breathed a sigh of relief, glad to have avoided a quarrel.

"Good," he said warmly. "Hope I can talk you into something else tomorrow."

She laughed. "Hmmm . . . . It all depends on what you ask me . . . ."

Chapter Eight

Carole woke on Thanksgiving morning, feeling something cold and wet on her nose. She opened her eyes to see Belle's nose in her face. Then she felt the soft lapping of her tongue as the puppy licked her cheek.

"Happy Thanksgiving to you, too," she said, giggling as the puppy's wet kisses tickled her.

Already a routine, she pulled on jeans, a tee, and canvas sneakers, hooked Belle's leash to her new collar, and remembered to grab a plastic bag to collect shells. As they left the condo's portico and began walking, Carole realized they were only five minutes from the cove the scouts had cleaned. She broke into a grin when she spotted Estrella waving to them.

"Ready to find starsnail shells?" called Estrella

"Sure am," Carole called, holding up her empty bag.

"Come on," Estrella said, motioning to follow her into the wooded area that paralleled the shoreline. "I know a shortcut."

Carole trailed behind, ducking beneath low branches and pushing undergrowth out of the way. Belle scouted out and rolled in every muddy spot she could find and then brushed against Carole's legs.

"Where are you taking us?" Carole asked after several minutes of scrambling over craggy rock outcrops and tree roots.

"You'll see," Estrella said, turning her head.

"Is it far?" Knitting her brow, Carole checked her watch, planning her schedule. *Have to get back before Nick arrives at nine. Then we're meeting Gabby at twelve.*

"You've got to let go," said Estrella. "Relax and follow your star."

Carole paused, thinking. "Isn't Estrella Spanish for star?"

The girl grinned. "We should be there in just another minute or two."

Snickering, Carole made a moue. "Mm-hmm, you just want me to follow you."

"Here we are," said Estrella, wearing a cheerful smile and holding back the overhanging branch so it didn't smack Carole. "Watch your head."

Belle ran ahead to investigate. As Carole emerged from the undergrowth, she looked around the hidden cove. Other than the rabbit trail Belle had discovered, no paths appeared to lead to the small beach.

The sound of surging waves crashing against the rocks caught her attention. Judging from the rough surf, Carole surmised the reef didn't extend to this part of the island. White spume topped every breaker like heads on drafted beers. Rough-hewn boulders rose at steep angles to the sea in a crescent pattern around the shoreline, leaving only a tiny patch of sand between surf and stone. Nautically or otherwise, there appeared no easy entry to the private cove.

"This is charming," said Carole, taking in its raw beauty. "Your own little beach."

Estrella smiled.

Carole looked at the smooth, unmarked sand leading to the beach and turned back toward her little friend. "No footprints. This really is an isolated beach."

"Forgotten, not isolated," said Estrella, shaking her head. "Few people remember how to get here anymore."

"How did you ever find it?"

"I followed *my* star . . . ." Estrella grinned as she left her answer hanging.

Carole chuckled. "Seriously, how did you find it?"

When Carole continued to stare, waiting for an answer, the girl suddenly scampered away. "Weren't we going to collect starsnail shells?" With an urchin's smile, she rushed from shell to shell. "Look, here's one, and here's another. Carole, bring your bag!"

Carole held out her bag as Estrella gently deposited each shell in it. Then, taking off her shoes, Carole got caught up in finding her own shells as Belle sniffed and examined every rock and shell. Within half an hour, the bag was full to bursting.

Carole thought of leaving, but the morning and beach were too beautiful to waste. She surveyed the crescent cove, searching for a reason to stay. Just then, Belle started barking at something in a tide pool at the edge of the beach. Crouching, her front legs pushed out in front of her, Belle growled and barked at something in the craggy area.

Estrella and Carole walked toward the tide pool, where the receding sea had left behind a tiny microcosm of sea life—several kinds of clams and sea anemones. Belle was barking at a hermit crab crawling about in an oversized shell.

Getting down on her knees, Carole moved the hermit crab to safety after first inspecting it with Estrella. She laughed as the hermit crab walked across her hand.

"It tickles," she said as she carefully handed it to the young girl.

Cocking her head, Carole looked at her. *She's a free spirit the way I used to be.* She looked down at her bare feet as she knelt at the rocky tide pool's edge and snickered. *What do I mean, 'used to'? I feel like a girl again.*

Then she remembered she had to get ready for Gabby's Thanksgiving dinner and, before that, Nick was coming at nine. She hugged herself, thinking of what he would say, what he would ask.

"What?" Carole said, realizing Estrella had said something.

"I said, 'last one up the hill is a rotten egg'," called Estrella, racing up the sand dune.

Carole laughed as she picked up her bag of shells, pulled on her canvas sneakers, and gave chase.

Five minutes later, she caught up with Estrella and Belle, panting as she scrambled over the craggy rock outcrops and tree roots. They walked silently, Carole and Belle following Estrella's lead until she led them out of the wooded area and back to the beach.

"See you tomorrow morning?" she asked.

"Sure, are you leaving?" Looking around, Carole got her bearings as she recognized the Boy Scouts' cove. Carol looked at the girl, wondering where she went, where she came from. *She looks healthy, but so thin.* "Are you all set for Thanksgiving dinner with your family?"

"I have to go," said Estrella, retreating into the undergrowth. "Remember, follow your star," she called.

"Happy Thanksgiving," Carole called, eyes narrowing as she wondered where she lived, how she lived.

Belle woofed, but the girl was out of sight.

A few minutes later, as they approached the condo, Belle began sniffing a clam shell half buried in sand just in front of the condo's beach entrance.

"What have you got, Belle?" Carol put down her bag of starsnail shells, reached for the clam shell, and caught her breath. It seemed intact. Then she saw the 'shell' was a gold-rimmed case. Her brows furrowing, she looked left and right to see if anyone had dropped it, but the area was empty.

"What have we here?" She gently opened the hinged case and found a gold starfish on a chain. A tiny, typed note read, "Follow your star." She cocked her head and looked around again.

Nick appeared from behind the bougainvillea and sea-grape bushes, grinning, pointing toward the sea.

She raised her eyebrow. "What?"

Silent, pressing his lips together tightly, Nick continued to point toward the sea.

"Why so mysterious?" She narrowed her eyes, trying to give him a stern glance, but her best attempts ended in a girlish giggle.

"Look for yourself."

She walked toward the shoreline and gasped. There, written in the sand, were the words, "Marry me, Carole?" Instead of a heart encircling the words, a star shape surrounded them. She stared, speechless, recalling Estrella's parting words—follow your star.

She had been expecting Nick to propose, but . . . *Now that it's here . . . .* She thought of the waiting, the long weekends, the solitary meals. Gritting her teeth, she recalled the three times this week he had chosen business over her, cutting short their evenings. Then a smile lifted the corner of her mouth as she remembered how he'd dropped what he was doing to help her with the Boy Scouts and the video.

She looked at his face, saw the love in his eyes, and realized why she had waited those lonely nights in New York, why she had turned down dates with other men.

His eyebrows knit quizzically and his eyes smiled, silently asking the question in the sand.

Tears began to form. Cupping her face in her hands, she swallowed hard. Then she reached out to Nick, hugging him. She held tightly onto his shoulders, crying into his chest, inhaling the scent of his sun-warmed shirt.

Nick hugged her back tenderly, returning her tightening grip with his own. When her tears passed, she looked at him, sniffling.

He asked, "Will you take my sand in marriage?"

Her shoulders shaking, her sniffles turning into a paroxysm of laughter, she nodded and said, "Yes."

From his pocket, he took out a smaller gold-rimmed case and opened it so she could see its contents—a diamond ring. He carefully removed it and, easing her from his arms, placed it on her finger.

"It's . . . ." Carole wiped away her tears to better see the ring. "It's a star."

Nick nodded. Wearing a lopsided smile, he said, "The salesgirl called it a star-cluster ring. It's a round, brilliant-cut diamond, surrounded by five pear-shaped diamonds."

She held it up in the sun, admiring its sparkle. "It's beautiful!" She waved her hand to and fro, her eyes following its reflected facets in the sunlight. "I'm following my star." Smiling, she hugged him closer, kissing him, tasting a hint of cinnamon and salt. *What a Thanksgiving.* "Nick, I love you so much."

"I love you," he murmured against her lips. As their kiss ended, he pulled back his head and looked at her, his eyes twinkling almost as much as the ring. "Now, the second most important question . . . ."

'Yes?" she said, eyeing him expectantly. "Don't keep me in suspense."

"When should we set the date?"

She broke into a grin. "The sooner the better. I've been waiting too long as it is."

He picked her up, squeezed her tightly, and twirled her around as Belle growled playfully. "My thoughts exactly," he said, grinning. "How about we follow the Christmas star?"

"A Christmas wedding," she said in a hushed voice. Then she looked into his eyes. "On Christmas Eve?"

"Perfect."

She looked at the shell case in her hand. "Where did you ever find this?"

"The case or the starfish necklace?" he asked, grinning.

"Yes." She grinned back at him. "And this ring . . . where did you get it?"

"A friend of mine's a jeweler. I don't know where the idea came from, but something told me a star motif would appeal to you. Does it?"

She looked at the ring, then looked up into his face and kissed him. "Oh, yes." Remembering Estrella's words, she added, "Maybe even more than you thought." Opening the case, she studied the necklace and then handed it to him. "Would you put this on me?" She turned around and swooped up her hair, presenting her neck to him. Grinning, she said, "I want to dazzle everyone with my starry jewelry."

He chuckled as he fastened the clasp and turned her toward him. Surveying her, he said, "People might compliment your jewelry, but it's the stars in your eyes they'll admire."

At noon, Nick parked his golf cart in front of Gabby's house. Carole carried a fruit salad in one hand and held Belle's leash with the other. Nick toted an ice chest as they walked up to the door and knocked.

"Come in," Gabby said, holding open the door. "What have you got in there?"

"Fresh lobster, caught this morning," Nick said.

"Fire up the grill," Dante called, wearing a chef's apron and emerging from what appeared to be the kitchen. He transferred the spatula to his left hand and shook hands with Nick. "I'm Dante."

"Nick. We met at the beach clean-up."

"Who's this adorable puppy?" asked Gabby, crouching down to pet her.

"This is Belle," said Carole, tightening her grip on the leash.

"And what's this?" asked Gabby, wide-eyed, eye level with the ring. Taking the leash from her, she grabbed Carole's hand and studied the ring. "Is this something new?"

Carole felt the heat rise in her cheeks as she nodded. Everything had happened so quickly—she was unprepared to announce their engagement.

Standing up, Gabby studied the ring as she took the salad from Carole's free hand and handed it to Dante. "When did this happen?"

"About two hours ago," Carole said, finding her voice. She looked at Nick and shuddered.

"The blushing bride to be," said Gabby, grinning. "When's the wedding?"

"Christmas—"

"Christmas! What a perfect time for a wedding!" She gasped. "Oh, I have to be the coordinator." Carole started to demur, but Gabby broke in. "I won't hear another word on the subject. It's decided. I'm going to be your wedding coordinator, and that's that." Focusing on her ring again, she added, "A star . . . I've never seen anything like it. It's gorgeous!" Gabby became serious as her eyes focused on Carole's. "Follow your star."

Carole paused. "You're the third person today to say that."

"Let go, let God."

"You'd better *Belize* her," said Dante, wearing a big grin. "After all, Gabriela means messenger of God."

"How would you know that?" asked Carole, chuckling.

"She's told me enough times."

As they shared a laugh, several other people crowded around to admire Carole's ring. "These are my parents, José and Belén," said Gabby, making introductions. "They live in Tulum and are here for the holiday."

Carole spoke to the couple. "I'm Carole, Gabby's coworker." She turned toward her. "So that's where you stayed when we were shooting in Tulum."

She nodded. "It's very convenient."

"So you're Mexican then, not Belizean?"

Gabby gave a vague smile.

Carole thought she had not heard, so she tried again. "Your English is perfect. I would never have realized Spanish was your first language."

Gabby gave Carole a bland smile. "You haven't met my cousin," she said, pulling over the girl standing behind her. "This is Asunción." After they made introductions, she said, "Dinner should be in about an hour. Carole, Mama, Asunción, let's go into the kitchen. Papá, why don't you take Nick and Dante to clean the lobsters?"

"In that case, you can take this." Dante handed the bowl back to Gabby.

"It's fruit salad," said Carole. "Hope that fits into your menu."

"Perfectly."

"What are we having?"

"Pork *Pibil*—"

Carole repeated it. "What's that?"

Belén said, "It's pork marinated with habanero peppers, wrapped in banana leaves, and baked slowly. Traditionally, it was baked underground like in a Hawaiian luau."

"Sounds wonderful," said Carole, looking forward to sampling Belizean fare.

"We brought *darasa*," said Asunción, "a traditional *Garifuna* dish made of green bananas and coconut milk."

"*Garifuna*," repeated Carole, crinkling her forehead as she wracked her brain. "I'm not familiar with that word."

"The *Garifuna* are descendants of Arawaks and Caribs, South American indigenous tribes, who intermarried with West Africans. Their food is a blend of the various cultures and cuisines," said Gabby.

"Sounds delicious. I didn't realize Belizean cookery was such a melting pot of cultures," said Carole.

"If you're looking for exotic food," said Gabby, a mischievous twinkle in her eye, "we're also having turkey."

"Turkey?" Carole asked. "I didn't know turkey was a traditional Belizean dish."

"It isn't," laughed Gabby. "But with all the expat Americans, the custom's spread to Belize."

"Don't forget the grilled lobster," called Dante.

"It sounds like enough food to feed an army, but there are only six, seven of us," said Carole, counting heads.

"People are just starting to arrive. We're expecting twenty-five for dinner," said Gabby, grinning, "not counting kids."

"With twenty-five side dishes and desserts," said Belén. "It's a small group—only immediate family and a few friends."

Grinning, Carole caught Nick's eye. "We're in for a real treat."

Before dinner, everyone stood as José said grace. Gabby's family ended by crossing themselves while Carole, Nick, and Dante looked on. The scene conjured memories of church when she was a child, and Carole became pensive.

She whispered to Nick, "Maybe we should start going to church?"

Nick shrugged as they lined up buffet-style to serve themselves and then sat down to dinner. Using every chair, stool, and step available, with several nieces and nephews making a picnic of it on a beach blanket, they all found seats. Carole looked at the amiable congregation, smiled at Nick, and squeezed his hand.

Sitting on Carole's other side, Gabby said, "Asunción and her husband, Luis, also work for Damon."

"Really?" said Carole. "I haven't seen you in the office. Where do you work?"

"My husband and I have a delivery service," said Asunción. "As shipments come into Ambergris Caye, we deliver them." She rested her hands on her rounded stomach. "Now that we're expecting our first child, Luis is expanding the business."

"Congratulations," said Carole, her eyes widening as her interest piqued. Instead of an alien topic, the concept of pregnancy sounded suddenly less foreign, less suburban.

"They've just invested in a boat to transport the cargo," Gabby said, affectionately hugging her cousin.

Carole nodded and then peeked at Nick, wondering if they'd be contemplating a family any time soon. *How quickly life can change.*

"Now that tourist season is here, business will be good," said Asunción.

"What do you mean?" asked Carole, switching mental gears. She frowned as she tried to equate cargo transportation with tourism.

"In the US, autumn announces itself with falling leaves and bird migration, right?" Gabby asked, grinning. "Here, we note the changing seasons by the number of tourists. Thanksgiving's the beginning of high season."

"And the more tourists, the more shipments," said Asunción. "Tourism's good for business."

"Guess I hadn't looked at it that way before," said Carole.

"If you thought you hadn't seen much of me before," said Nick, a smile playing at his lips, "watch how busy I'll be during the next seven months."

Taking a deep breath, Carole raised her eyebrows and silently sighed.

"Technically," said Gabby, "June through November is hurricane season—"

"Don't worry," interjected Asunción, winking her reassurance. "August through October is the most likely time for hurricanes, and that's behind us."

"Now we're entering the busiest tourist season—the Christmas holidays," said Gabby. "Basically between Thanksgiving and Epiphany."

"Is Thanksgiving a holiday in Belize?" asked Carole.

"Not really," said Gabby. "Schools and banks are open, but, with the influx of American expats, it's becoming a *de facto* holiday."

"What are all these people doing here if it's not an official holiday?" asked Carole, surveying the group.

"You, Dante, I, and several others are off because we work for American companies. For Asunción, her husband, and many of the others, the reliance on American trade slows down business enough to take a long lunch."

"What about your parents?" asked Carole.

Gabby glanced at them and smiled. "They're nearly retired. One of my brothers all but runs the business for them."

"And tomorrow?" asked Carole. "I take it that's not a holiday here in Belize."

Gabby grinned. "No. I'm told you have the day off because you work for a New York firm, but it's back to the old salt mines for Dante and me."

"And it's back-to-back dives for me " said Nick. "Damon's got me booked solid until well into January."

"I hope you can take off Christmas to marry Carole," said Gabby, feigning concern.

Nick grinned. "A cruise ship of scuba divers couldn't keep me from those coordinates."

"I should hope not," said Carole, leaning over to give him a chaste kiss.

Chapter Nine

Monday, back at the office, Carole showed Damon the layout for the next campaign. As she turned the page, her engagement ring glinted in the morning's light.

"What's this?" he asked, catching her hand to better view the ring. "Do I detect something new?"

Smiling, Carole nodded. "Nick proposed Thanksgiving day."

Damon paused. A smile came to his lips, but his eyes remained hard. "Congratulations." He gave a hollow laugh as he let go of her hand. "Apparently I'm not keeping Nick busy enough if he has time to court you."

Unsure how to respond, Carole tipped her head to one side as she studied him. "They tell me this is the start of the tourist season." She flashed a curt smile.

"Oh, yes, this is just the beginning."

She caught his eye. "You almost make that sound like a threat."

Eyes narrowing, he sneered. "More of a promise." He pressed the intercom button. "Gabby, call the hangar. Tell them to have my plane ready in a half hour."

"Where are you going?" Gabby asked.

"A flyover of the property." Then, as an afterthought, he said, "And tell them to fill the tanks. I may have to fly into Houston later." He clicked off the intercom and raised his voice. "Dante, can you come in here?"

"What's up, boss?" Dante winked at Carole.

"Bring the car around. Carole and I need to go to the airport."

Carole chewed her lip. "Will we be gone long?"

"Maybe." Damon shrugged. "Why?"

"I have to let Belle out—"

"Dante will take care of that, won't you?"

"Sure, boss." Dante grinned as he looked at Carole. "Don't worry about Belle. We're old friends."

"How will you get in?" Carol asked.

"I've got the master key." He gave her a grin. "She'll be just fine."

Carole mentally reviewed the alternatives.

"Would you feel better if I brought her back to the office with me?"

"Yes," she said, the word morphing into a relieved sigh. "Could you watch her until I come back?"

"No *problemo*," said Dante.

"I really appreciate it. Without knowing when I'll be back, I'd hate to have her cooped up waiting for me." She grabbed Dante's shoulder. "Thanks for putting my mind at ease."

"I doubt it'll be necessary," said Dante slowly, as if choosing his words carefully, "but just in case you're late getting back . . . ."

"Yes?" Carole suddenly became concerned. *Dante never beats around the bush.*

He scratched the back of his ear. "Well . . . rest assured, I'll keep her with me until you get back."

What's he not saying? She studied him, trying to read between the lines. *How long does he think I'll be gone?*

She turned toward Damon. "We'll be back before dark, won't we?"

"Sure."

She scrutinized Damon. *He'd spoken a beat too quickly.*

Under her gaze, he added, "I'm not certified to fly at night." Then he added, "Don't forget to bring your laptop."

She turned to Dante, who gave her a reassuring smile. "Like I said, I'll keep her with me 'til you get back."

"Thanks." She rewarded Dante with a grateful smile, relieved that Belle would be in safe hands. *Now if I could only feel that way about myself.*

An hour later, they were in the air, circling the development site. Carol could see the changes occurring before her eyes. Below them, laborers bustled about in earth-moving equipment that looked like Tonka toys.

"Wow," she said, studying the scene. "I can't believe how much work's been accomplished this past week."

"The entire site's nearly cleared and leveled," said Damon as he banked the plane, tipping its right wing for a better view. "Starting tomorrow, they're laying the foundation for phase one."

"That's fast."

"As I said, there's a lot of PR work we need done over the next year or two. Eastwood Enterprises can give you as much business as you can handle." He glanced at her, his expression direct. "That is, *if* you can focus"

She inhaled deeply, reading more than a business proposition in his expression. She moved her eyes from his, turning her head to look at the beach. "It's obvious that you're moving fast."

"What?" He looked at her sharply. Then he glanced below at the site. "Oh, you mean with the construction . . . ." He watched her from the corner of his eye. "Yes, we're right on schedule, which is why I want to ensure you stay . . . focused."

Tired of his innuendoes, she fixed him with a stare. "If you're implying that my engagement to Nick will impact my job performance in any way, you're out of line. I have no difficulty separating business from pleasure."

In answer, he leveled out the plane and set his bearings to northwest.

"Where are we headed?" she asked.

"Houston." With a grin, he added, "It's time you meet the board."

Carole had to think fast. While they were still within range, she texted Nick their destination, adding that they might be back late. She then sent the same information to Gabby, asking her to let Dante know.

An image of Estrella suddenly popped into her mind. With a wistful smile, she wondered why she'd thought of the little girl. *Wish I could let her know . . . know what? That I might not be back for our morning walk?*

Frowning at the disturbing thought, she turned to Damon. "Will this be a short meet-and-greet with the board?"

He shrugged. "I want you to deliver the same campaign presentation that you gave me this morning." He turned toward her with an expression that almost passed for a smile. "That shouldn't take long, should it?"

"Even a full presentation shouldn't last more than an hour." She stared hard at him and tried to keep her tone light. "So we should be back by five."

"Sure."

Again, she had the uneasy feeling that he had answered a little too quickly.

Despite feeling underdressed in her island-casual sundress and sandals, Carole thought her presentation went well. *Almost too well.* Checking the conference-room clock, she had watched the hour hand go around a second time before she finished answering the board's questions about her proposed PR campaign. Nearly two o'clock, and she had not eaten since breakfast.

"Excellent presentation," said the last of the board members, shaking her hand. "Your proposal literally brings a breath of salt air to the project."

"Thank you," she said with a smile, trying to ignore her growling stomach. "I really do appreciate your support."

"Impressive," said Damon with a congratulatory chuckle. Lounging against the corner of the conference table, he crossed his arms. "You've won them over—not an easy accomplishment."

She drew in a deep breath. "That's good to hear." As she tucked the laptop into its case, she added, "I really hadn't prepared a formal presentation—this was just a work-in-progress I thought up over the weekend. I wanted to run it past you this morning for your feedback."

"I think you got your response. I love your idea, and, from all indications, so does the board. Technically, they have to vote on it, but that's a formality. If Jeff called your presentation 'excellent,' the vote's been cast."

"Who's Jeff again?"

"The president of the board, the last member to leave the room." Damon stood up and stretched. "What do you say we have a bite to eat and then fly back to Belize?"

"Okay," she said slowly. "Will that give you enough daylight time to fly back?" Despite her hunger pangs, she added, "I don't mind skipping lunch and heading back now."

"Nonsense," he said, chuckling. "I can hear your stomach growling from over here."

She laughed. "Fruit and yogurt only take you so far."

Holding the door open for her, he added, "Besides, we've got plenty of time."

They lunched at a modest restaurant near the office then caught a cab to the airport. But three miles from their destination, they ran into a detour, complete with bumper-to-bumper traffic. Carole glumly monitored their slow progress, feeling as bleak as the gathering clouds. "At this pace, we'd make better time if we walked," she said, forcing a smile.

Keeping an eye on her watch, she saw three o'clock come and go. She tried to stifle a sigh as the cloud cover increased. Finally, she couldn't stand the suspense any longer. Turning toward Damon, she asked, "What's the go/no-go time?"

He looked at her blankly.

"When's the latest we can leave Houston with enough daylight to return to Ambergris Caye?"

He thought for moment. "Sunset's at about five-fifteen. To be on the safe side, we shouldn't leave any later than three-fifteen."

She showed him her watch. "It's nearly that now."

"How much longer to the airport?" he asked the driver.

The man turned to face them. "That's anyone's guess." He turned back to check the odometer and clock. "It's taken us nearly forty-five minutes to go a mile and a half, and we have another mile and a half left. You do the math."

With a silent groan, Carole slumped in her seat. "At this rate, we won't get to the airport before four o'clock. Suggestions?"

"There's really only one alternative," he said, pausing. "Check into one of the hotels near the airport and fly out first thing in the morning."

Carole felt the heat rise in her cheeks as she noticed the cabbie watching for her response in the rearview mirror. Her eyes narrowing, she turned toward Damon. "How . . . convenient . . . ."

"You don't—" Damon cleared his voice and started again. "You certainly don't think I planned this, do you?"

Snorting sarcastically, she shook her head. "I don't know what to believe at this point. All I can say is I'm *very* disappointed to be detained overnight."

As if she'd slapped him, his cheeks paled. Damon sat up straight and caught the cabbie's eyes reflected in the rearview mirror. "Do you mind?" he said, raising his voice. The driver looked away.

The pupils of his eyes tiny pinpricks, Damon glared at her as he composed himself. Blinking and lowering his voice, he said, "Let me assure you I didn't plan this delay." He gestured to the highway's gridlock. "That is, unless you blame me for the detour."

Her chest heaving, Carole thought of his insistence that they have lunch before leaving. Then she looked at the traffic and detour signs. "No, the detour's out of your control. But flying here and back in one day during daylight hours, even under the best of conditions and especially after leaving so late this morning, is using questionable judgment."

His shoulders rose with a deep sigh. "To be honest, I forgot about the shorter days and daylight savings in Texas." He looked at her with a lopsided grin and raised his right hand. "Regarding your comment about using questionable judgment, guilty as charged." Chuckling, he added, "I throw myself on the mercy of the court."

"I'm concerned about Belle and—"

"Don't worry," Damon said, taking out his cell phone. "I'm calling Dante now. He'll take care of everything." He held up his hand for quiet.

"Dante, Carole and I have been detained in Houston. Can you pet-sit Belle overnight?" He paused as Carole heard a voice answer. "Good. Appreciate it. And can you ask Gabby to make reservations at my usual hotel?" Again Carole heard the hum of a voice. "Yes, that's right . . . two rooms," Damon said, emphasizing *two*, "for tonight only. Thanks. See you in the morning."

Damon hung up and turned to her. Grimacing, chin dipping to his chest, he said, "I really am sorry about this mix-up." He sighed. "You're right. I should have thought it through. Look, at least let me make it up to you with dinner—"

"No, no," she said, shaking her head. "Thanks, but I'll just order from room service."

"No need to hole up. Just meet me in the lobby for a quick bite. Nothing fancy, just the hotel restaurant."

She had to admit, with his forehead all crinkled up, he did look penitent. Taking a deep breath to clear her head, she said, "Why not? Let bygones be bygones."

"Appreciate your understanding. Meet in the lobby at seven?"

Checked into her room, the first thing Carole did was reach for Nick's cell phone. It was out of range, so she picked up the room phone and dialed direct using her call card. "Hi, Nick?" she said, glad to hear his voice. Then she realized it was a new recording. "Very realistic message," she said after the beep. "You might even say lifelike. I was hoping to talk to the real you. Long story short, I'm in Houston and won't be back until tomorrow morning. Call me when you can. Miss you . . . and," she paused, still shy about expressing it over the phone. "Nick, I love you."

As she hung up, she heard a polite knock at the door. *Now what?*

"Who is it?" she called.

"Room service."

I haven't ordered anything. "Just a minute." Skeptical, she peeked through the peephole and saw a maid with a cart.

First locking the safety latch, she cracked the door. "Yes?"

"Champagne," said the woman with a smile, stepping back to show the chilling bottle in the ice bucket. "Compliments of Mr. Eastwood."

Disgusted, Carole noted the two champagne flutes on the cart. She looked up and down the hall, expecting Damon to just happen to pass by, but the hall was empty.

The woman held up a small envelope. "He said to give you this."

Leaving the safety chain latched, Carole took the envelope, opened it, and read the handwritten card.

> *Please accept my sincerest apologies, Carole.*
> *Consider this small token a peace offering.*
> *See you at 7:00.*
> *Damon*

She reread the card, trying to decide if this was a no-strings-attached gift. Again she looked up and down the hall, but Damon was nowhere in sight. Shrugging, she unlatched the safety chain.

As the woman started to wheel the cart into the room, Carole said, "Thanks, I've got it." She grabbed a bill from her purse, handed it to the woman, and started to close the door.

"Don't you want me to open the bottle for you?" The maid stood in the doorway, looking perplexed.

"No, I'm good. Thanks again." Carole quickly shut and locked the door. Half expecting Damon to come knocking, she latched the safety chain as an added precaution. Only then did she take a deep breath. *Why am I so suspicious of him?* She scoffed. *That is, aside from this trumped-up reason to stay overnight in a hotel?*

She rethought her position. The contract with Eastwood Enterprises was what had enabled her to stay in Belize. Basically, it was the reason Nick had proposed. If she broke the contract or allowed anything personal to interfere with her work, it would jeopardize their fast-approaching marriage, her career, and even her country of residence. It would impact every aspect of her life—and Nick's. Eastwood Enterprises also happened to be Nick's biggest customer.

Taking a deep breath, she understood she needed to proceed with caution, but she felt so keyed up. She looked at the champagne and then at the clock. It was two hours until dinner, surely enough time for a glass of wine to wear off.

She decided to open the bottle and try to relax before dinner. She needed to calm down and put things in perspective. The bottle opened with a pop. She slowly poured its fizzing contents into the fluted glass, and then held it up to her lips, enjoying the bubbles as they tickled her nose. She smiled to herself, beginning to relax.

No sooner had she taken a sip than she heard a tap at the door.

No . . . . Shoulders slumping, she silently sighed, dreading a confrontation with Damon. She decided to pretend to not be there. The person tapped at the door again, this time calling out, "Housekeeping."

Still not trusting that it was hotel personnel, she kept quiet.

Then she heard a key in the lock. She crept to the door and peeked through the keyhole. A uniformed man was trying to open the door.

"Yes," she called in a stern voice.

"Apologies, ma'am," said the man, removing the key, and holding up fluffy, oversized towels. "I thought your room was empty. I was just delivering extra bath towels."

"I'll take them." She set down her glass, cracked the door, and beneath the latched safety chain took the towels from the man.

"Sorry again for disturbing you, ma'am," said the man.

"Thanks," she said curtly, shutting and locking the door.

This is ridiculous. I'm getting paranoid. Maybe reading will help me relax.

She took another sip of champagne, grabbed her laptop, sat on the bed, and read until dinner.

At seven o'clock, she stepped off the elevator into the lobby. She still felt apprehensive about meeting him for dinner but figured little could happen in the hotel's restaurant.

Damon was seated, waiting for her.

Rising, he said, "Right on time."

"I believe in punctuality," she said sarcastically.

"Ouch," he said, wincing. "Guess I deserve that." He grinned. "Are you hungry?"

Analyzing his open smile, she detected no hidden agenda, no innuendoes. He simply looked like a coworker meeting her for dinner on a business trip. She decided it was safe to drop her guard.

"Sure."

"This way," he said, extending his arm, pointing.

She smiled and started to walk into the restaurant.

"No, this way," he said, indicating the main door beyond the restaurant.

She narrowed her eyes, scrutinizing him. "I thought you said we were eating in the hotel restaurant."

He grinned mischievously. "No, I said we were eating in *a* hotel restaurant. I didn't specify which one."

Cocking her head to one side, she said, "What are you trying to pull?"

"Nothing," he said, holding out his arms. "What? This is simply a misunderstanding. You thought I said 'the' restaurant, but I said 'a' restaurant. What's the big deal?"

Rolling her eyes, she let out an exasperated groan. "Look, room service is sounding like the wiser choice at this point. Why don't I say good night, forget this ever happened, and meet you right here in the morning for our flight back?" She gave him a curt smile and turned on her heel.

"Oh, come on, Carole. Don't be unreasonable. We're simply going for a bite to eat, nothing more."

She hesitated, debating if she was overreacting.

"Besides, you haven't lived if you haven't had steak at Brayburns. Prime beef, choice cuts, aged to perfection." He smacked his lips. "The best in Texas."

Her back still to him, she sighed as she fought a mental dispute.

"Come on, don't make me eat alone. Please?"

His voice sounded earnest, even pleading. *Could he simply be lonely?* She turned to see his expression.

"Thank you," he said with a slight bow. "I'm sorry. I guess I'm just making one blunder after another." He scratched his forehead and sighed. "All I wanted to do is to make up for the delay, and instead I'm putting you on the defensive. My apologies." Chin to his chest, he stood back. "If you'd feel more comfortable eating in your room, I completely understand."

She looked at his humble posture and sighed. "Maybe I've been too hasty," she said, pursing her lips. "Sure. If you want to eat at another restaurant, fine. Let's go." She forced a smile.

"You mean that?"

"Yeah," she said hesitantly. Then realizing how hollow it sounded, she repeated it, forcing enthusiasm she far from felt.

"Wonderful. Thanks, Carole." He smiled warmly. "This way." He rushed ahead of the doorman to open the main door for her.

As she stepped outside, she saw a silver, Hummer stretch limousine. A uniformed chauffeur hopped to attention when he spotted Damon and opened the passenger door to the executive area.

Sharply inhaling, glaring, she turned to him. *Now what's he up to?*

Hunching his shoulders, he innocently spread out his arms at his sides. "It's the least I could do, Carole. I just wanted to give you a comfortable ride to and from dinner. That's all." When she continued to scowl, he added, "What?"

With an exasperated grunt, she asked, "How stupid do you think I am?" Not waiting for an answer, she tried to push past him into the lobby.

He blocked her way. "Carole, it's not what you think. I simply wanted you to enjoy Brayburns in style. Look, if it makes you feel any better, I'll dismiss the limo and have the doorman call us a cab." His eyes wide as he appealed to her, he said, "Whatever you want. Your call."

Biting her lip, she heaved a silent sigh. *This is ridiculous*. She grimaced and said, "Good night." Pushing past him back into the lobby, she heard him tell the doorman to call a cab.

Rolling her eyes, she hesitated, but then continued toward the elevator.

"Carole, I'm doing what you want. Please don't make a scene," he called loudly.

Heads turned. Conversations stopped.

She was suddenly aware of the eyes watching their drama—the doorman's, the chauffeur's, and those of several guests coming into and leaving the lobby. Upset by the embarrassing position he had put her in, she paused mid-step, debating whether to simply walk away and risk him making a bigger scene here—or worse, retaliating in the workplace—or to quietly get into the limo and drive off.

She did an about-face. Glaring at him as he smugly held the hotel door open for her, she took the chauffeur's extended hand as she stepped into the limo's interior.

She felt compromised, realizing he had orchestrated her unwilling consent. He had outmaneuvered her, and she resented it. She sat on the hand-tooled, leather upholstery smoldering, her chest silently heaving. Discreetly defiant, she refused to speak to or look at him.

Teeth grinding, she studied the limo's interior. Custom woodwork lined one side. An inset bar was set up with champagne chilling on ice. A row of hand-cut cup holders protected the monogrammed glasses. A folded napkin imprinted in silver with the logo Hi Ho Silver, Inc. peeked out of each fluted glass. A stereo system played Willie Nelson in the background.

Lips pursed, Carole fumed. She pulled Nick's phone out of her bag and then put it back, recalling its reception did not extend to Texas. All she wanted was to be back in Belize with Nick.

Then it occurred to her. *That's why I'm doing this.* By trying to maintain the status quo and not upset the applecart, she was protecting her situation and her relationship with Nick. She breathed deeply, letting that knowledge seep into her soul.

"That's better," said Damon, smiling, reaching for the champagne. "You're relaxing. Good."

The man's an imbecile—a master at manipulation, but an imbecile.

She averted her eyes and studied the matched pair of cylindrical aquariums on the bar. Backlit with black lights, they cast an eerie glow as the shadows of the fish swam past. They reminded her of Nick. He'd know what kind of fish they were. Missing him, she swallowed the lump in her throat.

As she hunched her shoulders, she looked down and noticed the polished wood flooring. She shook her head, wondering how much this debacle was costing Damon, or rather, how much it was costing the company. *What a waste.*

"Here you go," he said, holding out a glass of champagne.

She glowered at him.

"Go on, take it. You're here. You might as well enjoy it."

"Pu-lease." Her lip curled as she spoke.

"Come on, Carole. All we're doing is going to dinner in style. Lighten up."

She chewed her lip—wanting the ride, the dinner, the night to be over. Yet she hesitated, debating. *Do I play along? Do I pretend to cooperate? If so, to what degree?*

As if sensing a change in attitude, he again held out the champagne flute, this time with a napkin.

She debated, staring at the napkin's logo until it was imprinted on her brain. Then drawing a deep breath, her lips taut, she gave him the semblance of a smile as she finally accepted the glass. She took small pleasure in letting the napkin flutter to the floor, wishing she had the moxie to drop the glass instead.

"To a great evening," he said, clinking his glass against hers. He tipped his head and finished the wine.

She made no move.

"Come on, Carole. Drink up." He refilled his glass and tried to top off hers, but she covered the glass with her hand. "Don't be such a party pooper, Carole."

His repeated use of her name irked her. She recognized the standard technique for business intimidation.

"Damon, I'm simply not thirsty, Damon. So Damon, why do you keep asking me, Damon?" She sneered at him.

He grinned. "Busted." He shook his head. "You're too fast for me, Car—"

She glared at him.

"You know the game too well," he said, chuckling. "I like that. You keep me on my toes." His tone changed along with his expression. "Seriously, I admire your business acumen." Raising his eyebrow in punctuation, he clinked his glass against hers. "Let's drink to your success. You wowed the board today, and it takes a lot to impress that group."

She tried to read him. Taking her cues, she decided this was the extent to which she would play along. Clinking her class against his, she put its rim to her lips without so much as tasting the champagne.

It seemed to be enough. He reverted to his usual business behavior.

Watching his response, she concluded it was the right tact, the right amount of mock cooperation.

The restaurant gleamed—from its polished aluminum, mirror, and Plexiglas walls to its contemporary chandeliers. Every surface shone. Linen tablecloths and globes of giant blue hydrangea graced the round tables. One waiter held her chair for her while another opened their oversized napkins.

A polished aluminum ice bucket with a chilled bottle of champagne instantly appeared. A third waiter poured their wine while a fourth handed them menus.

Carole glanced at the other patrons in formal evening wear. Still in her casual sundress, she felt underdressed and out of place. *Haven't ordered yet, and I wish the night was over.* She sighed grimly.

"Would you care for an appetizer while you decide?" asked the waiter.

Looking at the menu, Damon said, "Let's start with an order of the Chile Calamari." He lifted his eyes above his menu to look at her.

Carole stifled another sigh as she ducked behind her massive menu.

"Very good, sir." He left with a nod as another waiter poured their water.

"Here's to a great evening," he said.

She peeked over her menu.

Holding up his glass, he said, "To a memorable evening."

"Cheers," she muttered, not making a move toward her glass.

He gulped his champagne and set down his glass. "What looks good?"

She mumbled under her breath.

"I know what looks good to me . . . ."

She couldn't let the tone of his words pass unexamined. Raising her eyebrow, she peered at him over her menu.

His eyes twinkled as he said, "The dry-aged prime rib."

With a grunt, she returned to her menu.

The waiter placed a small saucer in front of each of them and a sizzling platter of calamari between them. Another waiter refilled Damon's glass.

"Do you like squid?" he asked. When she didn't answer, he smiled mischievously. "I've found calamari a better aphrodisiac than oysters. Have some."

Rolling her eyes, she said, "No thanks."

He raised his champagne flute. "To us."

"Cheers," she repeated. She set down her menu, picked up her water glass, and took a sip.

"Come on, Carole, loosen up." He drained his glass. "Have some champagne."

"I'm the designated driver." She smiled blandly.

He chuckled as the waiter refilled his glass.

"Can I take your orders?" asked the waiter, looking first at Carole.

"I'll have the petite filet mignon," she said, handing him her menu.

"And for you, sir?"

Damon looked at her before answering. "Hold off on the entrées until we finish the calamari." He paused. "What kind of oysters have you got?"

"Oysters on the half-shell with tarragon mignonette, sir."

"Bring us an order of that next." His eyes met hers.

"Please bring my entrée when you bring the gentleman's hors d'oeuvres," she instructed the waiter.

"What's the matter?" asked Damon, his eyes glittering coldly. "Aren't you in the mood for," he paused, "seafood?'

She rolled her eyes. *It's going to be a long night.*

"A little more coffee, sir?" asked the waiter, setting a plate with two chocolate mints between them.

Damon held up his hand. "No, thanks, I believe I've had enough." He turned to her. "Carole, would you like more coffee?"

Resting her chin in her hand, she shook her head. With her other hand, she checked her cell phone. *Nearly nine o'clock.* She stifled a yawn.

"In that case, are you ready to go?"

She opened her eyes wide, glad to end the evening. "Oh, yes."

As she pushed back her chair, Damon said, "On second thought, I'd like an after-dinner drink." Turning to the waiter, he said, "Bring us a list, would you?"

"Certainly, sir," said the waiter.

Carole slumped back in her chair.

Draining his champagne flute, Damon said, "Drink up. You haven't touched your first glass." He inspected her glass. "I see the problem. It's flat. Waiter," he called. "Bring us another champagne flute."

"Yes, sir."

"No, I don't want any more champagne. In fact, I don't . . . ." Curbing her annoyance, she simply said, "I just want to leave."

"After-dinner drinks to cap off the meal, and then we'll be on our way," he said.

What a control freak. She gathered her purse and stood.

"Sit down."

"Your power plays are getting old. Good night." With a curt smile, she turned toward the door.

"Where do you think you're going?" he shouted.

She held her head high as she tried to ignore the stares. "Please call me a cab," she told the maitre d'.

"There's a line of taxis idling in front of the restaurant, ma'am."

"No need," said Damon's voice as he grabbed her arm from behind.

She wrenched it away.

The maitre d' said, "If the lady wants to leave—"

"She's leaving," said Damon, "with me." Handing him a fifty, he added, "Now have my car brought around."

The maitre d' hesitated. "Ma'am, are you all right?"

She looked at Damon, trying to read him. Then she nodded to the maitre d'. "I'll be fine."

"Whatever you say, ma'am."

As he walked away, she turned to Damon. "Enough is enough."

"What do you mean?"

Tempted to tell him what to do with his contract, she composed her thoughts and thought it wiser to wait. *I still have to get back to Belize.* "We can discuss it in the morning. For now, just take me to the hotel."

"Now you're talking, sweet thing." Winking, he ran his hand up her arm.

"That's it!" Recoiling from his grip, she stomped out the door and found the line of taxis. She jumped in the first one, telling the cabbie the name of the hotel and to hurry. Just as Damon put his hand on the door, she said, "Step on it," and the cab lurched away.

Carole grunted as she lip-read his profanity through the back window.

Chapter ten

The next morning, Carole watched as Damon entered the coffee shop. As their eyes met, she steeled herself as he approached her table.

Hand combing his hair, he said, "Carole, I am so sorry. I don't know what got into me last night." He brushed his tousled bangs off his forehead. "I had too much to drink, and I behaved badly. I'm so sorry."

After having had several hours to think it over, she knew what she had to do.

"Mr. Eastwood, I don't see how we can maintain a business relationship after last night." Carole spoke quietly, allowing no emotion to enter her words. "C&G opens in ten minutes. I'm going to request that they send another manager to handle your account since I can no longer be contracted to Eastwood Enterprises." She breathed deeply. *Then somehow I have to work things out with Nick.*

He nodded. "I see."

"Of course, if you'd prefer to cancel the account, that's entirely your prerogative."

Again he nodded slowly, one eyebrow raised, apparently considering the option. "Are you planning on staying in the States, or do you trust me enough to fly you back to Belize?"

She wished he hadn't phrased it that way. Trust was not in the equation. She took a deep breath, collecting her thoughts. "I need to move out of the condo as soon as possible. It would certainly speed up the process if I flew back with you."

"There's no need to move—"

"Actually, there is."

Grimacing, his mouth downturned, he stared at his hands. "Okay, I'll meet you in the lobby in forty-five minutes." With a departing nod, he left the coffee shop.

I knew this account was too good to last. Carole sighed. *But how's this turn of events going to affect Nick's and my wedding plans?*

She had called him after returning from the steakhouse, but there was no answer. Then she had thought of emailing him the whole story, but decided it would be better to tell him in person. She wanted to see the expression on his face.

Finishing her coffee, she headed to her room to use the hotel phone.

She dialed C&G, dreading the impending conversation. "Good morning, Simon."

"Carole, you're up bright and early, but then, from what I'm hearing, you've been putting in a lot of extra hours on this new account."

"Yeah . . . ." Pausing, she chose her words carefully. "That's what I'm calling about."

"You don't sound very enthusiastic."

"Well—"

"If it were me, I'd be bouncing off the rafters."

She squinted. "What are you talking about?"

"Don't tell me you haven't heard . . . ."

She shook her head. "Heard what?"

"I just got off the phone with Jeff Winthrop, the president of the board of Eastwood Enterprises."

She frowned, trying to recall their brief conversation. "What was he calling about?"

"He couldn't stop talking about your presentation yesterday regarding your new campaign."

"You're kidding, right?"

"Not in the least." He chuckled. "In fact, Winthrop doubled Eastwood Enterprises' PR budget, and . . . ." He paused dramatically, leading in with a flourish. "*Ta-da*, on their behalf, he authorized issuing you a 10K bonus."

This was not the conversation she had expected. She opened her mouth, but no words escaped.

"Say something already."

"Simon, I called to suggest that another manager handle their account—"

"Oh, no—he was very specific. He wants you, and you alone, to head up the campaign."

What's Damon up to now? She drew in her breath. "I believe it would be better for everyone concerned if I stay in the background on this one. I'll plan it—even orchestrate the campaign—but someone else will have to implement it."

"No dice, Carole. Winthrop was adamant. Eastwood Enterprises is open to every suggestion but one. Their only caveat is that you remain onsite throughout the campaign." He paused. "And they hold all the cards."

In her mind's eye, she saw tiny spider threads encircling her ankles. Each filament could be easily brushed aside, but interwoven, intertwined, they were tightening into a web. She had the sensation of golden threads wrapping her in an inescapable cocoon. *Fight or flight?* All her instincts told her to run.

She shook her head. "Simon, I wouldn't broach this if I didn't feel strongly about it. Without going into detail, I'll simply say that I can't stay onsite any longer."

"That's final?"

"That's final."

He sighed. In the ensuing pause, she could almost hear the wheels of his mind grinding. Finally, he said, "I don't want to force your hand, but I have to play my ace in the hole."

"What do you mean?"

He started slowly. "You know C&G's a public company, right?"

"Yeah, so?"

"As of last week, Eastwood Enterprises bought the controlling shares. They hold all the aces."

Carole felt a sudden throbbing at her temples. Squeezing them between her thumb and forefinger, she closed her eyes and tried to understand.

"Okay, let me restate what I think you just said. Eastwood Enterprises bought out C&G—"

"Uh-huh."

"Basically, you're telling me that I report directly to its president, Jeff Winthrop."

"Not quite . . . you report directly to its owner, Damon Eastwood."

"No!" She felt the blood draining from her cheeks.

"Oh, yeah—he's the one holding all the cards."

She felt the golden threads uniting, merging into ever-tightening shackles around her ankles.

"So all the years, all the work I've put into C&G don't count for anything?"

"Sure they do. That's what's gotten you to this point. You've come up trumps. If it weren't for you, Eastwood Enterprises would never have heard of C&G."

"So I'm the one responsible for this." She snickered. "That doesn't make me feel any better."

"You should be proud of yourself, Carole."

"Proud isn't the word for what I feel." The pounding at her temples increased. She rubbed her forehead, trying to think what to do.

"You've been dealt a winning hand," said Simon.

"I don't feel like a winner." She paused, biting her lip. "I'm not sure what to do."

"Simply play cards."

"Play cards," she said dryly. "Oh, Damon would like me to play cards, all right."

"Look, you've got a winning hand," he said. "Play it out."

She took a deep breath. "I can't work on this account, Simon. Like I said, I'll plan its campaign and coordinate it, but let some someone else implement it. Let me work on my other accounts."

"I'll lay my cards on the table." He sighed. "A re-org's already underway."

Reorganization. She knew only too well what that meant—out with the old, and in with the new account managers. Tuning out the rest of his words, she realized she was now facing two specters if she left Belize and the Eastwood account—probably unemployment and potentially a broken engagement.

"Play the hand you're dealt. Hitch your wagon to this star."

His words cut into her thoughts. "What did you say?"

"I said, play the hand you're dealt."

"No, the other thing."

"Hitch your wagon to this star?"

"Yes, that's it."

The words reminded her of Estrella's advice—'let go and follow your star.' *Maybe this is all part of a plan. Maybe I need to let go, play the hand I'm dealt.* She took a deep breath. Suddenly, she felt safer, less vulnerable.

"So make your play. What are you going to do?"

She paused, asking herself the same question. Letting go was not easy. In the past, letting go had always meant giving in, giving up. In this case, it hinted at the distinct probability of being let go if she didn't cooperate. She disliked surrender and extortion equally.

"Carole, you're forcing my hand." He took a deep breath. "Okay, if it's this hard a decision for you, I'll up the ante." He took another deep breath. "Winthrop authorized issuing you a 12K bonus."

"I thought you said ten."

"I did, but I was bluffing."

She now felt unable even to trust her managing editor.

"Okay, *okay*, a 15K bonus, and that's my final offer. Take it or leave it."

"What?" Suddenly an image of Estrella flashed through her mind. In the vision, the girl was grinning, nodding. Interpreting it as a sign, a sense of direction, Carole smiled inwardly, willing to see where 'letting go' led. As relief flooded her, she started chuckling, then laughing.

"I'll take that as a 'yes.'" He gave an exasperated sigh. "Anyone ever tell you you're a born poker player?"

Damon met her in the lobby as she stepped off the elevator. Carole stared at him, waiting for him to speak first. He stared back as if waiting for her to make the first move. She wondered if Simon had called him about her decision, but she refused to play his game.

Instead she asked, "Catch a cab to the hanger?"

His eyes opened momentarily in surprise, and then heavy-lidded, he smiled crookedly, extending his hand toward the door. "After you."

Their working relationship needed definition with parameters firmly set in place, but Carole was beginning to view the concept of 'letting go' as a challenge. She wanted to see where her star led.

Inside the cab, Carole turned to him. "We need to get something straight."

"And what's that?" His eyes flickered in amusement as a lopsided smile crossed his lips and just as quickly passed.

"If you and Eastwood Enterprises want me to continue with this campaign, our relationship needs to be strictly confined to business. Are we clear on that?"

"Perfectly," he said, a hint of a smile gleaming in his eyes. Then his demeanor changed. Rubbing the back of his neck, he winced. He took a deep breath and met her eyes directly. "Look, about last night, I truly am sorry. I had too much to drink, and I was way out of line."

"That's the truth," she said. Uncomfortable, she felt her shoulders tensing.

"You have my word that I'll never try anything like that again." He looked somberly into her eyes. "Can you forgive me?"

She shrugged. She wanted to make her point, but the sooner they could get past this awkward moment and return to their previous business association, the better. "Sure," she said too quickly. "Let's let bygones be bygones." Her words sounded more magnanimous than intended. She pursed her lips, annoyed with herself.

"I'm glad you said that." His eyes softening, he smiled. "Those are my feelings exactly. Maybe the less said about last night, the better . . . for everyone involved . . . ."

She immediately thought of Nick. *What will I tell him?* If he knew what had happened, it would upset his business relationship with Damon and could morph into changed perceptions in their relationship—as well as her working relationship with Damon, Eastwood Enterprises, and C&G. She sighed. *This is getting tangled.*

She debated whether it was better to confide in Nick or keep it to herself. *Would discretion protect their peace of mind, protect their engagement?* She looked at Damon. Wide-eyed, he stared back at her earnestly as he listened for her answer.

"As long as it's in the past and never happens again . . . sure. As I said, let's let bygones be bygones."

A smile flickered at his lips and built until it lit up his face. He tenuously held out his hand. Reluctantly, she shook it lightly. Before she could let go, he gave her hand a subtle squeeze.

She recoiled instantly, drawing her fingertips into an enclosed fist and bringing it close to her chest. She studied his face for any indication of sexual overtures, but he had closed his eyes, appearing immersed in the moment.

When he opened them, he smiled innocently and nodded his head, almost in a bow. "Thank you."

She pursed her lips, trying to dismiss his grasp as her misinterpretation. "Now, about moving out of the condo, if Dante could—"

"Nonsense, there's no need to make any changes." He shook his head. "Nothing's happened, so let's simply continue status quo, shall we?" When she didn't answer, he lifted an eyebrow. "Deal?"

She worked her jaw, unsure.

"Deal?" he repeated, his eyes drilling into hers.

"Okay," she said finally, making a mental note to put chain locks on the doors.

That night, Nick char-grilled fresh tuna steaks, corn in the husk, and fingerling potatoes on the gas grill. They ate on the patio, watching the sun set over the sea. As the garnet-red sky turned deep amethyst, the stars began twinkling in the twilight.

Carole breathed in the fresh salt air, its scent intermingling with the bougainvillea and plumeria surrounding the patio. Belle curled up at her feet, Nick beside her, she sighed, feeling safe and secure for the first time in days.

"So how was your trip to Houston," he asked, slipping Belle a piece of tuna under the table.

"Where do I begin?" She thought about it for the tenth, hundredth time that day. *How much do I tell?* She shuddered. The perfect evening suddenly seemed chilled.

"Why don't you begin at the beginning?"

She told him about the whirlwind decision to fly to Houston, the presentation, the president of the board's apparent interest in her campaign. She went into detail about C&G's buy-out and the bonus. What she left out was Damon's behavior at dinner and his behind-the-scenes orchestration.

Shoulders drooping, she searched her conscience. Although she had done nothing wrong, she felt guilty and ashamed for not confiding in Nick. Discretion had seemed the better course under the circumstances, and she'd given Damon her word, but was it the better part of valor?

"You don't look very happy about it," Nick said, reaching for her hand.

"Just tired, I guess." She pursed her lips. *Another fib . . . or a lie?*

"I've missed you, you know." Swinging her by her hand, he pulled her into his arms, tilted back her head, and looked into her eyes. "I'm in love with you, Carole. Have been since we met. I'm just so glad we're together, finally. So glad things worked out the way they did." He kissed her gently, slowly, beginning at her neck and working his way to her lips.

His breath tickled, and she sighed, enjoying his nearness, his closeness. Yet his words nagged at her conscience. Whether or not she had done anything wrong, concealing Damon's lack of judgment from Nick made her complicit. She tried to swallow, but a lump prevented it. Instead of being happy in Nick's arms, she felt like crying.

Damon was stealing the joy from the moment. She cleared her throat, trying to rid herself of the guilt.

"Do you need a drink?" Nick asked.

His words broke into her internal conversation. "What?" She looked at him blankly. "Oh, no, I'm fine."

Tipping back his head, he peered at her skeptically. "You seem a million miles away. Is anything wrong?"

"No," she said quickly. Uncomfortable with his questions, she was anxious to get off the subject. She cleared her throat again, trying to swallow.

"Are you coming down with a cold?"

She hesitated. "Uhm, maybe. Yes, that's what it is." she said. She bit her lip. *Another white lie—I can't stand this.* She groaned inwardly. Withholding from him wasn't worth it. Taking a deep breath, she decided to get it off her chest. "Something happened that I—"

Nick's cell phone rang.

She tried to ignore it, but earlier, she had turned up the ringer. "Nick, I wasn't—"

Its shrill sound cut into her thoughts.

"Are you going to get that?" He loosened his grip on her shoulders.

She heaved a frustrated sigh. "No, first I really need to tell—"

The phone stopped mid-ring. She inhaled deeply and started again. "Last night—"

Belle gave a low, warning growl. Her fur bristling on the back of her neck, she began barking.

"What's wrong, girl?"

"Hello," said Damon, approaching the patio from the beach. In the twilight, she had not seen him coming through the bougainvillea and plumeria. He looked from her to Nick and back. "Hope I'm not intruding. I tried calling," he held up the phone, "but got no answer."

Then why did you come to the back door? She stifled a frustrated sigh as she shushed Belle.

Nick let go of her shoulders. Putting on a bland smile, he said, "No, we're just relaxing after dinner. Can I get you a beer?"

Looking at Carole, Damon said, "Sure."

Nick started to get up, but Carole said, "I'll get it."

When she returned a moment later, Nick asked, "Why didn't you tell me you had dinner at Brayburns?"

Her eyes flashed. She scowled at Damon, furious with him for first putting her through a guilt trip and then putting her on the spot.

"Brayburns has the best steaks in Houston," continued Nick. "I go there whenever I'm in town."

"Didn't realize you knew about it," she said, trying to recover from the jolt. She glared at Damon as she handed him the beer. *Thanks for opening that can of worms.* "Here, why don't you open this can, too."

"Thanks." Damon's eyes twinkled as if amused.

Carole debated whether to share the whole story now or wait until after Damon left. Discretion winning again, she sat beside Nick.

"What's so important that you stopped by?" She didn't care if it sounded impolite. She resented his intrusion. She wanted him to state his business and leave.

Damon's manner changed. Dropping his smirk, he became serious. "Carole, I wanted you to be the first to know, and, Nick, this applies to you, as well." Turning toward her, he said, "In no small part thanks to your video and presentation, Eastwood Enterprises has successfully completed its round-one funding for resort development of Paradise Harbor, raising its $50 million target. With an overall projection of $250 million, early indications look extremely positive for the project's second round."

"Congratulations," said Nick, hugging her.

Carole nodded modestly. Although proud of her role, she did not want to display any enthusiasm in front of Damon. She didn't trust his motives.

He turned toward Nick. "This is going to affect your business directly."

"How so?"

"For starters," said Damon, "the number of prospective investors will be quintupling, and that's only during construction. Once Paradise Harbor is completed, you'll have a steady stream of tourists and year-round retirees eager for your diving and snorkeling services. If you've ever thought of expanding, now's the time."

"Quintupling . . . ." Nick scratched his chin.

"I'm not exaggerating this opportunity. If you need any working capital to purchase another boat or remodel your dive shop, consider me your silent partner." Damon held out his hand.

"Thanks for the offer," Nick said, making no move to shake on the deal. He caught Carole's eye. "My partner and I need to talk it over." Then he turned back to Damon. "We'll let you know."

Maintaining a genial smile, Damon withdrew his hand. "Of course, wouldn't have it any other way." He drained his beer and stood. "My job here is done. Again, congratulations, Carole. Your expertise is what sparked this resort project to life." He turned back to Nick. "You're a lucky man, my friend."

Standing, Nick shook hands. "I realize that." He smiled warmly at Carole.

"See you tomorrow," she called as Damon retreated to the beach.

Nick sat down beside her, putting his arm around her.

When Belle relaxed, and she felt sure Damon was out of hearing range, she asked, "What do you make of that?"

"His dropping by or his offer?"

"Yes," she said, grinning. "I didn't appreciate his unannounced visit, especially via the back door."

"He was probably just anxious to share the news. I wouldn't worry about it."

She groaned. "Since we're both involved with Damon in business, I was going to keep this to myself, but I don't trust him."

"Why?"

"Without going into detail, let's just say," she drew in her breath, "he wasn't always the gentleman in Houston."

Stiffening, Nick sat up straight. "What are you saying?"

"Having to spend the night in Houston," she paused, shaking her head. "I can't help thinking it was all a ruse to get me into a compromising position."

Nick studied her. Finally, he asked. "Do I need to take any action?"

"No, I can handle this myself, but I just want you to be aware."

"You're a big girl," he said, giving her an encouraging hug. "You can take care of yourself. I trusted your judgment when you were three thousand miles away in New York. There's no reason to question your common sense when you're here, but, if and when you want me to step in, let me know. I'm always there for you." Pulling her close, he nuzzled her nose, tasted her lips. Then speaking so close to her that she felt his breath on her lips, he said, "That's something that will never change."

Carole pressed against him, giving in to his kisses, relieved that all was well again between them. "Hurry up, Christmas Eve," she whispered. Giving him a devilish grin, she added, "I can't wait until we're married."

Chapter Eleven

Later that night, after she'd crawled into bed and turned off the lights, the phone rang. Drowsy, she reached for the cell on her nightstand. "I had a great time," she murmured, yawning, expecting Nick's goodnight call.

Instead, she heard breathing.

"Nick?" She wondered if he were using his headset. "Is your headset too close to your mouth?"

More breathing.

She hung up and flipped on the lights. Belle looked up from the foot of her bed. "That was creepy. Glad you're here, girl." She gave the dog a friendly pat, grateful for her company. Then she double-checked that all the windows and doors were locked. She was too keyed-up to sleep, so she read until her eyelids got heavy. Yawning, she turned off the light.

The phone rang.

This is no coincidence. Both times the phone had rung at the exact moment she turned off the lights.

She decided not to answer it, figuring the caller would eventually tire of the game. The phone rang nonstop, its grating sound making Belle whimper and crawl up beside her. She muted the phone, but still its annoying buzz kept her on edge. She finally turned it off, but it was hours before she could fall asleep.

The next morning, she heard a knock at her back door. Carole looked at the time. *Eight o'clock!* She'd overslept. Then she remembered the bizarre phone calls that had kept her awake. She groaned, not wanting to deal with it.

The knocking got louder. Wondering who it could be, she pulled on her robe and peeked through the patio door's blinds.

"Estrella, what are you doing here?" She opened the door.

"I wondered where you were. You didn't come yesterday, so this morning I thought I'd come get you."

"I'm sorry," Carole said, feeling guilty she hadn't been able to contact her. "I was called to Houston unexpectedly, and then this morning . . . ." She paused, still disturbed by the caller but not wanting to share that.

"Why didn't you and Belle meet me?" she asked, bending to pet the dog.

"Just overslept," said Carole, downplaying the memory of the calls. She smiled too brightly, trying to project a self-assurance she far from felt. Then her concern for the girl overshadowed her own fears. "Have you had breakfast?"

"Not yet." Estrella's dark eyes lit up.

Again, she wondered about the girl's home life. "I've been thinking. How would you like a job?"

The girl giggled. "What kind of a job?"

"Instead of Belle and me meeting you on the beach every morning, why don't you come by here and wake us up? That way, I couldn't oversleep, *and* I wouldn't have to eat breakfast alone. You'd be doing us two big favors." She watched as the girl's face brightened into a smile. "What do you say?"

"That sounds great."

"Wonderful, today's your first day on the job." Carole smiled at her, glad she could provide at least one nourishing meal a day. "Do you like French toast?"

"You look terrible," said Gabby, looking up from her desk.

"And good morning to you, too," Carole said as she walked into the office.

"What, are you keeping bankers hours?" asked Dante, pouring a cup of coffee. He set it on her desk. "Here, you look like you could use it."

"Thanks." Catching his eye, she added, "And thanks for taking care of Belle on such short notice."

He grinned. "Aw, shucks, ma'am, 'tweren't nothing."

"I appreciate it."

Dropping his grin, he said, "You didn't have much choice." Then he clapped her on the back. "Glad to do it, any time."

"Seriously, you look awful. What happened?" asked Gabby.

Carole told them about the phone calls. "It was creepy." She shook her head. "I'm going to invest in some chain locks."

"Don't bother," said Dante, looking uncharacteristically serious. "I've got some in the cabinet. Where do you want 'em?"

"Thanks, but I'll get Nick—"

Dante shook his head. "That condo's Eastwood property. Don't worry about it. I'll take care of it. You just want chains on the exterior doors, right?"

"That would be terrific, Dante. Thanks." She smiled, grateful for his help. Somehow, the evening's fright didn't seem quite as intimidating with friends around.

"Besides, you only have to live alone for three more weeks," said Gabby. Then her eyes opened wide, and she squealed. "Three weeks until you get married! We need to start planning your wedding. Let's go shopping at lunch."

"I'm hearing wedding bills ringing," laughed Dante. "Quick, hide the credit cards."

"I know an adorable bridal shop where they can custom make your gown."

"Sounds great," said Carole, "but at what price?"

"Don't worry," said Gabby with a mischievous grin. "It'll be wholesale. My aunt owns the shop."

"What kind of wedding do you want?" asked Lilliana, Gabby's aunt.

"Ambergris Caye already *is* a destination wedding," said Carole, grinning. "That in itself should be enough."

"But there are so many other kinds of weddings," said Gabby. "Barefoot-beach and trash-the-dress weddings are popular."

"I'd always dreamt of a church wedding," Carole said, staring into space, recollecting, "ever since I was a little girl."

"Why not both?" asked Lilliana. "Start the big day with a champagne brunch in a secluded palapa at the end of the pier, just the two of you—"

"How romantic is that!" said Gabby.

"Get married in church and then have a civil ceremony on the beach," said Lilliana.

Eyes sparkling, Gabby added, "Then jump off the pier and trash the dress."

"Follow that with a champagne and candlelit beach reception," said Lilliana.

Grinning, Carole said, "I like everything but the trash-the-dress part."

"Leave that to me," said Lilliana, beaming.

Carole eyed her skeptically. "What do you mean?"

As if telling the women a ghost story or a corporate secret, she lowered her voice and gathered them near. "I'll make a white . . . white, you want white, right?"

"White, off-white, bisque, ivory—anything in that color range will do."

With a knowing nod, Lilliana continued. "A sleeveless, full-length, bisque wedding sheath with a graceful back cowl that I'll make out of synthetic fabric—"

"So it's washable?" asked Gabby.

"Exactly!" Lilliana turned toward Carole. "That way, after the ceremonies and pictures, you can jump off the pier in it, wash it, and wear it again."

Catching the excitement of the moment, Carole pictured the image and grinned. "Perfect, but a full-length gown would need a full-length veil to offset it."

"How about a full-length *and trailing* veil?" asked Gabby.

"Even better," chimed Carole and Lilliana, laughing that their thoughts were in sync.

"A full-length sheath and trailing tulle gown," repeated Carole, staring into space, picturing it in her mind's eye.

As the image came into focus, her excitement began mounting. No creative visualization exercise—this was reality. She felt butterflies.

"And the groom—"

"Nick," interjected Gabby.

"Nick will wear off-white chinos and a white Mexican wedding shirt," said Lilliana. "Also wash-and-wear."

"Very island chic," said Gabby.

Carole envisioned it. Then she trained her eyes on the women. "I can see it. I'll carry vivid flowers, a *huge* bouquet of the brightest blooms available."

"And for the beach ceremony, you can stand under an arch of palm fronds sprinkled with purple and red flowers," said Gabby.

"Black orchids, heliconia, and red ginger," said Lilliana.

"Don't forget hot lips," said Gabby.

"Hot lips?" Carole repeated, squinting skeptically. "Is that a flower or a joke?"

"It's a flower with bright red or hot pink petals that are wide and shiny, almost waxy," said Gabby. "Like the wax lips we used to buy as kids."

"But beautiful when mixed in with the other flowers," added Lilliana.

"In fact," said Gabby, "that would be a perfect combination for the bridal bouquet *and* the table arrangements at the reception." She and Carole nodded in agreement.

"With a black orchid for the groom's boutonniere," said Carole, picturing Nick walking up the aisle. Suddenly, Estrella popped into her mind. "And a miniature bouquet for a flower girl."

Later that night, before going to bed, she double-checked that all the windows and doors were locked. Silently blessing Dante, she hooked the chains on the front and back doors.

Nervous that the obscene caller would phone again tonight, she tried to unwind with a cup of herbal tea during Nick's good-night call.

"Relax," he said. "It was probably just some kid making prank calls."

She disagreed, but said, "Hope you're right."

After they hung up, she crawled into bed and read until she could stay awake no longer. She turned off the light and rolled over. The phone rang. Her eyelids flew open as she listened in the dark, debating whether or not to answer.

Calm down, this could be a legitimate call. She reached for the phone, intending to answer it, but self-preservation shouted down her voice of reason. Instead, she turned off the ringer and lay in the dark, too keyed up to sleep. Stirring at every sound, she was anxious that someone was outside, watching, waiting.

When Belle growled a low, warning growl, Carole crept toward the front door in the dark. Belle dogged her heels. Suddenly, fangs exposed and saliva frothing, Belle began barking ferociously at the door. Carole grabbed the only thing within reach—a vase. She stood poised, ready to smash it over the head of anyone who tried to break in.

After several tense minutes, Belle's barking subsided, and Carole set down the vase. She waited in the dark, listening. Only the dog's calm presence soothed her nerves. She petted Belle beside her, glad for her company. It was an hour before she went back to bed. Even then, she lay there, wide-eyed and stirring at every creak.

Suddenly, she heard a pounding. She bolted out of bed before she opened her eyes and saw it was morning. *Didn't know I'd fallen asleep.* Then, chuckling to herself, she checked the clock—seven-thirty. She heard the knock again and peeked through the peephole—Estrella. She pulled on a robe and unlocked the door.

"Am I glad to see you," she said, undoing the chain. "Come on in."

"Ready for our walk?" the girl asked. "I know where we can find some cowrie shells."

"Sounds good," said Carole, "unless you'd rather eat breakfast before our walk."

"After's fine," Estrella said. Then she opened her hand to show its contents. "I found this just outside your door."

In her hand was a book of matches with the Brayburns embossed logo.

Carole stiffened, recognizing it from the Houston restaurant. *Damon.* She wanted to scream but swallowed instead, trying not to alarm the girl.

"Thanks, a friend must have left them." An involuntary shudder passed through her body when Estrella gave her the matchbook. As if it were on fire, she tossed it in her purse. "Give me a minute to dress, and we can be on our way."

"Okay, I'll play outside with Belle."

Carole nodded as she picked up her phone and turned it on. Missed call, it read. She checked the time—seven-thirty, the moment she had jumped out of bed.

She forced herself to breathe deeply, slowly. This game of his had gone too far.

As she dressed, Carole devised a plan. First, she needed to confront Damon. Then she had to change the phone number. She speculated how he knew when she went to bed and got up. *Eastwood Enterprises owns this condo. Is it bugged?*

She clutched her robe to her as her eyes swept the room, scrutinizing every nook and cranny for a hidden camera. Later, she would check thoroughly, but, for now, she thought it wise to dress in the bathroom.

When she got to work, a vase of blue hydrangeas was waiting on her desk.

Stopping in her tracks, Carole felt the blood drain from her cheeks. First the matchbook, now the flowers—both were reminders of their Houston dinner together.

"Nick sure is thoughtful," said Gabby, slowly shaking her head in admiration.

Relief flooded Carole. "Oh, they're from Nick?"

Gabby shrugged. "I guess so. Actually, I didn't look."

Carole set down her laptop and searched for a card. Nothing.

Joking, Dante asked, "Who's the secret admirer?"

"That Nick," said Carole, smiling, putting on a facade. "He thinks of flowers but forgets to write a note."

"You're one lucky girl, Carole," said Gabby, teasing. "You two have such a trusting relationship. Nick doesn't have to add his name—you know who it's from."

"Yeah," she said dryly, "I know who it's from, all right." Carole drew in her breath. Keeping her tone as light as possible, she asked, "Is Damon in yet?"

"No," said Gabby. "He called to say he's flying to Houston today."

"Know when he'll be back?"

Gabby shook her head. "He didn't say."

Nick met her for lunch at a local restaurant. The open-air structure was topped with an immense, thatched-roof palapa. Huge columns of tree trunks and beams held up the roof of dried palm leaves, and sea breezes swept through the airy building. They chose a round table with rattan chairs near the perimeter's railing where they could watch the sea *al fresco*, yet be shielded from the sun.

After serving the drinks, the waitress invited them to help themselves to the local-food buffet—plantains, mangoes, papaya, rice, beans, and a wide selection of salads, side dishes, seafood, and desserts.

The palapa kept the restaurant quiet and private, enveloping them in an intimate shelter. As Carole began to feel safe, she began to relax. Rather than skim over the events as she had previously, she told Nick about the phone calls in detail, describing how they occurred the moment she turned off the light each evening and rose each morning.

"It's time to get your own phone," he said, lips tight, white. "I'll pick one up for you today. In the meantime, give me back my phone. Let this guy call *me*." He grunted his scorn.

"Sounds like the best approach," she said, reaching into her bag and handing him his phone.

He caught it, holding her hand, fingering it in his. "You know, you're the most important part of my life." Shaking his head, he groaned. "I never should have let things go this far."

"There's more," she said, taking a deep breath before she took the plunge. "This isn't just a prank caller. It's Damon."

He dropped her hand. "What?"

With her now free hand, she reached into the bag and pulled out the matchbook. "This was at my door this morning, and, when I got to work, a vase of blue hydrangeas was on my desk."

"Okay, I get the connection with the Brayburns matchbook, but I don't understand what the flowers have to do with it."

"There were blue hydrangeas on the table in that restaurant."

"That . . . ." Nostrils flaring, he bit his lip, keeping his thoughts to himself.

She waited until his labored breathing subsided. "I didn't want to tell you—"

"Why not?" Both his words and scowl interrupted her.

She blanched as she saw anger sweep across his face. "Where do I begin?" She held up her hands, gesturing ineffectively. "He's your primary customer. Basically, he's my boss—as well as the reason I can stay in Belize. Let's face it—my being here is probably the rationale for your proposing, the basis for us getting married. It's what's allowed us to both keep our careers yet be together."

"You have a point . . . actually, several."

She looked up into his eyes. "I didn't want to upset all that for something I may have imagined or the possibility that he'd had one drink too many in Houston. I had to be sure. Until this morning, I wasn't certain. Can you understand why I waited to share this?"

Nodding, he picked up her hand and kissed her fingertips. He looked into her eyes. "The question is, what are we going to do about it?"

When Carole returned from lunch, she asked if Damon had called again.

"Yes," Gabby said. "He's going to be detained in Houston for several days."

Carole took a deep breath, both glad she would not have to work with him, yet sorry she could not confront him.

"He wants us to get started on the next video with Mario."

"Our videographer," said Carole, nodding. "Okay, when's Mario coming?"

"He's at the site now," Gabby said. "Dante's going to drive us over."

A half hour later, they turned off the main highway onto a freshly cut road. Carole saw the bulldozed trees hastily pushed aside, their roots left exposed. She looked at the sliced hillsides, their multicolored layers of sand a geographic genealogy of the centuries in their making. All that was left of a lush forest was stumps and litter.

"When did they cut this road?" Carole asked.

"A week ago," said Dante, his eyes on the road as he steered the converted golf cart around the tree branches and muddy ruts.

"All this in a week . . . ." Carole took in the devastation.

"Yeah, the road crew really made good progress," said Dante with a congenial laugh.

Carole cringed at his words. She met Gabby's eyes, and both women looked away, keeping their thoughts to themselves. *Wonder if she feels the same way I do.*

As they approached the building site, Carole recognized the activity she had seen from the air when Damon had circled the development site. Now, instead of working far below them in equipment that looked like Tonka toys, laborers bustled about in monster-sized, earth-moving machinery.

"Wow," she said, studying the scene. "I can't believe how much work's been done."

"They finished laying the phase-one foundation," said Dante, parking the vehicle. "It should be dry enough to walk on."

They stepped over wood chips and muddy puddles as they crossed toward the immense foundation. Squinting, Carole looked around the area. *Something's familiar.*

"You're looking at a hundred thousand square feet of concrete," said Dante, chuckling.

Carole surveyed the cement sea before her. Then the sound of surging waves crashing against the rocks caught her attention. She looked toward the shoreline, trying to get her bearings.

Estrella's cove! Only it looked so different.

"Yeah," said Dante, following the direction of her view, "not much of a beach, is it?"

"I think its raw beauty's beautiful," she said quietly.

"Yeah, easy on the eyes, but no place to swim or snorkel. No way for boats to get in, but the engineers will take care of that."

"What do you mean?"

He pointed down the shoreline to the left and right. "First, they'll take out the mangroves to open up the view. Then they'll widen the channel so boats can maneuver. Finally, they'll haul in white sand, extend this beach out to the rocks."

Carole tried to imagine the altered geography. "Won't it destroy the reef's ecosystem?"

Dante shrugged. "It'll change it, that's all."

"What about Eastwood Enterprises' active environmental stewardship?" asked Carole, standing hand on hip. "Are their words nothing but lip service?"

"Eastwood Enterprises observes internationally-accepted best practices for sustainable tourism," said Dante. He grinned. "But first you got to have the tourism."

"At what cost to the environment?" Carole looked at the mud-choked tide pools.

"Eastwood Enterprises supports the conservation of the environment and natural attractions."

She grimaced. "Interesting . . . that's exactly what Damon said." Tilting her head, she appealed to his better judgment. "What about the reef, Dante? What you're proposing here will destroy the beach's ecology."

"We're helping establish a Coral Propagation Corps. Students from the upcoming Aquatic Biology School will conduct research on coral transplantation."

"Propagation Corps? That's the same propaganda Damon fed me," she said, shaking her head. "What he couldn't tell me is when this school would be built."

"Plans are in the works."

She heaved a sigh. "When?"

"Carole, ecotourism's the lifeblood of Belize. One in four people works in the industry." He gestured toward the laborers with his thumb. "That's not counting the construction industry that supports it. Look around you. Eastwood Enterprises is providing jobs, hiring Belizeans at every level. That all increases the tax base, funds the infrastructure, and eventually helps build the school."

"But at what cost?" She looked at the muddy rubble below her feet, at what had recently been a sandy beach. She picked up a smashed starsnail shell. "What about the sea creatures that depend on this cove to survive?"

He made an attempt at his trademark grin. "Let them move down the beach a few feet."

Carole surveyed him. "Dante, this doesn't sound like you. I can't believe you really feel this way."

Gone was his grin. His mouth set in a grim line, his eyes homed in on hers. "We all work for Eastwood Enterprises, and we all have to follow orders." She shook her head. In her mind's ear, she heard Estrella's words. *Follow your star.* "There comes a point when you have to follow your conscience."

He grimaced. "You have to follow orders if you want to get paid."

She looked at the broken starsnail shell in her hand, wondering what other wildlife would die. The link between cause and effect was obvious— the resort's construction and the beach's destruction. Worse, she recognized her role in its devastation. Clasping the starsnail shell to her chest, she made a decision.

"It shouldn't be 'all in a day's work'," she said. "There's more, much more at stake. Corporate social responsibility shouldn't be optional."

"It's all about the bottom line."

"I disagree." Pressing her lips together in a thin line, she shook her head. "In fact, I just read a study showing that ninety percent of consumers support corporations that endorse environmental stewardship."

"Talk about lip service," said Dante with a cynical snort. "Consumers are only looking at what it costs them, not what the hidden costs are to the environment. They're bargain hunters wanting the most bang for their bucks."

"I don't buy that," she said. "Business models can be sustainable, both environmentally and financially."

"In books, maybe," his grin was condescending, "but not in real life."

"I can give you plenty of examples—"

"People want luxury condos at tenement prices. They want the best for less. Our job's to provide them what they want . . . at the price they want." He shrugged. "It's business."

So you pave paradise and put up a parking lot? Losing patience, she realized debating economics was a waste of time. She had to act.

"Is the board aware of these construction methods?" she asked, trying another tact. "I was under the impression Eastwood Enterprises is a green builder."

"Is that what Damon told you?" Eyes twinkling, Dante chuckled mirthlessly. "It's all about the net gain."

"But they liked the first video I did—and my storyboard for the next one."

"Sure, you're good at what you do—convincing prospective investors that Eastwood Enterprises is a green builder."

Feeling like the wind had been knocked out of her, she whispered, "I believed it." Her shoulders slumped as her self-respect plummeted. "I thought they believed in it, too."

He attempted a half-smile. "Which is why you were so Belizable."

She pulled in a deep breath and then slowly released it in a sigh. "And now that I know better, how do I deal with this job?"

He shook his head sympathetically. "You have to get through the Mondays to get to the Fridays."

She grunted at his analogy.

"Mario's on the phone," said Gabby, stepping over a pile of debris to join them. She pointed to a rocky overlook. "He's up there, ready to start filming when you are."

Carole stared at her, wondering if the intern struggled with her conscience.

Gabby held out the phone to her. "He tried calling your cell but got no answer."

"Oh, yeah," Carole said, remembering the prank calls, the other reason she was unhappy with Eastwood Enterprises. "I've changed my number."

Gabby raised her eyebrow and opened her mouth as if to ask a question. Instead, she said, "Mario wants to know how to shoot the scene."

Carole cringed inwardly. The last thing she wanted to do was direct the videographer to tape the development and film around the devastation. She couldn't tout Eastwood Enterprises' environmental policy, not any more. *What do I do?*

As she searched her soul, she glanced at the starsnail shell in her hand. Again Estrella's words came to mind. *Follow your star.*

"Hello, Mario," she said, accepting Gabby's phone with a tight smile. "Use a telescopic lens for this scene."

"You want a long shot?"

Not sure where she was going with this, she nodded. "Yes, start with an overview of the building site and then seamlessly home in on the machinery as it cuts the road. I want this video to capture the effort that goes into building a premier, luxury resort. In the quest to provide their clients the best for less," she turned toward Dante so he could overhear as she spoke into the phone. "I want to document that Eastwood Enterprises leaves no stone unturned."

When Carole answered the knock at her door that night, Nick presented her with flowers.

"They're lovely," she said, inhaling their fragrance as she kissed him. "Thank you."

"And this," he said, handing her a new cell phone. "The number's unlisted, so you shouldn't have any more trouble with prank callers."

Her eyes roamed around the room, warily focusing on the woodwork's nooks and crannies. "Now, if only I felt there weren't a camera hidden here somewhere . . . ."

"Glad you brought that up," said Nick. "You mentioned that it's when you turn out the light or first get up in the morning that you've gotten calls, right?"

"Yes," she said, nodding. "If there's a camera anywhere, it's got to be in the bedroom."

"Let's do a manual sweep of the room," he said, starting for the bedroom.

"Just give me a minute," said Carole. "I want to put these flowers in water." Belle woofed.

"Hello, girl." Nick reached down to scratch her neck. "You want to help?" Belle woofed and pranced.

"Okay, I'm back," said Carole. With a grimace, she glanced up at Nick. "Hope you don't think I'm being paranoid."

"I think you're being cautious. Self-preservation's a good thing." He took her in his arms. "I'll just be glad when we're married, and you can move out of this place and in with me."

She gave him a bear hug. "Me, too!" She reached up to kiss him, savoring his nearness.

Belle barked.

"Oh, you're jealous, are you?" she asked, letting go of Nick, scratching Belle behind her ears. Chuckling, she asked, "Ready to search?"

"Sure," he said with a crooked grin. "Look for anything that seems out of place. You know, pictures placed at odd heights or in weird places or lampshades that don't quite sit right."

They checked underneath the desk and shelves. They inspected the crown molding. Nick even used the miniature screwdriver on his pocket knife to unfasten the light switch and outlet covers, but they found nothing.

As it started to get dark, Carole flipped on the light.

"No, turn it off a minute," Nick said. "I thought I saw a tiny red light."

"Where?"

"Somewhere over here," he said, again checking behind the picture's frame.

Belle barked again.

"Shush, girl," Carole said, but the dog began barking loudly at the picture. She looked at Nick. "What is it? Do you see anything?"

Weaving back and forth in front of the picture, Carole could make out a nearly imperceptible red light barely glimmering from an inner corner of the picture frame. "Here!"

He took the picture off the wall and laid it on the bed. Probing with his pocket knife, Nick found a loose mitered joint. He gently pried it loose, and they saw a tiny round object, emitting a faint, red light.

"An LED light," he said, studying it.

Carole lifted it out. "The camera's a quarter the size of my thumbnail."

"Whoever installed this did a sloppy job. They never deactivated the power-on indicator light."

Holding it up to her face, she spoke into it. "You son-of-a-bitch, see if you like this angle." Tossing it to the floor, she crushed it beneath her shoe, taking pleasure as she ground the camera to pieces.

"That's it," he said. "You're moving out of here tonight."

"But where?"

"In with me," he said gruffly.

"We've waited this long," she said, conflicted. More than anywhere else, that's where she wanted to be—with Nick, especially now that her suspicions were confirmed. Someone was watching her, stalking her, yet she had waited this long to be alone with him. She locked her eyes on his. "Can't we wait another few weeks? Until we're married?"

"You can have my bed." Running his hand through his blond hair, he added, "I'll sleep on the couch. You'll be safe."

She grinned. "It's not you I'm worried about."

Grinning back, he rubbed his chin. "Then check into the hotel where you were staying."

She looked at Belle and back at him, shaking her head. "They don't allow dogs."

"Well, there must be someplace on this island that allows them. We just have to find it." He took her in his arms and bent his head to kiss her, his sun-bleached hair sweeping against her cheeks.

She met his lips with hers, wrapping her arms around his neck and pressing against him.

When they broke apart, he said, "I don't like the idea of your being here alone."

"Belle's here, and Dante put chains on the doors. I'll be fine. Plus the camera's gone, and Damon, or whoever the stalker is, can't call me on the new cell phone you got me."

"I'd feel better if I could stay here tonight, but I've got a late dive." He pulled out his cell. "Maybe I can get Fedro to cover for me tonight . . . ."

Shaking her head, she covered his hand with hers. "I promise I'll find another place to stay tomorrow, but I'll be fine here tonight." She led him into the kitchen. "There's Chinese takeout warming in the oven—let's eat dinner before it gets too late."

Over chopsticks and open containers, Carole told Nick about the building site.

He shook his head. "If they dredge that beach and haul in sand, the reef will be destroyed. The cloudy water will deplete the seagrass, and the sea turtles will lose their feeding and breeding grounds."

"How would cloudy water affect the reef?"

"No sunlight," he said. "No coral or seagrass growth."

"I knew burying it under sand would destroy it," she said, "but it never occurred to me that muddy water could damage it."

He nodded. "Sedimentation suffocates the reef, but turbidity during dredging stresses it to the point of no return."

"Reefs look rock-hard," she said, tasting the *moo goo gai pan*.

"But they're only a thin veneer of delicate tissue. Despite their vulnerability, they support a quarter of all marine fish species, not to mention us two-legged creatures." He grinned. "Speaking of which, you've got to try this *kan-shao* shrimp." Using his chopsticks, he fed her a shrimp.

She moaned in pleasure as she sampled it. "Oh, that tastes good," she mumbled, her mouth full. Swallowing, she added, "Reefs sound like rainforests, only underwater."

He looked up from his takeout carton with a half-smile. "I like that comparison."

"So now that Eastwood Enterprises has broken ground and laid the foundation, is it too late to save the reef? Has the damage already been done, or is there anything we can do?"

"Good questions." His eyes hardened as they met hers. "As you saw today, there's already been a direct loss of coral habitat within the project's footprint."

Nodding her head, she sighed. "Oh, yeah."

"But it's not too late to lower the impact with good construction management."

"Like what?"

"Like the operating policies and choices of equipment. Impact depends on the scale, duration, and frequency of shock to the ecology." He studied her. "If you could convince the board to modify its construction methods, it's not too late to save that reef."

"It must be badly damaged, even after a week," she said, pursing her lips grimly.

"Absolutely, the damage from the project's been done." He reached for her hand and gave it an encouraging tug. "But coral's resilient. It can recover from temporary impact. It's the long-term demolition that destroys it. What you have to do now is persuade the board to change its processes—and the sooner, the better."

She met his eyes. "Damon's going to be the issue, both personally and professionally. I get the feeling he'll fight me every inch of the way, and frankly, I don't know how the board will react to my proposals. It's possible they support him. They could even back his methods, although something tells me they'll listen to reason." Her chest heaved in a silent sigh. "I'm not even sure that I can trust Dante." She hesitated. "He's a company man." Raising her eyebrow, she flashed Nick an ironic grin.

"What about Gabby?"

She shook her head slowly. "I'm not sure. I sense she's against the destruction, but she hasn't said or done anything to indicate how she feels one way or the other."

"Who can you depend on ... " he paused, his eyes crinkling, " ... besides m—"

"Mario," she said, cutting him off in her enthusiasm. "I have the proof from his footage today! That video contains all the evidence I need to persuade anyone who's concerned." She sighed. "I just hope the board truly cares. In fact, I'm counting on it—which brings up another subject . . . ."

"Which is . . . ."

"Can I count on you?" She watched him closely.

"Of course." He sighed patiently, a half-smile playing at his lips.

Carole thought he answered a little too quickly. "There's good reason to believe my taking this evidence to the board will lead to my contract being terminated."

"We'll manage."

"That could mean having to return to my job in Manhattan. We need to face that possibility." She peered into his eyes, trying to read his thoughts. "We're where we were when I got here."

"Carole," he drew in a deep breath, "let's not borrow trouble. We'll face it when and if we have to, but there's more than enough to focus on without worrying about that prospect."

Inwardly, she groaned. *He's avoiding the inevitable by not confronting this likelihood or even taking the coward's way out. On the other hand, he's right. Within the next twenty-four hours, I somehow have to create a presentation, submit it to the board, find a place to stay, move out, and hopefully not have to deal with the stalker. I really can't spread myself any thinner.*

Chapter Twelve

The next morning, Carole awoke to banging on the back door. She looked at the clock—seven. Though the rosy blush of dawn was penetrating the draperies, Carole turned on the light to test whether the stalker had hidden another camera in the room or had discovered her unlisted number.

No phone call. She took a deep breath. *What a relief.*

The knowledge energized her. She smiled, ready to face the day. Belle at her heels, she jumped out of bed and pulled on her robe. Peeking through the peephole, she saw Estrella.

True to her word, Estrella was on the job.

"Good morning," she said brightly, undoing the chain and unlocking the door. "Come right on in."

"Hi." As the girl entered, she held out her hand. "I found this just outside your door."

Carole looked at the napkin imprinted in silver with the logo, Hi Ho Silver, Inc. She recalled the last time she had seen those napkins tucked in the limo's fluted glasses. *Damon.* She looked left and right of the door, wondering if he were there, hidden in the bushes, watching, smirking.

Gone was the joy of the morning and, with it, her energy. She slumped, suddenly exhausted.

"Is anything the matter?" asked Estrella, looking up, worry furrowing her young forehead.

"Oh, no," fibbed Carole, trying to snap out of the sudden doldrums. "Come on in." As she closed, locked, and chained the door, she remembered the disfigured building site. "Actually, there is something bothering me." She looked into Estrella's young, trusting eyes. Hesitating, she wondered how to broach the subject, wondered how the girl would take the news.

"Do you mean the starsnail shell beach?" asked Estrella.

"Yes," said Carole. Surprised by the girl's insight, her calm, she asked, "You knew about it?"

The girl nodded. "I watched them cut the road. In fact, I saw you there yesterday."

Carole wasn't sure which line of questioning to pursue first—the girl's apparent truancy or her uncanny knowledge. Point-blank, she asked, "Estrella, don't you go to school?"

"Sure," said the girl.

"Then how are you able to take time off—"

"Teachers' conference," she said.

Carole worked her jaw, unsure whether or not to believe her. It was a plausible, if convenient, excuse—as well as one difficult to check out. She sighed, knowing she had been outmaneuvered, and tried the second line of questioning.

"How do you always seem to know what's going on?"

The girl smiled mysteriously. "I follow my star."

"You follow your star," Carole repeated, tongue in cheek, as she tried to repress a smile.

"Mmm-hmm," she said, her dark eyes twinkling, "and, after breakfast, there's something I want to show you." She grinned.

Estrella led them along the beach, this time heading toward town instead of away from it.

Carole thought it strange since the girl usually took them to out-of-the-way coves where they beachcombed for shells. 'Treasure hunts,' Estrella called them.

"Where are you leading us?" Carole asked, recognizing her old apartment complex and some of the local restaurants.

"Keep following," said Estrella, grinning. "We're almost there."

Within moments, they stopped in front of an ornate, cement structure. Small palm trees and a Marian grotto graced the entrance. Carole read the sign—San Pedro Roman Catholic Church. She looked at the girl.

"Why are we stopping here?"

"They're holding a Christmas Bazaar here to earn money for the school."

Perplexed, Carole stared at her. "I still don't understand."

"We can make Christmas ornaments out of the shells and sell them at the bazaar," said Estrella.

"Earn money for you?" asked Carole, still puzzled.

"No," giggled Estrella. "Give the money to charity."

Carole grimaced, embarrassed that a child had to remind her. "Good idea!"

"We've got two weeks to make the Christmas ornaments," said Estrella. "But first you have to sign up." Taking her by the hand, Estrella added, "Over here." The girl led her around the building to a courtyard where several women were gathered at a table, talking.

"Carole," called a voice.

She looked up and saw Gabby. "Hey, what are you doing here?"

Gabby introduced her to the women and said, "I'm chairing the Christmas Bazaar. Want to join our group?"

Carole inwardly cringed. It had been years since she'd gone to church.

"Oh, I don't know about joining," she said. Then she remembered Estrella. "But my little friend and I would like to help by making Christmas ornaments out of seashells and donating the proceeds."

"That's a wonderful idea," said Gabby, wearing a big smile.

"It's all Estrella's idea," Carole said, wanting none of the credit. With her thumb, she gestured toward the girl at her side.

"Who?" asked Gabby, looking around.

"Estrella, my little friend," said Carole, turning toward the girl to introduce her.

But the girl had vanished. Only Belle looked up. Looking left and right, Carole chuckled self-consciously. "She was just here." She shook her head. "She must have wandered off, but this is Estrella's bright idea."

"It's wonderful."

"I didn't know you were active in the Church," Carole said. "It's always odd to work with someone and then see them in a different place, a different light."

"There's often more to people than meets the eye," said Gabby, her smile stilted.

Carole wasn't sure how to respond, so she shrugged and agreed. Then she remembered the next item on her to-do list. "You don't know of any apartments for rent that accept dogs, do you?"

"Why?" asked Gabby. "Don't you like your condo?"

Leaving out the details of the matches and napkin—anything that would directly implicate Damon—Carole told her about the stalking, surveillance camera, and phone calls.

"That's awful." Gabby's eyes narrowed. "I'd suggest asking Damon or Dante for a different condo, but perhaps you'd be better off finding something that isn't the property of Eastwood Enterprises."

Carole surveyed her, a respectful grin creeping at the corners of her mouth. *What a shrewd woman.* Without her mentioning the details, Gabby had surmised the situation.

"What do you . . . . " Carole started to ask Gabby her opinion about the construction methods used at building site, but then thought better of it. She still didn't know where Gabby's loyalties lay. No sense in 'laying all her cards on the table,' as Simon would say.

Instead, she asked, "Do you know of any apartments near here?" Looking around, Carole saw that it was only blocks from the office. If she lived closer to town, she wouldn't need the converted golf cart. The less reliant she was on Eastwood Enterprises, the better.

"Actually, I think Martina may know of something." She turned toward the group. "Martina, hadn't you mentioned an apartment for rent near you?"

The plump woman nodded. "A small efficiency, but it's only available until the first of the year."

"That's perfect," said Gabby, her eyes dancing. "My friend's getting married on Christmas. She only needs it a few weeks."

"Does it allow dogs?" asked Carole, scratching Belle's ear.

"Yes."

Carole shared a gleeful smile with Gabby. "Is it ready to move in?"

"Yes, I can introduce you to the manager now, if you like."

"Sounds great, I'd love to see it," said Carole.

Then she remembered Estrella. Carole was reluctant to leave without the girl, or at least without telling her where she was going. Looking around, she spotted her near a group of children on the beach. She waved, and the girl grinned and waved back.

"Who are you waving at?" asked Gabby, looking in the same direction.

"Estrella, my little friend," said Carole. "See her with that group of kids?"

"Which one is she?"

Carole tried to describe her, but realized the description fit at least three of the girls in the group. She motioned to Estrella to join them, but the girl shook her head.

Chuckling, Carole turned back toward the group. "I wanted my little friend to come along, but apparently she's too busy playing. Sure, if you have time, I'd love to see the apartment."

"Don't worry about coming into work late," said Gabby with a wink. "Take your time. Damon's still in Houston, and Dante's showing properties to prospective clients."

By ten o'clock, Carole had signed a week-by-week lease and moved her few belongings into the furnished apartment. After she parked the golf cart in front of the office, she dropped its keys and the condo's keys on Dante's desk.

Only then was she able to breathe. She told Gabby about the morning's events, finishing up by saying, "And it's only five minutes away, so I can let Belle out every few hours."

"I prayed it would work out for you," said Gabby, smiling softly.

Carole's shoulders tensed. Talking of prayer or anything else smacking of religion made her uncomfortable.

"Yeah, well, thanks," she mumbled before changing the subject. "Any word from your aunt about my wedding dress?"

"I'm glad you asked," said Gabby, eyes dancing. "Lilliana said the dress is ready for a fitting. It's a sleeveless, full-length, bisque wedding sheath with a graceful back cowl."

"Just the way she'd described it," said Carole, feeling butterflies in the pit of her stomach.

"Are you excited?"

She couldn't restrain the gleeful grin. "It's been a long time coming, and, despite the recent events—maybe partially because of them—I can't wait to marry Nick." She hunched her shoulders. "Oh, yeah, I'm excited!"

"Maybe we can stop by Lilliana's shop after work," said Gabby.

Carole nodded. "I'd like that."

Gabby paused before saying, "There's something else I've been meaning to ask you . . . ."

From Gabby's reluctance to broach the subject, Carole surmised she shared her opinions about the destruction at the building site. "I think I know what you're going to say. You're wondering how I feel about the Eastwood Enterprises' construction methods."

Gabby's jaw dropped. "Actually, no," she said slowly, as if choosing her words carefully. She cleared her throat. "I was going to ask you about reserving your wedding date at the church. Christmas is a busy season, and I'd hate for you to be disappointed."

"Ohmigosh." Carole thumped her head. "With everything else that's been going on, I nearly forgot." Her eyes widening, she looked at Gabby. "Do you think it's too late to set a time?"

"Well," said Gabby, "it's not only setting the date. You need to sign up for a pre-marriage workshop."

"What?" asked Carole, squirming, her breathing labored as she tried to hide her discomfort.

"It's not hard," said Gabby, rushing in, "but it does take time, and we only have a few weeks. Besides," she added with a grin, "as your wedding coordinator, it's my duty to make sure you get hitched without any hitches."

Carole chuckled, relaxing at her joke. Then, pressing her lips together, she faced Gabby. "I don't know anything about this religious stuff. Can you . . . ." she hesitated, biting her lip. "Can you guide me through it? Can you go with me to ask the priest?"

"Sure," she said with an easy smile, "but wouldn't you rather Nick went with you?"

"Eventually, yes, but just go with me to set up the logistics." She laughed uneasily. "I'll ask Nick to go with me later for the workshop."

"Okay."

Carole took a deep breath, letting it out slowly. "Thanks."

"We can stop by the church office during lunch."

Carole felt the tightness of breath again. "Maybe tomorrow."

"You really don't have much time." Gabby shook her head sympathetically. "The sooner we get the process started, the better your chances for a Christmas Eve wedding."

Carole weighed the odds. Finally, with a sigh, she nodded her head. "Okay. I'll call Nick, give him a heads up of what to expect. I'm sure he wasn't figuring this into the mix."

At noon, they walked to the church office and caught Father Francis just as he was leaving for lunch. An American expat, he reminded Carole of her Uncle Oscar.

"In a nutshell," said Carole, talking fast—partly not to delay Fr. Francis any longer than necessary, and partly because she was nervous. "Nick and I would love to get married on Christmas Eve."

"Are you both Catholic?" he asked.

"No . . . well, yes, but . . . ." She paused, trying to remember if Nick had ever mentioned being Catholic.

"You don't know?" he asked, a twinkle in his eye.

"I am." She winced. "At least, I was, but I don't think Nick's Catholic."

"You were baptized? Confirmed in the Catholic faith?"

She nodded. "Oh, yes, and I made first communion."

"Let me guess," he said gently, "you're no longer a practicing Catholic."

She squirmed, recognizing it was better not to lie and compound sins she'd have to confess later. She sighed. "Not really."

"First things first," he said. "Christmas Eve, you say?" She nodded. "That's a busy day. Let's see if any time's available in the schedule." He rubbed the bridge of his nose as he checked the computer.

Carole shot Gabby a nervous smile as they waited.

"There's one spot open," he said.

Carole inhaled deeply, unaware she had been holding her breath. "When's that?"

"Following the morning mass."

"Noon?" asked Carole, feeling a weight lift as relief replaced angst. "That would be ideal."

"No, mass is at seven. There's an hour available between eight and nine. Would that time work for you?"

"Perfect," said Carole, sharing a grin with Gabby. *That will give us plenty of time for the follow-up beach wedding.*

"Now for the important matters." He again checked his schedule, scrolling through the pages of entries. "There's one pre-Cana workshop before Christmas." He surveyed her with a stern lift of his left eyebrow. "It should be taken six to twelve months prior to a wedding," his eyes glinted as his expression softened, "but love can be impetuous."

She smiled, feeling more at ease.

"It takes place over the course of two evenings, two hours each—one evening this week and one the next." He studied her. "Can I count on you and your fiancé to attend both sessions?"

She nodded solemnly. "I'll be there."

"And your fiancé?"

"He'll be there, too. I promise." She mustered a smile. "When does the workshop begin?"

"Tomorrow at seven. Here," he said, handing her a printout. "This is a Marriage Preparation Checklist. I'll need copies of your baptismal certificates a week prior to the wedding."

Carole scanned the sheet. "So you'll need them by December seventeenth." Raising her eyebrow, she said, "I'll do my best."

"I need better than that." His eyes unyielding, his thick brow puckering, he stared at her. "These are prerequisites. Without them *and* the completion of the pre-Cana workshop, I can't perform your wedding ceremony. This is a covenant you're entering into. It's not a contract, not a license you sign. Marriage is a vocation, a lifelong commitment, and it can't be undertaken lightly."

Biting her lip, wishing she hadn't thought out loud, she nodded. "I understand. I'll get them for you."

Apparently satisfied he had made his point, his disposition lightened. With a warm smile, he shook hands. "I'll expect you and your fiancé here tomorrow at seven."

Reprieved. She felt she had just been let out of detention. "We'll be here, Father," she said with a relieved sigh. "Thank you!"

As she and Gabby left the church office, Carole turned to her. "He's quite the disciplinarian, isn't he?"

"Actually, he's a very sweet man He just loses patience if he thinks people don't take marriage seriously.'

"Really? That's what's behind it?"

Raising her eyebrows, Gabby nodded. "He's had to deal with more than a few bridezillas recently. It's amazing what transformations take place between 'Will you marry me?' and 'I do.'"

"I'm beginning to get an idea." Carole laughed at herself as much as her fellow brides. "I never realized how many details go into a wedding. It isn't a walk down the aisle—it's a marathon!"

Gabby threw back her head and laughed. "You haven't even begun." Counting on her fingers, she said, "You've got to make an invitation list, buy and address the invitations, send them out, order the flowers, cake, and food, and book the musicians and reception area. Then you have to find a minister or justice of the peace to perform the second wedding ceremony on the beach. First things first—you have to reserve rehearsal times, book a restaurant for the rehearsal dinner, make arrangements for the honeymoon, invite friends and relatives to serve as wedding attendants, readers, ushers, greeters, and altar servers. Don't forget you have to select Scripture readings and get a marriage license."

Carole stared at her. "You're not kidding when you say 'I haven't begun.'" Paralyzed with panic, she stopped in the middle of the sidewalk. "Can you help me?"

Gabby laughed. "Of course! That's why I'm your wedding planner!"

As they began back to the office, Carole spotted Estrella with a group of children. She waved, and Estrella waved back, grinning.

"There's Estrella," she said pointing.

Gabby shielded her eyes from the sun. "Which one is she?"

"The one in the blue top. See her? Behind that large boy? Come over with me, and I'll introduce you." Carole started toward the girl with Gabby following.

Gabby's phone rang, and she stopped to answer it. "Hi, Dante. I'm five minutes from the office. What do you need?" She waved Carole on. Covering the receiver, she whispered, "Meet you back at the office."

Carole nodded and continued on to Estrella alone.

"Hey, what happened to you this morning?" asked Carole. "I felt bad leaving you here, but you seemed to be enjoying yourself with the other kids."

The girl shrugged. "Just hanging out."

"A lot's happened since you left—"

"You moved. I know," said Estrella with a nod.

"Oh." Carole blinked, wondering how she knew. Then with a smile, she nodded. *It's a small island. She must know the women in the group and have heard about the move.* "It's nearby. I hope you can still come by mornings to wake us and join—"

"Sure," interrupted Estrella. "How about starting on the Christmas decorations tomorrow morning?"

"That's a good idea . . . another one." She started to leave and then turned back. "You know where my new apartment is?"

"Yeah, on Webster Street," said Estrella with a nod. "Apartment 14B, right?"

Scratching her ear, Carole nodded. "Yeah, that's right. How did—"

"See you tomorrow morning," said Estrella with a smile and a wave.

Chapter Thirteen

The next morning, Carole heard knocking. *What time is it?* Half-asleep, she reached blindly for the clock. After several unsuccessful attempts of groping for it on the nightstand, she opened her eyes and looked around the small, furnished apartment. She gasped. *Where am I?* Then Belle began licking her face, waking her up, and Carole remembered the move.

"Thanks, girl." She scratched the dog's neck as she looked at the time—seven o'clock. The knocking got louder. *Estrella?* She grabbed her robe, peered out the door's peephole, and smiled. There stood Estrella holding a plastic bag. "Come on in," she said, yawning as she opened the back door. "What've you got in the sack?"

"Baby starfish shells, see?" She opened the bag for Carole, displaying the inch-wide shells. "I thought after breakfast we could start making the Christmas ornaments."

"Oh, yeah," said Carole, stretching, remembering their conversation. "Lilliana gave us yards and yards of leftover white, champagne, and gold silk ribbons—all the scraps she had from her bridal shop—and I've got scissors and hot glue here somewhere. Everything we need—that is, if we can find it." She winced as she looked at the stacked, unpacked boxes. "Tell you what." She pointed to two large boxes. "Why don't you take Belle for a walk and then start looking through those. See if you can find the scissors and glue while I start breakfast."

A half hour later, Belle had been walked, the breakfast dishes had been cleared away, and the craft materials were laid out on the kitchen table.

Sitting across from Carole, Estrella said, "Let's make the bows first." She nimbly wound the silk and lace snippets around her fingers, creating rosette bows. "Then we can glue them onto the shells and add ribbons for hanging them."

"Another good idea." Carole smiled as she chose a combination of a narrow, ivory satin ribbon and a wider gold chiffon ribbon, creating a multi-layered effect. "You know, working with these wedding materials reminds me—Nick and I were wondering if you'd like to be the flower girl at our wedding."

Estrella's dark eyes opened wide. "Would I ever!"

Carole chuckled at her enthusiasm and then remembered her real reason for bringing up the topic. "'Course, we'll have to check first with your mother to see if it's all right with—"

"Oh, it'll be all right." Estrella kept her eyes steadily on her ribbon, never meeting Carole's eyes.

"Just in case," said Carole, closely watching the girl's reaction, "we really should ask your mother. When's a good time to visit?"

Never raising her eyes from her handiwork, Estrella said, "She works odd hours, no real schedule. It's hard to catch her."

"Hmmm . . . ." Pursing her lips, Carole studied the girl. "Then what if I call her? What's your phone number?"

"Oh, the phone isn't working just now. The number's out of order."

"I see . . . . Then what's your address, so I can at least mail your mother an invitation and ask her permission about your being our flower girl?"

"It's Post Office Box 222," said Estrella, momentarily looking up from her work to peer at Carole's eyes and then looking down, focusing on her ribbon.

"Estrella, I'd really like to meet your mother to ask her permission in person."

"You'd have better luck writing to her."

"Okay." Calling her bluff, Carole got up, rifled through a nearby box, and brought back the invitations. "Post Office Box 222, right?"

Estrella nibbled her bottom lip as she gave a terse nod, never looking up. Carole addressed the envelope and wrote a short note on the invitation.

As she was about to put a stamp on it, Estrella said, "That's all right, I'll take it to her to save you the trouble."

"It's no trouble."

"I'll save you the stamp." Estrella nimbly reached for the envelope and put it under the pile of bows and rosettes she had made.

"Estrella . . . ." Carole started to scold the girl but instead said, "Be sure to bring me back her answer."

"No problem." The girl looked up with a mischievous smile. "So you're marrying Nick on Christmas Eve?"

"That's right," said Carole, frowning. "How did you know the date?"

"I read the invitation upside down." Carole raised her eyebrow, but said nothing. "Do you love him?"

"Estrella, what a question!" Carole gave a self-conscious laugh. "Of course, I love Nick. I wouldn't be marrying him if I didn't."

The girl nodded thoughtfully as she wound the ribbon into an ornate bow. "How did you meet him?"

Eyes on her half-made bow, Carole smiled to herself as she recalled the chance meeting. "It was in Cape May, New Jersey." A snort passed for a private chuckle. "I was working with a client on a marketing campaign."

"My brother's visiting this weekend. Hope you don't mind, but I asked him to join us for lunch."

"Of course," said Carole, closing her notebook. "The more, the merrier. After strategizing your account all morning, we've earned a little R and R."

"The restaurant's just across the street—a little seafood bistro that's Nick's favorite," said Joe. "He says its atmosphere reminds him of the island."

"The island?" Carole furrowed her eyebrows.

"Nick just moved to an island in Belize." He held the office door for her. "He's starting a diving business on Ambergris Caye."

Carole nodded. "Sounds intriguing."

As they approached the columned entrance, Joe waved to a man standing beneath the striped awning. "That's him. Nick!"

Carole appraised the tall, tanned man. As he stepped out from under the awning, the sun highlighted his blond hair.

"Carole, I'd like you to meet my brother, Nick. Nick, this is Carole, the woman I mentioned who's masterminding the PR campaign."

Smiling a toothy grin, Nick reached out to shake hands. White teeth flashed against a bronzed, angular face. His cerulean blue eyes shimmered in the sunlight.

"When Joe told me how attractive his account manager was, I pestered him to invite me along for lunch."

"Pleasure to meet you," she mumbled, shaking hands, distracted by his captivating blue eyes.

"I see you've been diving this morning," said Joe, fingering Nick's soggy, open collar.

Water wicked from his still-damp hair onto his shirt. In the noon sun, she noticed the temporary lines on his face left from his diving mask.

"You know me too well." Turning toward her, he grinned sheepishly. "I can't be around open water without wanting to dive in." He turned back to his brother. "Besides, I wanted to see some of Cape May's artificial reefs. They were just a few nautical miles out, and then only at a depth of sixty-five feet."

"Surprised he hasn't sprouted gills and a dorsal fin by now," said Tom, pretending to check his brother's back. "He's always been more at home under water than above."

"Gills and fin, huh? If you're *fin*ished sharing family secrets," said Nick, opening the door, "let's have lunch. See if I can't *fin*esse Carole to sit beside me,"

"*Fin*agle her between us, if you don't mind," said Joe.

Inside, a swordfish graced the wall, seemingly swimming above the booths. Dark paneling, seascape paintings, brass, and recessed lighting created a nautical motif.

"Table or booth?" asked the waitress.

"Booth," said Nick, eyes twinkling, a millisecond before Tom said, "Table."

Carole smothered a grin as the waitress led them to a corner booth. She sat down, and Tom slid in beside her, barely beating out his brother. Nick heaved a silent sigh and sat across from them.

She couldn't help chuckling. "Are you two always so competitive?"

"Old habits die hard," said Tom.

"Friendly rivalry," said Nick, shrugging. "Besides, Tom's a happily married man. Trying to outdo each other is just a game we've played since we were boys."

The waitress handed them menus and began pouring their water.

As Carole looked at her menu, she found herself peeking over it. From her vantage point, she studied Nick's thick, blond hair, widow's-peak hairline, and high forehead. She noted his smile lines, quick grin, and laid-back attitude. During light banter with his brother, she watched his charismatic eyes light up. They seemed to glow, as if lit from within, and she caught her breath when they met hers.

With a self-conscious grin, she lowered her eyes and resumed reading her menu.

During lunch, Carole caught him watching her. She met his eyes, and they both smiled. This time, neither looked away.

Over dessert, Nick caught her eye. "Have you ever gone dolphin-watching?"

"Nope, can't say that I have."

"Would you like to go this evening?"

"Now, just a minute, bro," said Tom, his hands raised as if to stop Nick's advance. "Thanks to Carole's PR campaign, my business is finally taking off. Don't jeopardize it."

"My brother seems to think I'm being too forward." Nick looked at her, his blue eyes locking onto hers. "Am I?"

"Forward? Definitely. But *too* forward?" She rolled her eyes and, humming, pressed her lips together, pretending to give it thought. Then, with a smile, she shook her head. "No, not *too* forward."

"If my brother, Simon Legree, will let you out of the office by six, there's a sunset dolphin cruise around the harbor. Would you like to go?"

Taking a deep breath to ground herself, Carole turned to Tom. "Think we'll be finished by then?"

"What happened then?" asked Estrella.

"We went out that night—and the next." Carole put the finishing touches on her bow, stacked it on her mounting pile, and started another. "Then the next morning, I had to return to Manhattan."

"How did you ever find time to fall in love?"

Carole studied the little girl. "How old are you?"

A mischievous glint in her eye, Estrella smiled without looking up from making her bow. "Old enough to know that falling in love takes time." She added the bow to her pile and began another. "So how did you fall in love?"

Carole stared off into space, smiled at the memory, and took a deep breath. "We exchanged email addresses and phone numbers. We got to know each other by typing or talking. Long distance has its advantages."

"How?"

"I got to know Nick better because we shared our thoughts and dreams—shared our *minds*—before we spent time together. In some ways, I prefer long-distance courtship, but . . . ." Her smile wavered and then drooped. "I hated the lonely nights and weekends." Grunting, Carole shook off the memory.

Half-made bow in hand, Estrella looked up from her handiwork. "So what you're saying is, the less time you have together, the more you appreciate each other."

Tilting her head to one side, Carole mulled that over. "Yes. In fact, the only time Nick and I argue is when we're in the same room. Distance doesn't separate us. Familiarity does." Then she scrutinized Estrella and asked once again, "So how old are you, anyway?"

Chapter Fourteen

That night, Nick met her for an early dinner in an open-air palapa. Cooled by balmy sea breezes, they ate grilled tuna steak and salad.

"It wasn't easy getting Pedro to fill in for me at the last minute," said Nick. "Is it really necessary to take this pre-Cana workshop?"

"It is if we want to be married in the Church."

"Why don't we simply get married on the beach?" He gestured at the seascape surrounding the palapa. "What's wrong with this?"

"Nothing, the beach is beautiful." She lightly rested her hand on his arm. "And we will get married here . . . after we get married inside the church."

"I don't get it." He shook his head. "Why do we need two weddings?"

"The Catholic Church can marry us only on consecrated ground. After we're *really* married, we can have a beach wedding."

He raised his eyebrows and sighed. "I don't know about this."
"Don't worry." She reached for his hand. "It'll be fun."

Carole met Nick in *Boca del Río* Park. Her heart leapt at the sight of him. After the years of separation, simple moments together were a luxury. She glanced at the faces of others around her—vacant, blasé. These people appeared so used to each other's company, they didn't treasure their time together. They seemed to take their loved ones for granted. *I'll never tire*

of being with Nick. She wrapped her arms around him in a tight hug, feeling his heart beat.

He leaned his head toward her in a kiss, his hair brushing against her cheek.

"Missed you." She sighed, snuggling into the crook of his arm.

He answered by turning her so her back was facing him and putting both arms around her, squeezing her in a warm embrace.

The sound of Christmas carols drifted toward her from a children's choir. Lights hung overhead began twinkling in the twilight.

"Hungry?"

She nodded, inhaling the scents of barbeque and grilled chicken wafting in the breeze. She looked toward the booths that had been set up for the block party and holiday lighted boat parade.

"I'm starved."

"Nearly every restaurant in San Pedro has a booth set up." Taking her hand in his, they began strolling toward the food stands. "Have you ever tried pupusas?"

She made a sour face. "No, they sound awful. What are they?"

Nick chuckled. "They're grilled, stuffed corn pancakes with your choice of filling—delicious."

"Never heard of them. Are they traditional Belizean food?"

"Actually, El Salvadorean," he said. "With ten different ethnic groups on this island, Ambergris Caye boasts more multicultural menus and holiday celebrations than anywhere else I know."

"Today's December sixth, St. Nicholas' day." Playfully swinging his hand, she looked up at him and grinned. "Since he's your patron saint, you choose, 'saint' Nick."

"Pupusas, it is."

They walked up to the grill and watched the owner cup a masa-dough pancake in her hand. Into that, she spooned the filling and then covered all with more dough, making a fat pancake of the mixture. She placed the dough on a griddle and heated it until the cheese melted and the dough browned.

Carole breathed in the aromas wafting from the grill. "It smells wonderful."

"What flavor do you want?" asked the woman, pointing to the choices written on cardboard posters.

After studying the options, Carole said, "Pumpkin and cheese sounds interesting."

"All right," said the woman, already stuffing the mixture into the cupped dough. "And for the gentleman?"

"Pork and cheese, my favorite."

Within minutes, the woman served the steaming pupusas on plates with side orders of carrot-cabbage slaw drizzled with vinaigrette dressing.

They ordered Belikin beers and found a table on the beach.

Carole groaned as she bit into the pupusa. "This is wonderful," she mumbled, hand covering her full mouth. "An excellent choice."

"Glad you like it." His teeth flashed white in the fading light. "And we've got a good view of the sea. Those decorated boats will start parading past here from Wayo's dock," he pointed, "to Caribbean Villas, but they'll end right here at the park."

"Glad I have insider information." She sampled the slaw. Again she groaned. "This is delicious."

As the twilight faded, the red, orange, green, and blue holiday lights on the regatta contrasted against the dusk. The first evening stars began to glimmer when a streak of light caught her eye. She looked overhead as a shooting star arced across the sky. "Nick, look! A shooting star!"

"The Geminids."

Carole drew in her breath. Wordlessly, she reached for his hand.

"Beautiful, isn't it?" His tone hushed, he squeezed her hand as a drum roll interrupted the stillness.

"Ladies and gentlemen," announced the emcee. "Welcome to the Holiday Boat Show! Leading the regatta is Captain Claus and his Ship-Shape Elves, sponsored by the Lions Club." Five costumed and white-bearded men waved from the boat. "Give them a big round of applause."

Turning to watch, she pulled her hand from Nick's to applaud. Canned music started playing *Feliz Navidad* over the intercom.

One decorated boat after another glided past the crowds gathered on the beach and piers—each boat twinkling with strings of lights and swinging lanterns, their decorations reflected on the water, doubling the spectacle.

"Look at that one." She pointed to the boat passing in front. "Are those backlit parasols stacked on top of each other?"

"Maybe they're supposed to be snowmen. See, the sizes are graduated. A little one's on the top for a head, a medium one's next for the body, and the biggest is on the bottom."

"Whatever they're supposed to be, these floating light displays are eye-catching."

"Be-decked, you might say." Nick grinned.

She snickered and reached for his hand. "No wonder you like it here. Belize is charming."

"Think you'll like living here?" Nearly dark, she sensed more than saw his eyes watching her response.

"I'll love living with you." Squeezing his hand, she looked at her surroundings. "This is paradise. Who couldn't help but like living here?"

Inside the church hall, they met Father Francis and two other couples.

"Have a seat," said Fr. Francis, gesturing toward the chairs set up around the table. He shook hands with Nick, introduced himself, and handed him a booklet.

Carole squeezed Nick's hand as they sat on the metal folding chairs.

"Pre-Cana classes are a Catholic marriage preparation program to help strengthen your bond as a couple," Fr. Francis began. "Some of you might wonder what's allowed and what isn't in a Catholic marriage ceremony."

Carole hid a grin as she half-turned toward Nick. He gave her hand a friendly squeeze under the table.

"Tonight we'll cover ceremony planning—where I'll answer your questions and explain the traditions behind the answers. We'll also discuss the spirituality of marriage. Married life has stages that can be compared to Jesus' Transfiguration, Crucifixion, and Resurrection. Although you may be in love now, no marriage is without conflict. We'll discuss how marriage is a sacrament that teaches couples to die and rise again and again." Fr. Francis chuckled. "Yesterday, I renewed the vows of a couple who've been married for fifty years. 'It feels like fifty minutes,' said the white-haired bride, *'under water.'*"

Carole laughed along with the group, feeling some of her nervous tension lift. She moved her chair closer to Nick's.

"We'll talk about the effect your family had on you growing up and how that will impact your upcoming marriage, as well as the family that you'll be starting."

She glanced at Nick's profile, wanting to see his reaction. He didn't flinch. *Not five minutes into this class, and already we're into unexplored territory. I think this'll be good.*

"We'll go over communication skills—listening, sharing emotions, and being assertive. We'll discuss the differences between the way men and women communicate."

"Mars and Venus," Nick whispered in her ear. She swallowed a smile.

"We'll cover conflict management, how to handle disagreements in a positive way, and how to forgive each other."

Nick tugged at her hand.

"Then we'll end tonight's discussion by understanding the meaning of marriage. Remember, you're entering into a permanent union that's rooted in Scripture. Marriage is more than a legal contract. It's a covenant, a sacrament, and a vocation. Now," said Fr. Francis, demonstrating, "if you'll open your booklets, you'll see that there are doubles of most pages, one for him and one for her. We'll take turns reading the exercise as a group. Then you'll write your answers privately, and each couple will discuss their answers with each other." He turned to the couple nearest him. "Josie, would you read the first exercise for us?"

She nodded. "List the top three things you think are important in a successful marriage. Discuss your answers with your partner and prioritize them. Then, as a group, compile a list of what you believe is important in marriage."

Carole thought about it and wrote love, friendship, trust.

After a few minutes, Fr. Francis said, "Okay, now share your answers with your spouse-to-be. If your answers don't match, discuss the differences and why you feel these traits are the most important."

Nick turned toward her. "What did you write?"

Carole showed him her list. "Trust is the most important."

"Why?"

She chewed on her lip as she gathered her thoughts. "You're already my best friend, and I love you. But trust is what's bound us together these years we've lived apart. We couldn't have come this far without it." She stole a quick kiss. "What did you write?"

"Love, faithfulness, and truthfulness," he said, turning his paper so she could read it.

She asked, "Why did you write truthfulness?"

"Without truth, you have nothing," said Nick. "If I didn't tell you the truth, I'd be lonely because you wouldn't know the real me." His eyes hardened. "My father had an affair when I was a kid. He lied about it and kept it hidden for months. He told me about it years later, but I recall the time. The atmosphere in the house was strained. My parents didn't talk or even kiss each other hello. My father said by the time he confessed it to my mother, the marriage was ruined. Their relations were never the same after that." Nick stared into her eyes. "I believe truth is fundamental to a solid marriage."

As he walked her home, Carole said, "You never told me that story about your father."

He lifted an eyebrow and sighed. "I don't like talking about his infidelities, but his cheating," he turned toward her, "and then his lying about it shaped how I feel."

"I can see that."

"It changed my parents' marriage."

"But they're still married."

"In name only. They barely live together. Weeknights, my father stays in town. He goes home on weekends, but they sleep in separate rooms."

"That reminds me. It's St. Nicholas Day—your saint's day and the beginning of the Christmas season." She stopped walking and turned to him. "But you haven't given me your list yet. We've got to get those invitations out."

Wearing a lopsided grin, he said in a nasal voice, "Yes, dear."

She groaned. "You know what I mean. Our wedding's less than three weeks away. Who do you want to invite?"

"Okay," said Gabby, holding her hand over the receiver. "It's the bakery. They're confirming they can make a triple-layer wedding cake with a nautical theme."

"Great! What will they use for the topper?" Hands poised over the keyboard, Carole looked up from her computer.

"Sterilized sea shells layered on a seashell mounting."

"It sounds perfect!" Carole's eyes twinkled at the thought. Then she recalled Nick's one request. "Can they make it in Italian cream with custard cream filling?"

Gabby shook her head. "They can make it in Italian cream, but with either vanilla cream or lemon chiffon filling, not custard cream." She made a face. "Sorry. What should I tell them?"

Carole stared sightlessly at her computer, thinking. "Tell them vanilla cream. How different can it be from custard cream?" They laughed.

"Good point." Gabby relayed the message and turned back to Carole. "What about the frosting?"

"Buttercream. Nick loves buttercream."

"What color?"

Carole hunched her shoulders and spread her hands. "What do you think? Off-white frosting to match my bisque gown?"

"Classic choice," said Gabby, relaying the message.

"And can they can deliver on Christmas Eve?"

Gabby nodded. "They said they can deliver in plenty of time for the reception. They just need the address."

Carole grimaced. "Tell them TBD. We'll let them know as soon as we get confirmation from that palapa near the church."

After Gabby hung up, she shut down her computer and turned to Carole. "Ever onward."

"Huh?" Carole looked up from her computer.

"All set for your final fitting at Lilliana's?"

"It's five already?" She checked her watch, shaking her head. "There aren't enough hours in the day. Just give me a minute. Let me send this press release for the board's review, and I'll leave the rest for the morning." Carole gave the document one last look and hit send.

"Damon's not due back, and I'm not aware of any deadline." Gabby studied her. "Why do you push yourself?"

"Habit, I guess." Carole shrugged. "Aim for the stars. That's what my mother always said. Always give your best." Estrella's phrase shot through her mind—*follow your star*. She paused, noting the similarities.

"C'mon, let's talk on the way," said Gabby, holding the door, "or we're going to be late."

"I can't believe it's been a week since our last class." Carole shook her head as they approached the church. "It seems like we just left."

"Eleven days from today, we'll be back again," said Nick, looking around the church hall, "but as man and wife." He hugged her to him as she put her arms around his neck and squealed.

"Can't wait!"

They broke apart as another couple came up the sidewalk. Hunching her shoulders, Carole pressed her lips together in a tight, embarrassed grin as they approached.

"Hi." After they passed, she gave a nervous giggle.

Nick took her hand as they walked into the church hall and found chairs. She opened up their workbook to the next exercise.

"Good evening, everyone," said Fr. Francis. "It does my heart good to see you all back for the second night of our pre-Cana workshop." He smiled warmly. "I'm glad you're here. I'm glad *I'm* here," he added.

Carole shared a grin with Nick.

"Last week, we ended with discussing marriage as a covenant, a sacrament. This week, we'll go over sexuality and intimacy in marriage."

Several in the group giggled.

Fr. Francis wore a patient smile. "A loving sex life contributes to a lasting marriage. By talking through these sensitive themes now, during your engagement, you're positioning yourselves for a life of fulfilling intimacy."

Keeping a straight face, Carole playfully pinched Nick's hand beneath the table.

"The act of procreation is beautiful," said Fr. Francis, his normally jovial face now serious, "and that segues into the next topic—natural family planning. Maybe children are the last thing on your minds now, or maybe you're planning a family right away. Either way, it's important to discuss fertility and children at this stage so you'll have a clear understanding of each other's expectations."

Carole stared into space. *Children. I've always wanted kids, but is this the right time?* She peeked at Nick. *How does he feel about it?*

Fr. Francis said, "The next topic we'll talk about is how the body and soul are united. The physical body reflects the inner person. In turn, what we do to the body, we do to the soul. We'll examine the distinct roles of husbands and wives in marriage. Then we'll explore how the marital embrace is a selfless gift of love to each other—without separating the love-giving and life-giving natures of marriage."

Carole shivered.

"Cold?" asked Nick, putting his arm around her shoulders. She snuggled into the crook of his arm.

"Last but not least, we'll talk dollars and sense. Are you a saver? Is he or she a spender? What about buying on credit? Are you for or against it? Different opinions about money can lead to quarrels and bitterness."

"Two pockets," Carole whispered, "the same pair of pants."

Chuckling, Nick lightly squeezed her shoulder, drawing her closer to him.

"Capping off the evening and the workshop, we'll write a love letter and end with a closing prayer. That's tonight's overview," said Fr. Francis. "Now, if you'll open your booklets, we can get started. You'll have twenty minutes to complete your first assignment—sexuality and intimacy. As soon as you finish writing your thoughts, start discussing them with your partner."

"Not too many surprises," said Carole as they began comparing answers for their final topic—Finances.

"Seems all our phone calls and emails helped us learn about each other," said Nick with a wink.

"This is the only question I stumbled over." Carole pointed to the last question on her worksheet.

Everything we have is a gift from God. How will we share our gifts, time, talent, and treasure?

"Last one, and you didn't answer it." Nick searched her face. "Why?"

She shrugged. "I've been so busy trying to get my career going that I haven't taken time to share the gifts God's given me."

Nick nodded. "I had trouble with that one, too."

"What did you write?"

Wearing a sheepish grin, he showed her the one-word answer he had written. "Scouts."

She cocked her head. "What does that mean?"

"Remember the day you asked me to speak to the scouts about environmental stewardship?"

"Sure."

"I enjoyed sharing my knowledge with them." His eyes homed in on hers. "I'd like to work more with kids."

"Wow . . . ." *Stewardship and children.* She nodded slowly, internalizing the double meaning of his words. "That's quite a response."

"It wasn't any effort speaking to them. Just the opposite—it was fun, rewarding. Though I hope they learned something, I know I got a lot out of it."

She saw him in a new light, and it made him shine. "Tell you the truth, I'm a little envious."

"What do you mean?"

"You already know how you want to share your time and talent." She chewed her lip as she chose her words. "I don't have a clue, not even a direction. Worse, I work for a man that's destroying the reef under the guise of 'environmental stewardship.'"

"Maybe that's your north star to finding your direction."

North star. Estrella's words came to mind. *Follow your star.* She looked up at him. "You're right. Now I just have to figure out what I'm going to do about it."

Chapter Fifteen

That night as she lay in bed, Carole recalled the devastation of the beach and how something had prompted her to have Mario use a telescopic lens for a long shot.

Though it had made no sense at the time, an idea suddenly came into focus.

She flipped on the light and brought her laptop into bed. Belle wagged her tail and woofed until Carole absentmindedly patted the bed for the dog to jump in beside her. An idea was emerging. In her mind, Carole replayed her words to Mario and Dante. "I want to document that Eastwood Enterprises leaves no stone unturned."

The next morning at work, she asked Dante, "How's building going?"

"Not as expected. Two of the multi-terrain loaders broke down, and we're waiting for parts. We're trying to work around it, but, without those two critical earth-movers, there's nothing for the crews to do."

"Mind if we get some footage for the video while there's a lull?" she asked.

"Knock yourself out." Dante gave his trademark snort.

"Okay to borrow the digital wallet?'

"Sure, it's in the top left drawer of my desk."

"Gabby, do you have Mario's number?" she asked, slipping the digital wallet into her pocket.

"Way ahead of you," said Gabby, smiling, phone in hand. "He's on the line."

"You read my mind." Carole appraised the girl, wondering if she shared her opinion of Damon's building methods. Accepting the phone, Carole said, "Mario, can you meet us at the building site this morning? We need to document the progress."

"Not much of that," Dante informed her. "Progress, that is."

"Got a tight schedule today," said Mario. "Maybe tomorrow—"

"Shouldn't take long," said Carole. "Just a couple of still shots to integrate into the video. You won't even need to bring the video equipment."

Mario sighed. "I'll squeeze it in if you can meet me there in half an hour."

"Half an hour," Carole repeated for the others to hear, raising her eyebrows, looking for confirmation.

Gabby nodded, and Dante said, "Can't join you. I've got an appointment, but you can take one of the golf carts."

"Thanks, Mario! Gabby and I'll meet you there in half an hour."

As Gabby drove the golf cart, Carole worked up the nerve to ask her, "How do you feel about the construction site?"

Never taking her eyes off the road, she parried with another question. "In what way?"

Carole sensed Gabby was purposely being wary. Taking a deep breath, she decided to be more direct, even if it meant Gabby might inform on her.

"It disturbs me . . . deeply . . . to see a beautiful beach torn up in the name of progress." She turned toward the girl. "How do you feel about it?"

When Gabby didn't answer, Carole wondered if she'd heard, so she repeated it. "How do you feel about the building site?"

"It sickens me." Wearing a lingering grimace, she glanced at Carole and then returned her focus to driving. "What's to become of the reef if Belize's beaches are sold off wholesale, dredged, and stripped of mangroves?"

Carole took a deep breath, relieved they shared the same concerns. "My feelings exactly."

"What do you want to do about it?"

"I started putting together a video last night showing the early destruction of the beach. If Mario can get close-ups of the disturbed mangroves and other habitats, I believe we'll have enough evidence to show the board what's going on. I can't believe Damon's complying with Belizean green-building methods or internationally-accepted best practices for sustainable tourism."

"He isn't." Gabby shook her head. "Neither is he following Belize's environmental approval process. He's had no EIA done."

"No what?"

"He's had no environmental impact assessment done for the beach, let alone for building a large-scale coastal resort. He hasn't even performed a limited level environmental study or applied for any permits."

Carole looked at her friend in wonder. "How do you know all this?"

Abruptly swerving to the side of the road, Gabby parked. "It's time you knew. I hesitated telling you this because I didn't know whose side you were on."

"And I was afraid you'd blow the whistle on me." Carole laughed and then, seeing Gabby's solemn eyes, sobered. "You said, 'It's time you knew.' Knew what?"

"I'm not a grad student or an intern doing research," she said. "I work for the Belizean DOI."

Carole squinted. "The what?"

"Sorry, government jargon. The Department of the Interior. I've been assigned to collect evidence against Eastwood Enterprises—"

"I don't think it's Eastwood Enterprises that's at fault—I think it's Damon."

"I've come to the same conclusion—well, Damon and Dante," said Gabby, correcting herself.

"Dante?"

Gabby nodded. "You'd be surprised, but that's another story for another time."

"Wait a minute," said Carole, shaking her head, trying to clear it. "Let me get this straight. You're some kind of special agent, investigating Damon for the DOI?"

"Yup."

"I never would've guessed." Carole rolled her eyes.

"Well, good," she chuckled. "You weren't supposed to. And I wouldn't call me a special agent. I'm more of a researcher—an examiner. Just trying to find the facts."

"And protect the environment," added Carole.

"And protect the environment." Her eyes hardened. "I think you've found the way to bring evidence against Damon."

"He is devious . . . ." Carole took a deep breath. "As long as we're sharing secrets, here's the real reason I changed my phone number and moved." She told Gabby about the night in Houston, the prank calls, the hidden camera, the matchbook cover, and the napkin.

Gabby shook her head, and then asked, "Was there something about the bouquet of blue hydrangeas?"

"Oh, yeah. That was another of his little innuendoes."

"I suspected as much."

"We should've joined forces sooner. Just hope we're not too late to save that beach—speaking of which . . . ." Carole looked at her watch.

"No worries, we're two minutes away." Gabby pulled out into traffic and stepped on the gas.

"Mario," called Carole as they approached. She looked around the work site. Two laborers were stacking sand bags, but otherwise the site was devoid of activity. "Wow, Dante wasn't kidding when he said there was nothing for the crews to do since the multi-terrain loaders broke down."

"Who said they broke down?" asked Gabby.

Carole opened her eyes wide. "Sabotage?"

"I wouldn't call it sabotage. The crew just performed a little 'preventive maintenance,' that's all."

Carole laughed. "Don't ever let me get on the wrong side of you."

"Hey," said Mario, looking like a sea urchin with his camera and telephoto lens cases hanging off his shoulders at odd angles. "Where do you want to start?"

"The mangroves," whispered Gabby, pulling Carole aside. "Mangrove clearance requires a permit from the DOF." At Carole's raised eyebrow, she added, "Department of Forestry."

"What else requires permits?" asked Carole in a hushed voice. "Let's concentrate on the known violations."

"Dredging from the Department of Geology and building from local planning committees."

Mario joined them. "Where do you want to start?"

"First, let's get shots of the phase-one foundation," said Carole. "Then we can move on to the area they're planning to dredge. We'll finish up with shots of the mangroves."

They stepped over wood chips, broken branches, and muddied debris as they crossed toward the foundation. Surveying the sea of cement, she recalled Dante's words. 'You're looking at a hundred thousand square feet of concrete.' *And no permit.*

"Use a wide-angle lens, Mario. Let's capture the size of this resort." Lifting an eyebrow, she looked at Gabby. "We want to impress that upon our audience."

As they neared the shoreline, Carole smelled—before she saw—the heaps of sand, coral, decaying sea grass, and mangled crustaceans. A yellow bulldozer was parked on top, a mechanical crab with its dozer arms extended like massive claws.

"This must be where they were dredging," she said, glancing at Gabby. The girl nodded solemnly. "Okay, Mario, take photos of this from all angles. In fact, get close-ups of the crushed shellfish and coral."

He took his camera from his eye. "Are you sure Damon wants me to film this?"

"Eastwood Enterprises does," said Gabby. "I know. I'm the one who submits the statements to them."

He deliberated. "Doesn't seem—"

"If you want Eastwood Enterprises to sign your check, do as Carole asks."

Without another word, he raised his camera and began snapping. As he finished, he sucked his teeth and crossed his arms. "Next?"

"The mangroves," said Carole. "Just down the beach."

The stumps of trees, looking like bleached bones, stood inches above the water line. Where the mangroves' green canopy had recently sheltered minnows and filtered debris from entering into sea, the sun now beat down on the polluted water. Plastic bags, aluminum cans, potato-chip bags, and an old shoe littered the macheted stumps.

When Mario finished shooting, Carole said, "Mind if I download your photos? Eastwood Enterprises is anxious to get these shots."

"Don't have a cable." Mario did an about-face and started walking away.

"I do," said Carole with a tight-lipped smile.

"Yeah, but no computer."

"Got something better," said Carole, taking the device from her pocket. "A digital wallet."

With a wordless shrug, Mario turned back and handed her the camera. Carole plugged the USB-cable into it, attached it to the digital wallet, and downloaded the images. Before she unplugged the camera, she double-checked that all the pictures had transferred.

"Thanks." She handed him back his camera with a smile.

Eyes never meeting hers, he asked, "We done?"

Carole studied him. "Looks like it." She held up her hand in a wave. "Take care, Mario."

Without a backward glance, he stomped across the beach, following the bulldozed trail to the road.

"What was that about?" asked Gabby.

"Something tells me he's going to contact Damon." Carole rewound the USB-cable and slipped the digital wallet back in her pocket. "I wanted to make sure we got these photos before he did." She looked at her watch. "Let's get back to the office and put this documentary together before Damon finds out."

Back at her desk, Carole downloaded Mario's still shots into her laptop, integrating them in the video she had made earlier that morning. Using Mario's long shots of the building site from the previous week's shoot, she panned in on the destruction, homing in on the three areas where Damon was working without permits.

"Just to be on the safe side," Carole said, handing a thumb drive to Gabby as she pocketed a second. "Here's a copy of the video. Hide it."

"How 'bout I give it to the DOI instead?"

Remembering her conversation with Nick the night before, Carole nodded. "Good idea. We work for a company that's destroying the reef—let's do something about it."

"What are you going to do?" asked Gabby.

"Already did. I emailed a copy of the video to Jeff Winthrop, the president of the board, asking if he's aware of Damon's disregard for Belize's environmental laws."

"That's gutsy." Gabby's smile and slight nod implied her respect.

"Thanks," Carole said, "but it's something I—" Carole's phone rang. She held up her index finger. "Just a second while I get this." Stepping away, she answered.

"Carole, what's the beef down there?" She recognized the voice as that of her managing editor at Campbell and Glenrock, but not the tone—hostile.

"Simon? That's an interesting greeting. What's up?"

"That's exactly what I want to know. You're being eighty-sixed."

"What?"

"Booted, baby. You've crapped out."

"Okay, Simon." Feeling a headache starting, she pressed her fingers into the bridge of her nose. "English, please."

"You've been axed, dismissed, discharged, given notice, fired, let go. *Capiche?*"

She took a step back as if she had been slapped. *So soon?* "You're joking, right?"

"Nope, you've been banned from the premises."

"I just sent off—"

"I don't want to hear the details. Look, I'm just doing my job here—like you should have been doing yours." He sighed. "Sorry, kiddo. It sounds like you got a bad beat, but this is just a courtesy call. Expect someone to walk you out at any minute."

"Simon—" The line went dead. " . . . thanks . . . ." In a daze, Carole hung up.

Gabby lightly touched her shoulder, and Carole spun around.

"Are you all right? You're pale as a ghost. Who was that?"

"My managing editor from C&G." Carole rolled her eyes. "Scratch that— ex-managing editor. Apparently, bad news travels fast."

"What are you talking about?"

Dante burst through the door, Mario dogging his heels.

"Both of them are in on it," said Mario, pointing at them but not meeting their eyes.

Dante's snapping, dark eyes glared. The thunderous clouds gathered and broke in a torrent of words. "Who do you think you are, stealing Mario's photographs? Where are the images you stole?"

"I stole nothing. Mario's images are on the digital wallet."

"Which is where?"

"Which is back in your desk drawer, where I found it."

"You mean, where you took it."

"It's back where you told me to find it," she said, "after I asked your permission to use it." She stared him down.

Dante turned toward Mario with a mutinous scowl. Then he turned back to Carole. "Where's the video?"

"Check your inbox," she said, gathering her personal effects. "I copied you and Damon when I sent it to the board." She met his eyes as she picked up her laptop. "I'm not hiding anything."

"Take your things and get—"

"I'm way ahead of you," she said, walking past him and out the door.

Carole dialed Nick. When he didn't answer, she left a message. Anxious to share the news, she redialed a moment later. He picked up on the fourth ring.

"Nick—"

"Carole, can I call you right back?"

"Uhm . . . ." She bit her lip, trying to hide her disappointment. "Sure . . . ."

"It'll just be a few minutes. Thanks."

"Love you," she said, needing to hear his nearness, even if she couldn't feel it.

" . . . you, too," he said, lowering his voice. "Call you as soon as my meeting's done."

A half hour later at her apartment, her phone rang.

"Nick, am I glad—"

"You've behaved foolishly," said a familiar voice.

Damon. "You've got your nerve," she said, poised with her finger over the disconnect button, her lip curling.

"Same could be said for you." The tone was dark, intimidating. "You and I aren't finished."

"Oh, yes, we are." She took pleasure in disconnecting, but the satisfaction was short-lived. *How did he get my phone number?*

When the cell rang a moment later, she let voice mail pick up. Not until she heard Nick's voice recording did she answer.

"Nick," she sighed, "am I ever glad to hear your voice."

"Yours, too," he said, his warmth flowing through the line. "Sorry I couldn't take your call before. Let's just say, I've been doing a little Christmas shopping." He cleared his throat. "Correction—combination Christmas and wedding-gift shopping."

The sound of his voice, the thought of his eagerness to please her, relieved her bruised ego, the sting of being let go, Damon's threatening words. She breathed in the moment. *It'll all work out. No, it is all working according to God's plan.* The dread of dealing with Damon, the board, finding a new job all ebbed away as the joy of their upcoming marriage washed over her. "Let me guess. It's—"

"It's a surprise." His excited chuckle charmed her. "All I can say is, it's something I've given a lot of thought to, something I've considered for weeks—ever since you said you'd marry me. I hope . . . ." Again the warmth came through his voice. "Hope it makes you happy."

"*You* make me happy. Any *thing* is just icing on our wedding cake." She felt wrapped in his love, protected from whatever evils Damon, Eastwood Enterprises, or C&G could concoct. Still, seeing him and holding him would be so much better than 'reaching out and touching' by phone. "But I really would like to see you this afternoon."

"Can it wait 'til dinner?"

"Sure . . . ."

"I've got a two-tank, group dive this afternoon."

"Yeah," she tried to shake off her disappointment, "sure."

"Are you okay?" His tone changed. She heard his concern.

"Not a problem. Go." Swallowing her disappointment, she forced a smile. "The sooner you start your dive, the sooner I'll see you for dinner."

She had barely hung up when she heard a knock at the door. Belle woofed. Carole started to open the door but then, recalling Damon's phone call, looked through the peephole.

"Gabby," she said, swinging the door wide open, "what are you doing here?"

"Couldn't stand the suspense of waiting to get sacked." She grinned.

"Yeah, but, even if you were, you'd still have a job with the DOI. I'm unemployed from both Eastwood Enterprises and C&G."

"Cheer up. It simply means you'll have more time for your wedding preparations." Gabby handed Carole her purse and opened the door. "Come on, we have to stop at the florist and find musicians for both ceremonies and the reception. Chop, chop—time's a wasting."

Carole had to laugh. "You're a hard person to turn down."

"It's a gift."

"Can we bring Belle?"

"Of course! Dogs are always welcome, especially this sweet girl." Gabby bent down to pet Belle as Carole fastened her leash. "San Pedro isn't Manhattan."

Carole locked the front door, testing it to double-check. "Three guesses who called a few minutes ago, and the first two don't count."

Raising her eyebrows, Gabby asked, "Our friend, Damon?"

Carole nodded. "Just wish I knew how he got my new cell number."

"He probably bribed someone." She stifled a sigh. "That's how he got the beachfront property—and most likely how he's gotten by without environmental impact analyses, studies, or permits." Gabby stopped in her tracks and faced her, suddenly standing in her space.

"What?" Carole blinked, surprised by the sudden change in proximity.

"Just want to say that you did the right thing in exposing Damon." She took a deep breath. "That took courage."

"Just did what I felt I had to. Was simply following my—"

"Star?"

"Conscience is what I was going to say." Carole said as they resumed their pace. "But I like your version more." Her thoughts returned to Damon's call. "Do you think Dante's in on it? I remember you saying he's everyone's go-to man."

"It's true." Gabby nodded as they walked. "Whatever you need, he finds it. Whatever you need done, he does it—or he knows who'll do it and arranges to have it done for you."

"So you think Dante's in on this with Damon."

"Officially, I can't share any evidence, but I can tell you this . . . ." She stopped and looked around, as if checking whether anyone was eavesdropping. Lowering her voice, she said, "Dante's involved in it, although not necessarily by choice."

"What do you mean?"

They resumed their walk, but kept their voices low.

"Dante has a gambling habit." At Carole's raised eyebrow, Gabby nodded. "Remember, I keep the office books. Dante had a habit of 'borrowing' the weekly income from investors on Friday night instead of depositing it in the bank. Then, Monday mornings, he'd make the deposits. One Monday, I overheard Damon and Dante arguing in Damon's office. The door was closed, but you know the walls—paper thin."

Carole nodded. "What was the gist of it?"

"Apparently, Dante's luck ran out. He'd gambled away the previous week's investment money and couldn't cover his debts."

"How much was he in debt?"

"Two hundred and fifty thousand dollars."

Carole whistled. "In one weekend?" At Gabby's nod, Carole summed up her thoughts. "Wow!"

"Damon accused him of embezzling the funds, but Dante kept saying over and over again that he'd just 'borrowed' the money, that it had been 'a sure thing.' If Damon would give him time, he'd pay it back."

"What'd Damon say?"

"He said there wasn't time—that a third-party firm had been hired to audit their accounts."

"Was that true?"

"Who knows?" Gabby shrugged. "But he made Dante a deal. Damon said he'd bail him out financially if Dante would make the arrangements with Belizean officials to purchase the beachfront land and 'look the other way' regarding environmental impact assessments."

"Basically, he got Dante to bribe them." Carole met Gabby's eyes. "So that's why Dante seemed so blasé about the beach's destruction? I thought it seemed out of character for him."

"Dante's a nice guy," said Gabby, nodding, "but he's become Damon's pawn."

"You make it sound like he's sold his soul to Damon."

"He might as well have."

"What a shame." Carole shook her head. "Whether or not he shares Damon's scruples or agrees with his building methods, he's in just as deep."

"I'm afraid he is," Gabby studied Carol's face. "But this is confidential information. Please keep it to yourself."

"I will."

"Good because we're here." Gabby stopped in front of a weathered storefront.

Carole appraised the building's neglected exterior. "This is the florist?" she asked, noting several dusty-leaved plants in the otherwise bare storefront window.

"Wait 'til you get inside before you draw any conclusions," whispered Gabby, her eyes twinkling.

The moment they entered the shop, Carole was bombarded with the scents of lilies, carnations, roses, and dozens of varieties of flowers she did not recognize. Color was everywhere. Flowers inside tubs, vases, and containers lined three of the tiered walls and flowed over the ancient oak table. Behind the glassed doors of the refrigerator that covered the fourth wall, buckets of flowers stood at attention, waiting to be pruned, twisted, and shaped into bouquets and arrangements. But what fascinated Carole was the massive vine that grew up the sides of the refrigerator, was suspended from the ceiling, and gracefully cascaded down the walls.

"This is incredible," she said, unable to take her eyes from the greenery.

"I know. It isn't possible to take it all in at a glance. There's so much packed into this tiny shop." Addressing the woman behind the counter, Gabby said, "Chantal, my friend Carole's getting married on Christmas Eve. Think we can help her with her wedding flowers?"

"Be happy to," she said, reaching over the counter for Carole's hand. "Everyone calls me Chantal. Pleased to meet you. Carole, right?"

"Your shop is gorgeous," said Carole, nodding, still taking in the visual feast as she shook hands. "If your arrangements are half as elegant, I'll have the best bouquet and wedding flowers in Ambergris Caye."

"I'll do my best. What are you looking for?"

"For starters, I want a *huge* bouquet of the brightest blooms available—and several matching arrangements for the altar."

"And for the beach ceremony, we were thinking of an arch of palm fronds sprinkled with purple and red flowers," said Gabby.

"As I recall, black orchids, heliconia, and red ginger," said Carole.

"Don't forget hot lips," said Gabby. "Plus, we'll need coordinating table arrangements for the reception."

"And a black orchid for the groom's boutonniere," said Carole, visualizing Nick as she walked up the aisle, "and a miniature bouquet for a flower girl."

Gabby turned toward her. "Who's going to be your flower girl?"

"The little friend I told you about, Estrella."

"What about the bridesmaids and maid of honor?" asked Chantal, taking notes.

Carole's eyelids flew open. "Ohmigosh, I forgot to ask you. Gabby, would you be my maid of honor?"

"Of course! I'd love to be your maid of honor." She hugged Carole. "I'd have been insulted if you'd asked anyone else."

"My cousin, Rafael, is a wonderful musician," said Gabby. "He has his own band, plus he knows most of the musicians on the island. Let's ask him if he's available—or knows someone who is—for your wedding."

"Great idea."

"He's playing at the Black Cat Bar." She checked her watch. "He could be there now. Want to stop by and see?"

"Sure." As they walked toward the beachfront bars, Carole said, "You told me earlier that it had taken courage to expose Damon." Gabby nodded. "And I'd said it was something that my conscience made me do."

"Yeah . . . . " Gabby nodded.

"Well, I had a personal reason for doing it, too." Carole took a deep breath. "Deep down, I figured going to the board would terminate my contract . . . ."

"So . . . ."

"So I thought taking a break from my PR career and staying on in Ambergris would be my Christmas present to Nick."

"What do you mean?" Gabby squinted.

"Ever since Nick and I met, we've been at odds over our careers. It was the biggest hurdle to our getting engaged." She held out her right hand. "He wanted me to stay here for two years while he established his dive business." She held out her left hand. "I wanted him to come to New York for two years while I made a name for myself in the PR world."

Gabby nodded.

"I figured this would be the best gift I could give him."

"Staying here on Ambergris Caye?"

"Exactly." Carole bobbed her head in agreement.

"What will you do with your time?"

She grinned. "Maybe I'll write that novel I've always talked about."

"Today's events may have been a blessing in disguise. I think you're going to enjoy a furlough from PR work," said Gabby, positioning herself to better see Carole's eyes. "Come over here in the sunlight. You actually have stars in your eyes."

"Stars in my eyes." She repeated the words and thought of Estrella's motto. *Follow your star.*

Gabby's cousin, Rafael, was playing at the Starfish Grille when they arrived. Wavy rows of iridescent blue and aqua black lights lit up the bar. The effect was of being beneath the sea. Wooden, starfish-shaped candleholders added flickering glimmers of light on each table. They listened to Rafael's band play a set, and then Gabby called him over, introducing him.

"What kind of music did you have in mind? Jazz, Caribbean, steel drums, or party music?" he asked.

Carole blinked. "To tell you the truth, I hadn't given it a lot of thought."

"Can I make a recommendation?" asked Gabby.

"Please!"

"Rafael, we're going to need two, if not three, kinds of music." Gabby counted off on her fingers. "First, there's the church wedding. Then, there's the beach wedding, and finally, the reception."

His arms folded, his eyes staring but not seeing, lost in thought, Rafael nodded. "Okay."

"What about guitar music in church?" Gabby looked to Carole, who nodded. "Then how about Caribbean music for the beach wedding?"

"It sounds great so far," said Carole. "Do you have any ideas for the reception?"

"I'd suggest party music," said Rafael, "with a little jazz and Caribbean music thrown into the mix for local flavor."

"Perfect. Another one you can check off our list, Gabby," said Carole, beaming. "Rafael, your band sounds great. I can't wait to hear you play at our wedding Christmas Eve."

"Looking forward to it, and don't worry about amplifiers, wires, or anything else. We'll take care of all the equipment. All you need to do is enjoy your big day."

Chapter Sixteen

Despite the morning's rough start, Carole walked into her apartment humming one of the band's selections. "It's funny how things work out," she told Belle, removing her leash.

The dog woofed and licked her face in response.

She chuckled as she scratched Belle's neck and began humming *Kokomo*. After checking the refrigerator, she began chopping veggies for dinner. *Another few days, and I'll be making dinner for Nick every night.* She hunched her shoulders, hugging herself.

The doorbell rang, and Belle began barking. Carole shushed her as she wiped her hands on a towel and checked the peephole. *Nick.*

"I'm so glad to see you." She hugged him, pressing against him and lifting her lips to his.

He pulled away without a kiss and silently shut the door.

Suddenly, she felt a chill. Blinking, unsure what had happened, what had changed, she studied his face. His brows met in a deep V, his eyes were bloodshot, and he was scowling.

"Nick, what's wrong?"

His jaw firmly set, he ground his teeth before speaking. "This," he finally spat out, tossing her a thumb drive.

Caught off guard, she nearly dropped it. "What's on this?" She looked from the thumb drive to him and back again.

"You tell me," he shouted, glaring at her.

She involuntarily recoiled.

"Play it!"

Wordless, she plugged it into her laptop. She watched Nick's face for clues, trying to get a sense of what to expect. All she saw was his defiant stare and his angry, red eyes.

Suddenly, she heard her voice speaking from the thumb drive's recording. Her voice, her words, but jumbled. Her phrases had been taken out of context. Her inflexions were slightly off. Fragments had been pieced together, spliced, and remixed, but it was her voice—along with Damon's.

Despite the odd inflexions, she heard her voice telling Damon, "I can't believe how . . . good . . . that . . . feels."

"What about Nick? How do you feel about him?" asked Damon's voice.

"If you're implying that my engagement to Nick will, in any way, impact my . . . feelings . . . for you . . . you're out of line. I have no difficulty separating business from pleasure."

"Pleasure, huh? You like that?" asked Damon's voice.

"Oh, yes . . . yes." They listened to sound effects of kissing.

"How's this feel?" asked Damon's voice.

"Great . . . more . . . more," said her voice.

When the recording devolved into moans of lovemaking, Carole pulled the thumb drive out of its port.

How could Damon have sunk so low?

"I've heard enough." Disgusted, she turned to Nick. "You can't seriously believe I did or even said any of the things this recording suggests, can you?"

He continued to glare at her.

"Don't you recognize a second-rate remixing of my conversations into this hodge-podge of lies?"

Nick's chest heaving, he took a deep breath. "When Dante told me initially, no—"

"So it was Dante that delivered this to you. What? Damon was too squeamish to do his own dirty work?"

"When Dante first told me about you and Damon, I dismissed it, but when he played this for me—"

"You've got to be kidding. How could you believe something this poorly produced?" She rolled her eyes. "Just listen to my inflections. It's easy to tell my words were pieced together from various conversations and then remixed to *almost* sound as if I were saying those things."

"It's your voice."

"Yes, it's my voice, but, the words are so out of context, their sequence is a lie. Don't you get it?"

"I hear it. That's more than enough."

Groaning, she began rubbing her temples. "Okay, let me take a different approach. Forget the 'recording' for a minute, will you?"

"How can I?" His wounded eyes glared at her.

With a sigh, she gathered her thoughts. "Nick, I love you. How could you believe I'd ever do anything to hurt you?"

"I believe what I hear," he snapped.

"I just told you—this is all smoke and mirrors. Damon simply took recordings of my voice and used software to piece words and phrases together into sentences with completely different meanings. Everything was taken out of context and then remixed into this propaganda." When he didn't move, she gently touched his shoulder. "Don't you trust me?"

He pulled away with a contemptuous snort. "I did trust you, and look what it got me."

"Nick, a spliced soundtrack doesn't prove anyth—"

"Are you trying to deny that you cheated on me?"

"What?" *Who is this person?* She started to speak, but didn't know how to respond. Mouth open, she simply gazed at him in shock.

Finally, he said, "I want it back."

"The thumb drive? Here, take it." She held it out to him.

"No, keep that as a memento of Damon." His lip curled. "I want the ring."

She stared at him, speechless, blinking. She shook her head, trying to grasp how life could change so quickly. *Why won't he listen to reason? Can't he see I love him?* She studied his face, looking for signs of empathy, but all she saw was closed-minded irrationality. And defeat. *He's made up his mind. It's too late for logic.*

Okay, if this is what he wants to believe, I won't dignify his accusations by trying to change his mind. Swallowing the lump in her throat, she lifted her head to her full height. She held up her hand and stared at the engagement ring for the last time, moving her fingers to capture and reflect the light. *How can it still sparkle when my world's grown so dark?*

As she pulled off her ring, a thought flashed through her mind. She recalled reading that rings are worn on the left ring finger because the

Romans believed the *vena amori*—vein of love—directly connected it to the heart. *Maybe they were right. I don't feel I'm taking off a ring as much as cutting open a vein.* Her heart sinking, she handed it to him.

Not meeting her eyes, not touching her shaking fingers, he took the ring. Hunched over, grimacing, he clutched it in his closed palm, brought it to his lips, and sighed.

"I thought I knew you, but I don't. And you obviously don't have a clue about me." Crossing to the door, she threw it open. "Get out of here."

The next morning, Carole was awake when Estrella rang the doorbell. When Carole invited her in, Estrella looked at the mess of boxes and scattered clothes.

"What are you doing?"

"Packing," said Carole, folding clothes as they spoke.

Estrella's dark eyes dimmed as she looked up. "You're going away?"

"All good things must come to an end." Carole laughed silently at the irony.

"What about our Christmas ornaments? We're not finished, and the bazaar's Saturday."

Her tone made Carole look up. Seeing the girl's pout, she said, "We can finish them this morning. Tell you what. Take Belle for a walk. We'll have breakfast when you get back, and then we'll finish making the ornaments. Will that work?"

The girl nodded, her braided ponytail bouncing. "C'mon, Belle." She took the leash down from the wall. "Let's go for a walk."

They had no sooner left than the phone rang. Carole let the answering machine get it. When she heard Simon's voice, she picked up.

"What cheery news do you have for me today?"

"I was a little hasty yesterday." He cleared his voiced. "Jeff Winthrop . . . uh . . . the president—"

"Yes, I know, the president of Eastwood Enterprises' board." She let out a frustrated sigh. "Don't beat around the bush, Simon. What is it you want to say?"

"Jeff Winthrop emailed and called last night . . . ."

"And? Get to the point."

"He wants you to stay on as—"

"No."

"Before you say 'no dice,' hear me out."

"No. I'm simply not interested. Thanks, but no thanks. Now, if you'll excuse me, I'm in the middle of packing."

"Carole, Winthrop wants you to be the Communications Director for Eastwood Enterprises—not just for this project, but for the corporation." He took a deep breath. "Actually, if you take this position, I'll be reporting to you on this account."

It started with a grin, built into a laugh, and ended with tears running down her cheeks. Wiping her eyes, she said, "Simon, yesterday you, C&G, and Eastwood Enterprises fired me. Are you aware of the incongruity of this offer?"

"I know. This business is a crapshoot. C'mon, Carole. What's your answer?"

"What about Damon? Is he still the CO?"

"Oh," he coughed, "then you haven't heard."

"Heard what?"

"Damon's going to jail."

"What? You're kidding, right? Why?"

"He's being indicted for fraud and embezzlement."

"What for?"

Simon took a deep breath. "Sleight of hand. It sounds like he was deft at appropriating investors' funds. Anyway, Eastwood Enterprises is under investigation, and the board wants to improve its image—like yesterday. Hello? When can you start, Carole?"

"I didn't say I'd take the position."

"Will you at least consider it?"

"Simon, I'm not a ping-pong ball. You can't kick me out one day and promote me the next. It doesn't work that way."

"Duly noted."

"Was this because of my video exposé?"

"Apparently, the investigation's been ongoing for several months. Let's just say your exposé was well-timed."

"Just for the sake of argument, if I were to consider—"

"Then you'll take it?"

"I'm asking a question here, Simon. *If* I were to consider it, what are the board's expectations?"

He took a long breath. "Eastwood Enterprises had been under a lot of scrutiny because of Damon's embezzlement. Now, with your video and the DOI's inquiry, this resort is under investigation. The board doesn't need or want any more public scrutiny. It wants to dump the resort concept and improve its public image—fast."

"How fast?"

"Like I said, yesterday."

She took a deep breath.

"Before you say anything, did I tell you what Winthrop wants to start you at?"

"I don't—"

"Two hundred thousand big ones."

"It's not that I don't—"

"Okay, okay," he said, "two hundred and fifty thousand smackers."

"Simon, it's not about the money. Yesterday, you couldn't get rid of me fast enough. Now today—"

"Everything's about the money, Carole. Sheesh, you're a tough negotiator. Okay—and that is the final offer I'm authorized to make . . . $250K."

"Simon, that's not my point. I can't take being bounced like a bad check. I need security. I need to know that I'll have a job tomorrow. In other words," she took a deep breath, "if I were to even consider this position, I'd need an ironclad contract for the next twenty-four months."

Silence. Carole waited it out. She knew the next person to speak lost. The silence lasted so long, she checked her phone that they had not been disconnected.

Finally, she heard him sigh. "Let me get back to you. I've got to make a call."

Carole sliced the mushrooms and cheese. When Estrella and Belle returned, it took only minutes to make the omelets. Estrella buttered and sliced the toast, and they sat down to breakfast.

Carole was about to take a bite, when Estrella asked, "Why don't you say grace?"

"What?"

"Why don't you ever say grace before you eat?"

Carole shrugged. "I used to—just have gotten out of the habit, I guess."

Estrella folded her hands and closed her eyes. Carole followed suit, but peeked as Estrella said, "God is great. God is good. Let us thank Him for our food." She crossed herself, and Carole made a clumsy attempt to imitate her.

"Amen," Carole mumbled.

Estrella looked up at her. "Are you going away?"

"Yes. Well, maybe." She ran her fingers through her hair. "I don't know. I haven't made up my mind."

Estrella tilted her head and studied her. "Aren't you going to marry Nick?"

Carole took a deep breath and put down her fork. Pressing her lips together, she shook her head. "It doesn't look that way, not now."

"Why not? Don't you love him anymore?"

"It isn't as black and white as that."

"What do you mean?" Estrella's dark eyes looked up to hers.

She sighed. "Nick thinks I did something that made him very angry."

"Did you?"

"No," she shook her head, "but he believes I did. As far as he's concerned, it's the same thing."

Estrella squinted. "I don't get it."

"Someone told Nick a lie that makes me look guilty. He believes that 'evidence' more than he believes me."

"The truth is the truth," said Estrella, seeming wise beyond her years. She smiled and picked up her fork. "This looks delicious, Carole. You're going to make Nick a wonderful wife."

"But I'm not marrying Nick." Despite the sting of the broken engagement, Carole had to restrain a chuckle at Estrella's solemn words. *What a funny little girl.*

"Don't worry, Carole, you just need to follow your star. Everything will work out."

Carole rested her head on her hand as she studied the girl. "Why do—" The phone rang, interrupting her. "Excuse me." Carole took the call in the other room.

"Okay, Winthrop's serious about wanting you as Communications Director." Simon took a deep breath. "He authorized me to fax you a two-year, ironclad contract. That means that even if he fires you, you'll be paid for the entire two years. *Capiche?*"

"And at what price?"

"What we agreed on—$250K. Plus he bumped it up with a sign-on bonus of another fifty grand."

Wow! She inhaled deeply, thinking of the possibilities, debating. *Should I stay on Ambergris Caye? Move back to my apartment in Manhattan? Would the board want me to report to corporate headquarters in Houston?* Each option introduced more questions.

Finally, Simon broke into her thoughts. "Don't play hardball, Carole. This is as high as I can go. What do you say?"

"What would be my home base? Manhattan, Houston, Ambergris Caye?"

"Any of those, none of those … it's your choice since your position's virtual."

She raised her eyebrows. *This opens a lot of avenues.* "If—and I do mean *if*—I were to consider taking the position, Simon, when would I start?"

"The contract would be effective from the moment you sign it—which, by the way, I'm faxing to you as we speak. It's already been signed at this end. All you need to do is print out two copies, sign them both, keep one, and return the other. That's it."

She heard the whistling sound of the fax machine printing. "That's all there is to it?"

"Just sign and fax."

"And the board wants me to do what for this?" She pulled the contract from the fax tray and skimmed it.

"Smooth over this resort fiasco for them. They want to dump it—ASAP—and they want to come out smelling like roses. The more of a positive spin you can put on it, the better."

She breathed in deeply, grabbed a pen from her purse, scribbled her name on the contract, and faxed it back. "Okay, Simon. Eastwood Enterprises has their Communications Director."

"You've made a good move, Carole."

"Time'll tell. Talk to you later." She returned to the kitchen table and caught Estrella feeding the dog. The girl's plate was clean, and Belle was licking her chops. Unsure whether to scold or laugh, Carole decided to let it pass. "Business called."

Nodding, the girl lifted her eyes. "Does this mean you'll be staying on Ambergris Caye?"

"Are you psychic, or did you overhear my conversation?"

"Neither," said the girl. "You're smiling."

"So?"

"It's the first time you've smiled this morning. Does that mean you're not moving?"

Chapter Seventeen

An hour later, as she waved goodbye to Estrella, Carole asked herself the same question. She thought about her future as she carefully boxed the Christmas ornaments they had made.

Now that Nick and I are no longer a couple, is there any reason to stay on here? Then she printed out a copy of her signed contract and slowly read it. Taking a deep breath, she answered her own question. *Yeah, there is. I have to fix the board's dilemma. Where better to right Damon's wrong than working from Ambergris Caye?*

She dialed Gabby's number.

"Carole, I'm glad you called. So much has happened since yesterday."

"Ain't that the truth," she muttered.

"What?"

"I said, what happened at your end?"

"This morning, Dante told me to pack my things," said Gabby. "I smiled sweetly, emailed your video to the DOI, downloaded the investor transaction records onto my thumb drive, and waited outside until the police came to arrest Dante."

"You are one cool cucumber." Carole chuckled in admiration. "And you always seemed so nice."

Gabby snickered. "So how are you faring after yesterday?"

Where do I begin? She took a deep breath. "You know all the work we've put into making arrangements for the wedding?"

"Yeah."

"We'll have to cancel everything."

"What!"

"I'll buy the dress, of course, since your aunt has put so much time into it, but the cake, flowers, and music will have to be cancelled." Carole told her about Nick.

"All because he believed Dante's lies?"

"That and a doctored recording—at least, that's what he said." Carole shook her head. "I think he had cold feet, and this was just an excuse to back out of the wedding."

"No, I can't believe that. I've seen how he lights up when you're near him," said Gabby. "I wonder what happened to set him off."

"I don't know . . . ." Carole mentally replayed their breakup for the fortieth time. Then, remembering that Gabby was waiting for an answer, she swallowed her tears and cleared her throat. "I don't get it, either, but I can't think about it right now." She wiped away a tear that had escaped. "There's something I have to do, and I need your help."

"Other than making a few phone calls to cancel the wedding arrangements and writing a report for the DOI, I'm all yours."

"If all goes well, you'll have another report to file for the Department of the Interior soon." Carole told her about Eastwood Enterprises hiring her to repurpose the resort.

"You're kidding me, right?" Gabby snickered. "You were out of work for how many hours?"

"Getting hired was the one bright spot in the last twenty-four hours," said Carole. "So help me think. How could the DOI use this beach and the foundation that's been poured for the resort?"

"It's a beautiful location. Although the beach was damaged, by using green building methods from this point on—over time—its footprint could be reversed."

"What about using it as some kind of community learning center?" asked Carole.

"Since it's on the beach—maybe an environmental outreach center?"

Carole drew in her breath. "That's it! A marine-based environmental outreach center. Gabby, you're a genius." Carole began mentally composing press releases. "I can see the headlines—Eastwood Enterprises Funds Environmental Outreach Center. Or what about this? Star Quality: Eastwood Enterprises Recognized for Nature Conservation Leadership." She gasped.

"What?"

"I just had an idea. When Estrella first showed it to me, the beach was filled with starsnails. Hopefully, they'll return. What if we call it Starsnail Cove? Or how about calling it the Starsnail Center for Environmental Outreach?"

Gabby smiled. "You're the PR idea person. I'm just the one that knows which government forms to file for such an undertaking."

"Good point. First, we have to sell the board on this idea, although I think it'll be an easy sell. Then, we'll have to set up meetings between the DOI and the board."

"I know just who to invite," said Gabby. "One director in particular has been interested in building an outreach center, but the department could never get the funding. If Eastwood Enterprises will fund the project, I can just about guarantee Director Harding will support it."

"Perfect." Carole nodded as she planned her strategy. "Gabby, can you get started on the paperwork while I contact the board?"

"Aye, aye, captain." She giggled.

"Want to meet for lunch? Say noon at the Starfish Grille?"

"Sure, we can compare notes."

"Compare notes . . . while we listen to Rafael's band and cancel . . . ." In the excitement of brainstorming, she had forgotten about the broken engagement. As the memories flooded her, she squeezed her eyes shut, willing them not to tear up.

"How 'bout we go to the Pelican Palapa instead?" said Gabby softly. "I'll call Rafael."

"Thanks," she said in a strangled voice. "Yeah, the Pelican Palapa at noon, see you."

As she hung up, Carole thought about her future. *Not only was the wedding cancelled when Nick broke up with me, he cancelled Christmas, too. This holiday is going to be the worst.* Despite her best intentions, she started to cry. Belle rubbed against her leg, whimpering.

"Thanks, girl." She hugged the dog. "We'll be all right. I just have to keep busy, that's all."

Wiping her tears, she planned her morning. *First, call Jeff Winthrop, the board president, get his buy-in. Then begin writing the press releases . . . without knowing any details.* She laughed at the irony. *It won't be the first time I've written announcements without knowing the facts.*

She dialed Eastwood Enterprises' main number. "Jeff Winthrop, please."

After three rings, a recording said, "Jeffrey Winthrop is not available. To leave a message, press the star key."

The star key. Estrella's words popped into her mind. *Follow your star.* Taking it as a good sign, she took a deep breath and lifted her head. "Jeff, this is Carole. Please call me back at this number. I have an idea for turning the resort fiasco into a PR triumph."

"Absolutely," said Carole, "and if you get the legal department involved, I'll bet those smart folks can find a way to not only recoup the losses on the property, but get a tax write off. This contribution could offset any deficit . . . maybe even cover my salary."

"Sold!" Jeff chuckled. "Package it into a proposal, and I'll pitch it to the board."

"Expect it in your inbox by morning."

Carole stared at her surroundings, taking in the restaurant's turquoise and blue ocean-inspired décor, until the waitress brought the shrimp and red snapper ceviche. Suddenly, she realized she was hungry.

"I pulled in a few favors," Gabby said, eyes twinkling, "and I had a chance to talk with Director Harding this morning."

"Really?" said Carole, drizzling a halved key lime over her ceviche. "What did he have to say?"

"He's interested." Gabby's eyes lit up. "In fact, he wants to see the property as soon as possible."

"Today?"

"My friend's his assistant. Let me check if his schedule's open." Gabby took out her phone and texted. A moment later, she read the reply. "The director can't come, but his assistant, my friend, can be here at two o'clock." She looked up, grinning. "Will that work for you?"

"Will that work for me?" Carole repeated, mimicking her. "Hah!" She looked at her watch. "That's less than two hours."

"An hour and thirty-five minutes, but who's counting?" said Gabby as she texted back.

"This is Angel Ramirez," said Gabby, pronouncing Angel *On-hel* as she introduced her friend.

"Glad you could meet with us so quickly," said Carole, reaching out to shake hands.

"Opportunities like the one Gabby described don't come around often," he said with a wink at Gabby. He turned back to Carole. "Director Harding's very interested in this proposal."

"Wonderful," said Carole. "Let's grab a cab and see the building site."

Ten minutes later, they picked their way through the mud.

"This really is a beautiful cove," said Carole, "despite the damage that's occurred."

"I can see that," he said, catching Gabby's eye. "What do you think?"

Carole did a double take. Gabby's cheeks were tinged pink. Her eyes were bright, and she was glowing. Carole looked at Angel. He couldn't take his eyes off Gabby.

Well, well, well, what have we here? Friends, huh? She couldn't help but notice their obvious affection for each other, especially in the midst of her own cooling-off period with Nick.

"It's such a secluded location—away from San Pedro's sprawl, yet only ten minutes from town," said Gabby. "I believe it would make an ideal location for environmental education."

Maintaining eye contact, he nodded, obviously more taken with Gabby than her words.

Carole stifled a smile.

"Yes," he said, "this definitely has potential as an educational facility." He looked around, studying the natural environment. The grove of trees encircled the back of the cove while the sea shimmered in the front. "It could offer learning programs and training opportunities for all educational levels, from elementary and high schools to colleges and universities."

"There's been a loss of habitat within the project's footprint," Carole said, scanning the freshly cut road and the exposed roots and stumps of bulldozed trees. "But it's not too late to reverse the impact with good construction management from this point on."

"It's true," said Gabby, pointing to the construction equipment. "If these were replaced with machines that emitted fewer toxic gases, used biodegradable hydraulic fluid, and reduced noise levels, that would decrease the stress on this environment."

He nodded, internalizing her words. "I'm glad only the slab's been poured. That gives us choices to use recycled and natural materials in the building process."

Gabby pointed to the tree line between the site and the public road. "If we modify the construction methods, I believe this vegetation will regenerate itself."

Angel caught her hand. "Nature's resilient—don't worry. As long as it's temporary, it can recover."

Angel's words reminded Carole of Nick's summary the last time she had met him there, and her mind began drifting to better times. She swallowed hard. *I've got to focus on this project.*

"What we need to do next is persuade Director Harding and Eastwood Enterprises to meet—and the sooner, the better," said Angel.

"Why don't we set up a tentative meeting time for them?" Carole suggested. "Possibly the day after tomorrow?"

"What's wrong with tomorrow?" asked Angel.

Carole stayed up until dawn writing the proposal for the board. *At least it's delivered to Jeff's inbox. Just hope he can sell it to the board in time for this afternoon's DOI meeting.*

Yawning, she called Belle. "C'mon, girl. Jump into bed." As Carole turned off the light, she thought of Nick and was grateful for her exhaustion. *At least I won't lie awake thinking about him.*

A moment later, she heard the doorbell, followed by Belle's barking. Opening her eyes, she was surprised to see it was light in the room. She checked the clock. *Eleven?* She jumped out of bed and pulled on a robe. Peering through the peephole, she saw Estrella standing in the doorway.

"Good, you're up," said the girl.

"How did you know to come later than usual?" Carole yawned as she opened the door.

"Just did . . . plus, it's Saturday. Figured you'd want to sleep in."

"How about breakfast?"

"How 'bout I make it for us?" Dark eyes sparkling, Estrella grinned as she held up a bag. "Breakfast tacos. Why don't you shower and dress while I make coffee?"

Though half asleep, Carole regarded the girl with newfound admiration. "Okay, why not?"

Ten minutes later, Carole returned to the kitchen. Freshly squeezed juice and a platter full of yellow and green stars were waiting for her. The table had been set, and Estrella was pouring steaming coffee. Besides tacos, the girl had brought oranges, starfruit, and wildflowers for a centerpiece.

Who is this amazing, little woman? "Where'd you learn to do all this?"

Estrella shrugged and pulled out a chair for her. "Sit down."

Carole took her seat and began sipping her coffee. Estrella sat down, folded her hands, closed her eyes, and waited. Grimacing, Carole squirmed in her chair and set down her cup.

"God is great," Estrella began. "God is good. Let us thank Him for our food." She crossed herself, and Carole made a self-conscious effort to follow suit.

"Amen," Carole mumbled, again reaching for her coffee.

"Carole, the bazaar's tonight."

"Already?" She gulped her coffee.

The girl nodded.

"We're ready, aren't we?"

"We've finished the ornaments," said Estrella, "but we don't have any way to display them."

Carole furrowed her brow, trying to think what they could use. Her eyes roamed the kitchen, searching for something they could press into service.

Estrella's face lit up. "What about this?" She brought out a potted sea-grape bush she had hidden behind the table. "What do you think?"

"It's perfect." Carole shook her head in disbelief as she looked at the girl with respect. *What hasn't she thought of? What a remarkable girl.* "We can hang the ornaments on this tree to display them."

"And," Estrella beamed, "after the bazaar, this can be your Christmas tree."

After breakfast, they took Belle for a walk along the beach. Barefoot on the sand, they threw a Frisbee as Belle ran back and forth, barking as she chased and caught the disk. They waded in the water, not caring if their clothes got wet. With Estrella and Belle, Carole felt like a girl again, giggling, carefree. On the way back, they spotted a snow cone stand.

"How about a snow cone?" she said. *I haven't had one of those in years.*

"Sure." Estrella looked up with a big grin.

Carole shook her head as she surveyed the girl and Belle. *How would I have gotten through the breakup with Nick without them?*

They found a shady spot under a palm tree and sat on the sand. As Carole nibbled her shaved ice, Estrella said, "Tomorrow, we should go to the bazaar early to set up. I'll help you carry the shell ornaments and display tree."

Suddenly, Belle raised her head and began whining.

Estrella turned her head in that direction and called, "Hi."

Carole turned around to see who it was. *Nick!* She gasped and turned away, unsure how to respond. She looked at her damp, rumpled shorts and sand-speckled legs. With a sigh, she ran her hand through her tangled hair, trying to finger-comb it. *Nothing like catching me at my best.*

Belle stood up, whimpering, whining, and blatantly begging for attention.

"She wants to say hello," said Estrella, petting the dog.

Nick gave an uneasy laugh. "No, I'd—"

"Come on over," said Estrella. "Belle wants to say hi."

"No, I don't think I'm welcome here."

"Sure you are," said Estrella, her tone coaxing. "Belle wants you to pet her."

On cue, the dog wiggled, pranced, and woofed until Carole saw Nick's hand reach out to pet Belle.

"Hi ya', girl," he said, ruffling the dog's coat. As Belle rolled over to have her belly scratched, he knelt down on one knee, obliging.

Carole could see his outline in her peripheral vision, but she refused to look.

"Her name's Belle," said Estrella.

"I know." He cleared his throat. "We're old friends."

"Then you must be a friend of Carole's."

He grunted.

"Carole," said Estrella, "aren't you going to say hello?"

Keeping her eyes on her sandy legs, she took a deep breath. "'Lo," she muttered through clenched teeth.

"Hi." His tone was derisive, curt.

"Are you . . . ." Estrella paused so long, Carole raised her eyes to look at her. "Are you Nick?"

He gave an uneasy laugh. "Yeah, how did you know?"

"Just guessed." She studied him. "Nick, don't believe everything you hear."

"What?" Scowling, he looked first at the girl, and then he glared at Carole.

"Gossip is gossip," said Estrella. "Truth is truth."

"Estrella . . . ." Carole opened her mouth to scold, but she couldn't think of anything to say. *How do you fault facts?*

"Now you're recruiting children to defend you?" His tone accusing, he fixed an angry stare on Carole.

"Out of the mouths of babes comes truth." She sneered at him. "*That*, you should listen to."

He started to rise from his half-kneeling position, but Belle had other ideas. In one fluid motion, the dog rolled over and pounced on top of Nick, knocking him off-balance, pushing him backwards onto the sand. Sitting on his chest, snout to nose, the dog began licking his face.

When Estrella started giggling, Belle turned midair and playfully reached out a paw, spilling the girl's syrupy ice on Nick's shirt. As she responded to Estrella's shriek of laughter, the dog began wagging her tail, rhythmically bopping Nick's face and sweeping strawberry ice crystals across his shirt.

It started with chuckles and developed into belly laughs as Nick, Belle, and Estrella lolled together in the sand amid syrupy, shaved ice and a bad case of the giggles.

"Carole," said Estrella, laughing, catching her breath. "Quick, take a picture."

The girl's giggles were contagious. Grinning, Carole pulled her phone from its holster, but, as she brought up the app and looked through the viewfinder, Belle decided to help. Using Nick's chest as a launching pad, the dog leapt at Carole, knocking her into the milieu. The phone went flying, but Nick caught it mid-flight and snapped a self-picture of the four of them.

They erupted into paroxysms of laughter, each person unable to stop as Belle turned from one face to another, licking nonstop. Carole laughed until her stomach muscles ached. She wiped a tear from the corner of her eye as she caught her breath.

What a release! After these last few days, laughing feels good. She felt renewed, as if she had just woken refreshed from a deep sleep. She took a deep breath, feeling relaxed to her bones. The tension relieved, Nick caught her eye, and, for an instant, they connected and their eyes locked.

He opened his mouth, hesitated, and said, "Carole, it's—"

Her phone rang. Its sound pierced their bubble, deflating the moment, destroying the mood. As smiles hardened into scowls, they withdrew their white flags. Suddenly miles, not inches, separated them.

"It's for you." Lips pressed together in a thin, white line, he handed her the phone.

Brushing off the sand from her shorts with one hand, she took the phone with the other and stood up. In the time it took to answer, she had slipped into her business persona.

"Yes." She listened and then bobbed her head in a nod. "I'll join you at two." She turned back to Estrella and Nick.

"Date with Damon?" he asked. His eyes narrowing, he glared at her.

You bastard. "It so happens—" Angry words tumbled to the tip of her tongue, but she bit them back. Pressing her fingers into her forehead, she took a deep breath, counted to five, and then turned to Estrella. "Sorry, but I have to leave for a conference call."

"What about the bazaar?" the girl asked. "We have to set up our display table."

"Can you stop by at four?" Carole focused on her, refusing to look at Nick. "We can take everything over then."

Estrella said, "Maybe Nick can help us—"

"I'm sure he's busy." Carole warned him off with flinty eyes.

He turned toward Estrella. "Thanks, maybe another time."

Carole joined the conference call at two o'clock. As requested, she gave an overview of the project, virtually sharing her PowerPoint presentation.

"Director Harding, this cove is an exceptional location for an educational facility," she said. "The DOI could search far and wide, but it won't find another site that approaches it for convenience yet seclusion."

"My assistant confirms that," said the director. "What concerns me is the damage that's occurred to the cove."

"Although habitat has been lost within the project's footprint," Carole said, "it's not too late to reverse the impact with good construction management from this point on."

"In compensation for the initial damage," said Jeff, jumping in, "the board of Eastwood Enterprises would like to work closely with the DOI to devise an Environmental Compliance Plan."

"You mentioned the word compensation," said the director. "How do you plan to compensate Belize for the incurred environmental losses?"

"As a show of good faith," said the president of the board, "Eastwood Enterprises would like to make a tax-deductible gift of the property to Belize."

An attorney of Eastwood Enterprises spoke up. "Of course, *quid pro quo*, any real estate transfer would be contingent upon waiving all penalties, fees, and fines incurred against Eastwood Enterprises due to actions of Damon Eastwood, who allegedly worked as an agent of Eastwood Enterprises."

"What about the fines against Mr. Eastwood?" asked Angel.

"That would be for the civil courts to decide," said the attorney. "However, I wish it noted that Damon Eastwood worked autonomously—independent of Eastwood Enterprises. His actions in no way reflect the corporate ethics or values of Eastwood Enterprises which prides itself on active environmental stewardship."

Director Harding said, "You realize that the Department of the Interior and the courts will require documented proof that Mr. Eastwood was not in collusion with Eastwood Enterprises."

"Of course," said the attorney. "Copies of transactions and any other pertinent paperwork will be faxed both to the DOI and the courts as evidence. The documentation expunges Eastwood Enterprises of any knowledge of or collusion in Mr. Eastwood's alleged failure to comply with Belize's environmental standards."

"In other words," said Angel, "Mr. Eastwood acted in competition with this corporation."

"Exactly," said the attorney. "Damon Eastwood will be tried in a civil court."

"If the courts and the DOI find that the evidence supports these statements," said Director Harding, "I see no reason why Belize and Eastwood Enterprises can't find an amicable solution."

So Damon's the fall guy. It couldn't happen to a nicer person, but what about Dante?

Chapter Eighteen

Estrella stopped by at four, and they took a cab to the church.

"Have to let you off here," said the cabbie. "The street's closed to traffic."

"Why?" Carole leaned over the front seat to hand him the fare.

"For the Christmas Bazaar," said Estrella, her eyes dancing. "See, everyone can walk between the church and Friendship Park."

As they carried the boxes and potted, sea-grape bush, Carole looked at the rows of white, canvas booths being set up for games, crafts, local artists, food, drinks, and treats of all kinds. In front of each stall hung a luminous, red star. Strings of light bulbs crisscrossed the newly formed lane, creating an enchanting micro-cosmos where hours before only a street had existed.

"Carole," called Gabby, clipboard in hand. "I'm so glad you could make it tonight." Motioning to her, Gabby waved her to a booth six spaces down on the left.

"Estrella and I want to help with these seashell ornaments and donate the proceeds to the church."

"That's great," said Gabby, wearing a big smile.

"It's all Estrella's idea." Carole gestured toward the girl at her side.

"Who?" asked Gabby, looking around.

"Estrella, the little friend I told you about," said Carole, turning toward the girl to introduce her.

The girl had gone—again. Looking left and right, Carole insisted self-consciously. "She was just here, really." Shaking her head, she gave a nervous laugh. "She must have wandered off, but this is all Estrella's bright idea."

"It's wonderful that you're here." Gabby hugged her. "Maybe we can meet later, sit together during the Mariachi Mass for Our Lady of Guadalupe?"

Not fully grasping what was entailed in a Mariachi Mass, Carole nodded as she hugged Gabby goodbye. Then she called to Estrella.

"Here I am. What's up?"

"Where were you?" asked Carole.

"Right here," said Estrella, hunching her shoulders. "I just stepped away to say hello to a friend at the fishpond booth."

"No problem." Carole smiled. "Gabby wants us to set up at this booth. Here, why don't you set up the 'tree' while I unpack?"

From the moment they hung their beribboned ornaments on the sea-grape bush, customers flocked to their stand.

"We're a success, Carole." Estrella hugged her.

Carole placed her hands on the girl's shoulders. "The credit goes to *you*." Then she put both arms around Estrella and hugged her for all she was worth. "You're my Christmas angel. Thank you for getting me through not one . . . but several crises."

"Carole," said the girl, as their hug ended. "Follow your star. You'll be fine. It's all going to work out according to God's plan. You just have to believe."

Carole said, "I believe God sent you to me, but . . . ." Puckering her brow, she studied the girl. "I worry about you, Estrella. Like tonight, does your mother know where you are?"

"Oh, she knows." Estrella began rearranging the ornaments, never meeting Carole's eyes.

"I'd really like to talk with her," said Carole, closely watching the girl's reaction.

Never raising her eyes from the ornaments, Estrella said, "She works odd hours, nights mostly, and sleeps days."

"Hmmm . . . ." Carole studied the girl. "Then what if I call her? Is your phone working yet?"

"It's still out of order."

"I definitely want to escort you home tonight. I worry about you being out so late alone."

"I'll be fine. Don't worry, Carole. God watches over me."

"Yes, but—"

"Besides, I'm staying at my aunt's house tonight in town. See?" Estrella pointed toward a woman several stalls down the lane and waved. "See that woman in the striped blouse? Wave to her."

Carole's eyes followed Estrella's arm and beyond to a woman standing in front of the baked goods stall. She waved, and the woman smiled quizzically, waving back. Carole started toward her.

"Let's say hello. I'd like to introduce myself."

"I'll introduce you later at Mass." Estrella caught her hand. "Besides, we can't leave now. We have customers."

Carole glanced around but saw no one near their stall. "Where?"

A mischievous glint in her eye, Estrella smiled. "Here they come now."

As dusk fell, the strung lights lent a festive atmosphere to the area. Carole leaned against the booth, listening to the guitar music playing in the background. As people passed by, she heard laughter and congenial snippets of Belizean Kriol patois floating in the air.

What a perfect evening. A sea breeze swept through the bazaar, gently blowing, lifting her hair. She pushed it behind her ear, glancing at her bare, left ring finger. *Perfect, that is, except for being alone.* She sighed as she watched the couples, arm-in-arm.

"Did you sell all your Christmas ornaments?" asked Gabby, stepping out from the strolling crowd.

"What?" Her words caught Carole unaware, and she jerked in surprise. Chuckling, she switched mental gears. "Sorry, was just daydreaming." She pointed at their improvised Christmas tree. "Sold all but one." She reached behind the bush, picked up a small gift bag, and handed it to Gabby. "Estrella and I saved this one for you. Merry Christmas."

Gabby hugged her. "Thank you, that's so sweet." She looked around. "When am I going to meet this little friend of yours?"

Carole spun around, looking. "She was just here." Then she saw the girl standing by her aunt. "There she is," she said, pointing. She waved, and Estrella waved back, grinning.

"Where?"

"Right there—next to that lady in the striped blouse."

Gabby shook her head. "I must need glasses. I don't see anyone by that woman."

"She's right—" Carole stopped. Estrella wasn't there. "She must have scampered off."

"Introduce me later," said Gabby. "I want to show you the Shrine of Our Lady of Guadalupe. It's just over here."

Tucked between palm trees and sea-grape bushes was a well-lit but narrow booth draped in red and green canvas. A gilt-framed picture of the Lady of Guadalupe hung above a two-tiered altar holding lit votives.

"It's lovely," said Carole. "An island of solitude in this sea of humanity." She smiled, gesturing with a nod to the crowd just steps away. As she stared at the print, a sense of peace washed over her. She took a deep, cleansing breath, feeling refreshed, as if a breeze had swept away any nagging thoughts of what might have been.

A mariachi band struck up, catching their attention.

"That's my cue," said Gabby. "The band's going to serenade the Lady of Guadalupe."

"Why?"

"It's December twelfth, the feast day of Our Lady of Guadalupe." Gabby chuckled at Carole's expression. "Wait here. You've got the best seat in the house. The band will serenade the Lady before its procession into church. I've got to organize the procession, but I'll meet you here in a few minutes, and we can sit together at Mass."

Gabby hurried off, referring to her clipboard as she called to several people.

"Isn't this pretty?" asked Estrella, pointing at the colorful shrine.

"There you are," said Carole, startled. She turned toward the shrine. "Yes, and it's so peaceful."

The girl nodded. "I know what you mean."

As the mariachi band approached, music replaced the tranquility. Elaborately costumed men playing guitars, violins, and brassy trumpets led the crowd.

Carole stepped aside as the band serenaded the shrine. So close to the instruments, she felt the music as much as heard it. The sound waves reverberated in her chest, in her heart.

After the song ended, the band led the way into church for the Mariachi Mass for Our Lady of Guadalupe. Gabby caught up with her.

"Let's sit near the front, so we can see."

Carole nodded. "I want to introduce you to Estrella . . . ." The girl was gone. Looking around, Carole saw her with her aunt ten feet behind. Carole motioned to her to catch up, but the girl simply waved back, staying where she was.

"Where's this disappearing child you're always talking about?" Gabby grinned.

"She was just here." She gave a self-conscious laugh and pointed. "See, she's back there with her aunt in the striped shirt?"

Gabby shook her head. "Nope, I see a woman in a striped shirt, but I don't see any child with her."

"Right there, next to the man in the white polo shirt."

"Nope, sorry." Gabby made a face. "I see the white polo shirt and the striped shirt, but no little girl."

Sighing, Carole shook her head. *She's big as life. How could Gabby miss her?*

Again, she tried to point out Estrella, but the mariachi band started the entrance hymn, signaling the beginning of Mass. Gabby opened the hymnal and pointed to the lyrics until Carole found her place and joined in the singing.

After the blessing, they took their seats to listen to the word of God. It had been years since Carole had been to Mass. No traumatic experience had happened. It was just a gradual falling away. *It just wasn't important to me.*

From the corner of her eye, she watched as Gabby listened intently. She turned to see Estrella three rows back. The girl was so engrossed, she never noticed her, never turned to look. Even her aunt and the man in the white polo shirt were paying rapt attention to the readings.

What's wrong with me? Spiritually, romantically—why am I always on the outside looking in? With a sigh, she faced front and tried to concentrate on the biblical readings, not on herself.

When it came time for their row to go to Communion, Gabby rose along with everyone else in the pew. She gestured for Carole to join them, but Carole shook her head. *It's been years since I've been to Confession or Communion.*

Instead, she knelt, listening to the music—*Yahweh, I Know You Are Near.* The plaintive tune brought tears to her eyes. As she listened to the words— 'standing always at my side'—she almost sensed a presence beside her despite being the only person in the pew. Suddenly, it all made sense.

Omnipresent had meaning—'standing always at my side.' *God's everywhere and always with me.*

Deep in prayer, Carole didn't see Estrella until the girl lightly touched her shoulder. She raised her eyes.

"Don't wait for me, Carole," she whispered. "I'm staying with my aunt tonight. See you tomorrow." She waved, and before Gabby returned to the pew, she was gone.

The next morning over breakfast, Carole said, "The Mariachi Mass was beautiful. The music added another layer of meaning."

"When you sing, you pray twice," said Estrella.

"I believe it." Carole nodded absently, trying to remember. *It's been years since I attended Mass. When was the last time I went to Confession?*

"Carole, there's a Penance service tonight."

The girl's words yanked her from her reverie. Eyes narrowing, Carole scrutinized her. "Are you a mind reader or something?"

Estrella smiled mysteriously. "I'll pick you up at quarter to seven."

Following the service, Carole pointed to the church bulletin she had been reading. "What's *Las Posadas?*"

"It's a procession from the church to the first 'inn.'" Estrella's eyes shone even in the dim light. "It's like Mary and Joseph's journey as they searched for lodging."

"What happens? What do you do?" Carole hunched her shoulders. "How do you participate?"

"Meet me here tomorrow night at quarter to seven. See for yourself."

As they gathered in the twilight outside the church, each received a candle.

"What are these for?" Carole whispered, partly because of the hush over the crowd and partly because she was embarrassed to ask a child what appeared to be common knowledge.

"Candles mean the light of Christ coming into the world," Estrella whispered.

After an opening prayer, the deacon used a lit candle to ignite the candles of the people nearest him.

As Estrella lit Carole's candle, she leaned over and whispered. "Now we're spreading the light, chasing away darkness."

They turned and lit the candles of their neighbors, who, in turn, lit the candles of those nearest them. Within moments, everyone's candle flickered in the twilight.

Accompanied by a guitar, the music director led the group in a Christmas carol. Two people, carrying statues of Joseph and Mary, led the procession through San Pedro until they stopped at a house and knocked.

As a woman handed out fliers, Estrella whispered. "We're all *peregrinos.*"

"We're *what?*" Carole asked.

"We're pilgrims—going from inn to inn, house to house—looking for lodging."

Carole glanced at the figurines. "Like Mary and Joseph?"

Estrella nodded and pointed to the handout. "We sing this song, asking to be let in."

Carole glanced at the lyrics—*In the name of Heaven / I ask of you shelter / For my beloved wife / Can go no farther.* "I see, we're echoing Mary and Joseph's journey from Nazareth to Bethlehem."

"We sing one part, asking, and the innkeepers or people who live here, sing the other, answering."

"Antiphonal," said Carole, nodding. "A back-and-forth, give-and-take musical conversation."

"Exactly. It's the *Pidiendo Posada,* the Posada Song."

By the eighth verse, the 'innkeepers' had changed their tune. *Are you Joseph? / Your wife is Mary? / Enter, pilgrims; / I did not recognize you.*

After the pilgrims answered in song. the host family invited the group in.

The deacon blessed the procession, blessed the house, and blessed the food they were about to eat. Then the festivities began. The hosts led them to a table filled with Christmas cookies, homemade cakes, candies, lemonade, and a punch bowl filled to the brim.

Helping themselves to paper plates, Carole and Estrella got in line for the buffet.

"What's in that punch bowl that looks like eggnog?" asked Carole. "Rum popo." Estrella grinned.

"Which is what?" she asked.

"Eggnog with rum."

Carole began filling her plate, sampling one of each goodie. "What a great tradition."

"It's not over yet," said Estrella. "This is only the first night. It goes on for eight more nights."

"Here?" Carole looked at their hosts. "What generous people."

"No, we go to a different house every night with a party at each." Eyes sparkling, Estrella lowered her voice to a whisper. "And each host family tries to outdo the last one. If you think this party's good, wait until the last one."

Carole chuckled as she ladled rum popo into her cup. "Then what?"

"On Christmas Eve, we end our search for lodging at the church, and they have the Dance of the *Pastores*."

"The pastures?" asked Carole, popping one of the hand-dipped chocolates into her mouth.

"No, the *pastores* are the shepherds who visited the manger on the first Christmas." Estrella chose a sugar cookie from a heaping tray. "After that, we have the *Misa de Gallo*."

Carole shook her head. "The what?"

"The *Misa de Gallo* or the Mass of the Rooster is the midnight mass."

"Okay, this one you have to explain. Why would they call it the Mass of the Rooster?"

"Easy," said Estrella, grinning. "Legend says the only time a rooster ever crowed at midnight was the night Jesus was born."

Carole laughed at the idea. "I had no idea there were so many traditions surrounding Christmas. What fun!"

Suddenly, Estrella's posture straightened. "Gotta' go, there's my aunt." Pointing toward the doorway, Estrella said, "See you tomorrow morning."

"Wait a second," said Carole, motioning her back. "I want to meet her."

The girl waved as she disappeared into the next room. "See ya."

"Estrella," Carole called after her. "You left your cookie."

"Carole? What are you doing here?" Gabby gave her a hug. "I didn't expect to see you. Were you in the procession?"

Carole nodded. "Estrella's been introducing me to some of the local Christmas customs."

"Not this again." Gabby looked around, and then eyed her skeptically. "So where's this friend of yours tonight?"

"She was just here." Carole held up her plate. "See, this is her cookie."

Gabby exhaled quickly.

"I'm not imagining her." Pointing, Carole said, "She just went through that door."

"Okay." Gabby gave her a condescending smile. "Have it your way."

What is it with her? "If I didn't know better," she began in a warning voice, "I'd think you didn't believe—"

"Never mind, I was joking." Gabby waved it off. Then she lowered her voice. "Actually, I'm glad to see you. Angel called today with some interesting news."

"Really?" Carole instinctively moved closer. "What?"

"Apparently, our friend Damon is back at it."

"What do you mean?"

"He's managed to produce unrecorded paperwork that's predated to appear legitimate."

"Unrecorded?" Carole sneered.

Nodding, Gabby continued. "Until today, no agency and no department had received any of this paperwork, let alone had it on file."

"Yet he produced it today?"

"Remember how I'd mentioned he'd had no environmental impact assessment done for the beach, let alone for building a large-scale coastal resort?"

Carole nodded. "You'd said he hadn't performed a limited environmental study or even applied for any permits."

"Well, as of today, he has proof that he'd done all of that."

Carole narrowed her eyes. "How'd he manage it?"

Gabby ran her hand over her mouth. "I can only surmise, but all the paperwork had been signed by a director—who just *happened* to retire last week—and by Dante."

"No," Carole's eyes widening, she said, "do you mean—"

"Again, this is all conjecture, but," looking around, she lowered her voice. "It appears that somehow Damon blackmailed or bribed Mr.—"

"You said the man just retired?"

"Last week . . . unexpectedly . . . ,"

"However it happened, this director predated the paperwork—"

"And Damon either conned or blackmailed Dante into being the fall guy." Carole nodded her head thoughtfully. "I'll bet that's just what happened." She took a deep breath. "I wonder how this is going to affect negotiations between Eastwood Enterprises and the DOI?"

"I know for a fact that none of this paperwork existed during the time I worked for Damon. I also know that, as of a week ago, not one of these documents had been submitted to or filed with the DOI."

"So this paperwork is completely falsified?" Carole looked to her friend for confirmation.

Gabby gave a terse nod. "Yeah, but good luck proving it."

The next morning, Jeff texted Carole to call him.

"Yes, I heard," she said. "Damon produced the necessary paperwork."

"I just found out about it myself. How did you know?" asked Jeff.

"Damon's not the only one with insider information."

"How's this going to affect the dialogue between the DOI and Eastwood Enterprises?"

"From what I understand, Damon's paid off some director. On the surface, it 'looks' legitimate, but it's bogus." Carole drew in a deep breath as she gathered her thoughts. "From a PR perspective, this is good news. It does nothing but validate Damon Eastwood and, by association, Eastwood Enterprises."

"So you're thinking we should pull out of negotiations?"

"No," she said. "In the short term, this revelation will only make Eastwood Enterprises' offer appear more generous since, in the eyes of the law, no legal infractions have been committed. If no wrongs have been committed, no penalties, fees, or fines will have been incurred—so none will have to be waived."

"So are you saying we don't need to make any tax-deductible gift of the property to Belize?"

"Eastwood Enterprises definitely needs to follow through with this offer." Jeff grunted uneasily. "I'm not following . . . ."

"The truth will come out eventually," she said. "When it does, it'll destroy Damon's credibility. You don't want Eastwood Enterprises to crumble with him."

"So what do you recommend?"

"This information places us in a strong bargaining position for now," she said. "First, get together with the legal department to determine what concessions would benefit Eastwood Enterprises most, and then negotiate with the DOI to get all the tax breaks, write offs, and other incentives you can."

"But if donating the property to the DOI isn't necessary, I don't see why—"

"It *is* necessary," she interrupted. Frustrated, she counted to five and then explained once again. "Maybe it doesn't appear that way right now. In fact, the gesture sounds exceptionally charitable at this time. It increases our bargaining power." She sighed. "But the truth *will* come out, and, when it does, Damon will be indicted."

"So it's in Eastwood Enterprises' best interests to act charitably?"

Hello! She centered herself, putting aside the sarcasm before it colored her words. "It's not only in Eastwood Enterprises' best interests from a PR perspective, it's the right thing to do." *And it's the only way to protect the cove.*

"We're a corporation, Carole, not a welfare service."

"The founder of Eastwood Enterprises, Damon Eastwood, is guilty of using unsustainable development methods. He's a greed builder, not a green builder. He committed environmental crimes, and it's only a matter of time until he's found out. Don't let this corporation be guilty by association. Get out while you can."

"You're sure?" He groaned. "It's going to cost millions. Maybe we could just make a token donation—"

"You could save millions now, yes, but you'd lose millions later in penalties, fees, and fines, not to mention lose all credibility as a corporation with a conscience. What about Eastwood Enterprises' purported corporate ethics and values, its 'active environmental stewardship'?" She shook her head. "All right, let me put it this way. Donate the property, but get all the concessions you can. Done right, this can be a win-win situation for all. Eastwood Enterprises can profit, and Belize's reef will benefit."

Chapter Nineteen

Carole answered the phone.

"Are you sitting down?" asked Gabby.

Now what? She sat. "What's wrong?"

"That unrecorded paperwork Damon produced . . . ."

"Yes . . . ." She stifled a sigh. *Don't keep me hanging!*

"Your name's on some of it."

"What!" Carole jumped up. "What's he trumped up now?"

"Before you get too excited—"

"Too late for that!"

"Your name's not on any original paperwork, only on photocopies, so I'm assuming the signature's electronic."

She gasped. "Are you telling me Damon lifted my name from some document and created a forged electronic signature?"

"I'm saying your name appears on some of the photocopied paperwork, and that it's my guess he—"

Carole gritted her teeth and groaned. "Oh, that bastard! Trying to drag me into all this."

"Just thought I'd give you a head's up . . . and a word to the wise . . . ."

"Yes?"

"Get a lawyer."

"Jeff, how are negotiations going with the DOI?"

"Glad you called. Something's come up."

"Let me guess," said Carol. "Could it have anything to do with an electronic signature?"

"How'd you know?"

"Same little birdie told me."

"For now," he took a deep breath, "it might be better if you keep a lower profile."

"And by that, you mean . . . ."

"Join the calls, but stay on mute."

"Be a silent partner, so to speak."

He gave a twisted chuckle. "The money's just as green."

As she poured her third cup of coffee that morning, Carole glanced at the calendar. December twenty-fourth. *Christmas Eve, what a merry, marry Christmas* . . . .

The knocking roused her from her thoughts. With a loud woof, Belle rushed to the door, whimpering and prancing until Carole checked the peephole and opened the door. "Merry Christmas, Estrella."

"Merry Christmas." Wearing an elfin grin, the girl held out a star-shaped Christmas-tree ornament made from five, long snail shells.

"This is gorgeous, so delicate." Taking the ornament, Carole examined it. "Thank you. Did you make it yourself?"

Estrella nodded.

"Then I'll treasure it twice as much." She reached into her pocket and brought out a beribboned box. "This is from Belle and me."

"Thank you!" With wide eyes, Estrella looked from Carole to the dog and back again. "Can I open it now?"

"Sure."

She opened the box and gasped. "A charm bracelet with a star charm."

"Read it," said Carole, grinning.

"It says 'Lucky.'"

"That's because you're my lucky star, my good-luck charm."

"That's my name—Estrella." Beaming, the girl put on the bracelet, reached up, and hugged Carole's waist. "This is the best Christmas present I ever got."

"I'm glad." Carole hugged her back. "Are you hungry?"

She shook her head. "Carole, have you ever seen a Mayan Deer Dance?"

"No, what is it?"

"Come with me," said the girl, reaching for Belle's leash. "I'll show you."

"What about breakfast?"

Estrella shook her head. "I'm not hungry."

"You're never hungry." Frowning, Carole studied the girl's thin arms and legs.

"We can eat later, but we have to hurry. We don't want to miss the dance."

Carole relented with a sigh. "Okay, we can get something on the way."

As they walked along the beach, strains of *Good Morning, Miss Lady* wafted through the air. Carole found herself walking in time to the beat. As they approached the impromptu band, she noticed their medley of instruments—guitar, banjo, tambourine, washboard, kitchen fork and grater, donkey jawbone with teeth intact, bottle and stick, maracas, hand drum, and accordion.

"Kriol music with a *brukdown* beat," said Estrella, moving in rhythm to it. "But we have to hurry."

"Just a minute, I see a taqueria. Let me pick up breakfast tacos for us." She caught the girl rolling her eyes. "So we're a few minutes late."

Carole wolfed down her taco as they listened to the folk music. "Ready?" She turned in time to see Estrella feeding her taco to the dog. "That was supposed to be your breakfast, not Belle's."

"I can't eat any more," she said. "Just not hungry, I guess." She looked up at Carole with big eyes. "C'mon, they're starting the Mayan Deer Dance farther down the beach."

"What's the rush?"

"You've never seen a Mayan Deer Dance before," said Estrella. "I don't want you to miss it. C'mon!"

As the strains of the percussion faded, Carole began to hear marimba and flute music.

Estrella grabbed her hand. "Hurry, they're starting!"

They ran along the water's edge and within moments saw deer antlers above the crowd's heads. As they drew closer, Carole could see the antlers were attached to sophisticated masks and costumes—deer dancers. Some wore oversized bandannas, draping down their backs. Others wore Christmas-patterned material as diamond-shaped capes over their backs. All dressed in elaborately designed costumes, a few wore masks with human faces, but most dancers wore animal masks. Carole saw jaguar, monkey, dog, and deer masks. Red was the predominant color, but vivid yellows, blues, and greens competed for her attention in dazzling patterns. Men wearing bright, hand-painted masks and conquistador hats held on their chins with wide chin straps danced around the troop.

Three men played the xylophone as the dancers performed in front of it and little boys looked on longingly. Twelve dancers faced the marimba in two lines of six. Leading and following each line was a man dressed in red.

"That's the jaguar on the right," whispered Estrella, pointing, "and that's the deer on the left just behind the leaders in red. The dancers on the right are the younger brothers or sisters of those on the left."

"What are the ones wearing black?"

"They're the hunters," whispered Estrella, pointing. "The ones in red are the five Mayan cardinal directions."

"*Five* directions?" asked Carole, raising her eyebrow. "Don't you mean four?"

Estrella shook her head, counting off on her fingers, "North, south, east, west, and the center."

"I see, a kind of 'You are here' marker." Carole nodded, watching as the dancers used the four corners and the center of the space between the two lines.

The jaguar began dancing in the center and then around each of the dancers. Taking turns chasing and being chased by the men in red, the jaguar played the jester. He improvised, making fun of the hunters during the dance, stealing their rattles or their hats. Finally, the jaguar ran away and climbed a tree, where the hunters shot it with arrows. The dancer slipped out of his costume's skin and out of the dance as the hunters pantomimed killing and skinning the jaguar.

Carole groaned.

"Watch," Estrella whispered.

The deer danced next. It was graceful and noble, playing the king to the jaguar's jester. It leapt through the air. It grazed, making subtle leg movements that caused a rattling sound.

"What's that rustling noise?"

"Those are rattles sewn on his leggings. They're made of butterfly cocoons filled with tiny pebbles," whispered Estrella. "They're supposed to sound like noises of the forest, like deer stepping on dry leaves."

Really, Carole mouthed.

With fluid motions, the deer acknowledged the other dancers but then took cover in the trees. The hunters sent their dogs to chase it, finally capturing and killing it as the dancer stepped out of the deerskin.

Again Carole groaned.

Estrella pointed to another scenario. The jaguar and the hunters were taking turns trying to climb a greased pole nearby. After each slipped down, another and another dancer tried to shimmy up the pole, one at a time.

"How tall is that?" Carole whispered, shielding her eyes from the sun as she looked to the top. "It must be five, six stories tall."

"I heard the women say it was sixty feet high."

Carole gave a low whistle.

Estrella nodded. "It's made from a sayuc tree."

"Is that tree's wood naturally slippery?"

Estrella shook her head. "The women said it took two dozen, cut-up bars of soap mixed with three buckets of water. After the soap dissolved, they mixed it with melted lard. Then, before they raised the pole, they poured the mixture over it and rubbed it in."

"Amazing." Carole shook her head at the effort involved. "Why do they go to all this trouble?"

"It's no trouble. It's fun. Everybody works together, and it's a party." Estrella's smile showed off her gleaming, white teeth. "That's why I didn't want you to miss it."

Carole smiled, but then narrowed her eyes, thinking. "There's got to be more to it than that."

"They say the deer dance is about ancient Mayan hunters and how they connected with nature," said Estrella. "Once upon a time, hunters killed every deer they saw in the forest. The other animals became angry and chased the hunters away. It's a fairytale told in a dance."

"With a message, I'll bet." Carole smiled as she waited for the moral.

"Take only what you need from nature." Her tone solemn, the girl stared hard at Carole, as if making a point.

"Okay, I get it," said Carole. "It's a morality play about the environment."

Estrella nodded. "The ancient Mayans understood. People need to respect nature. If they don't, it strikes back—like when developers cut down mangroves for better views of the sea."

"When they remove the natural barriers," said Carole, "the sea reclaims the land, washing away the same beaches the developers were trying to improve."

She breathed in deeply, thinking how Damon had exploited Starsnail Cove and used everyone around him. She thought of Nick, their wedding, her reputation. *No matter what my personal losses, I did the right thing in exposing him.*

Then her whirling mind followed another line of thought. *What if the DOI and Eastwood Enterprises don't come to an agreement? What if the Starsnail Center for Environmental Outreach never gets built? Or worse, what if Damon builds his resort, after all? This will have been for nothing—*

"Don't worry," said Estrella.

Carole looked up from her fog. "What?"

"Everything will work out. You just have to follow your star." Grinning, Estrella held up her wrist, jingling her lucky-star charm.

Chapter Twenty

At ten-thirty, Carole met Estrella in front of the church.

"Okay," she said, "I'm curious about the Dance of the *Pastores.*"

"You're just in time," said Estrella. "They're lining up now."

Upbeat Calypso music started playing moments before women in ornate folkloric dresses began dancing with floral arches held overhead, while they lifted the flounces of their skirts and twirled, showing off the yards and yards of multicolored material. Men dressed in white costumes with mock patches held aloft stars perched on poles.

"The *pastores* are the shepherds who sang the first Christmas carols and brought the first gifts," Estrella said over the music.

Carol nodded as she watched the male and female dancers weave between each other and do-si-do according to ancient choreography.

Carole recalled that tonight was to have been her wedding night, but she shook off the thought and entered into the music, clapping and dancing vicariously.

At eleven, the lively dancers bowed, curtsied, and left.

"Next is the *Misa de Gallo*," said Estrella, leading Carole to a pew inside the church.

Within minutes, the church was filled to capacity and overflowing. Late parishioners gathered outside the open windows where they could watch and hear the Mass. Carole looked around her. Ornate, star-shaped chandeliers, handmade for the occasion, hung from the rafters. Families with sleeping children held and rocked them as they slept, everyone waiting for Christmas. Immersed in the culture, caught up in the oneness of the moment, she could not help but feel the urge, the longing for the stroke of midnight. She had never experienced the holiday like this.

This is Christmas! It's done in the community, not the privacy of your house. It's the difference between watching a movie in the theater or alone on TV. The energy's contagious. Your personal feelings intensify as you're swept up in the crowd mentality.

When it came time for Communion, Carole joined the line. She motioned to the girl to join her, but Estrella stayed kneeling, shaking her head, wearing her characteristic, patient smile. When she returned, the girl was gone. Carole looked around and saw Estrella sitting with her aunt. The girl waved and pointed to her aunt.

Estrella can't be running around the street at night. I have to do something about this. Bobbing her head, Carole came to a decision.

After the closing hymn, Carole tried to make her way over to Estrella and her aunt, but Gabby intercepted.

"Carole, I didn't expect to see you here." She linked arms with her friend. "C'mon, you're coming to my cousin's house for dinner."

She saw Estrella waving to her as she followed her aunt out of church. Carole waved back, uneasy about the girl having so little supervision.

"But it's after midnight," Carole protested, taking out her phone to look at the time.

"*Gringo,*" Gabby teased. "This is the night our Lord was born. We need to celebrate." Her tone became hushed. "Besides, you shouldn't be alone tonight."

Carole swallowed the sudden lump in her throat and looked down quickly, blinking back the stinging tears. "Thanks."

A short walk brought them to Asunción's house. "You remember Carole."

"Sure, join us! The more the merrier!" Asunción looked around. "Where's Nick?"

Carole and Gabby exchanged a look.

"He couldn't make it," said Carole, holding tightly onto Gabby's arm.

Asunción's eyes clouded over as she read Carole's body language. "That's too bad." Then her smile returned, and, opening the screen door wider, she gestured toward the dining room. "You both must be hungry. Go on in and help yourselves."

An immense platter of sliced ham filled half the table. Heaping bowls of rice, beans, rolls, and potato salad flanked the ham. What looked like a black fruitcake was set at the end of the table.

"What's that?" Carole pointed to the cake.

"That's a traditional Belizean holiday treat. Black fruitcake," said Gabby, "especially good with a dollop of rum or brandy." She winked.

Christmas morning, Carole woke to the sound of church bells. *Merry, marry Christmas . . . .* She sneered at her reflection in the mirror. *You sure know how to arrange things.*

Figuring Estrella would spend Christmas with her family, she made toast and coffee. As she sat at the kitchenette table, she looked at the empty chairs around her. She looked at the 'Christmas tree,' bare, except for the one ornament Estrella had given her. *Alone—is this how I'm going to spend the rest of my holidays? The rest of my life?* She snickered at herself. Belle cocked an ear, whimpered, and sat at her feet.

"You're right. I'm not alone. You're with me, girl." Carole reached down and scratched the dog's neck.

A knock at the door startled her. Belle woofed as Carole checked the peephole.

"Estrella," she said, opening the door, "what a surprise. I thought you'd be spending Christmas with your family."

"You're my family," the girl said shyly.

Carole felt a lump in her throat. *How could I have been feeling sorry for myself? This kid's mother doesn't even spend Christmas with her. I'm definitely going to see what the laws are here. Maybe—*

"Carole?"

Estrella broke through her reverie. "Huh?"

"Have you ever been to a Joncunu or Charikanari?"

"A what?" Carole squinted, mentally replaying the words, trying to make sense of the unfamiliar sounds.

"A Joncunu or Charikanari."

Carole shook her head. "Never heard of them. What are they?"

"They're Garifuna Christmas dances."

"Garifuna," Carole scratched her head, trying to recall. "Aren't they the descendants of shipwrecked slaves that married Arawak natives?"

Estrella nodded. "They dress in costumes and masks. They're so much fun to watch as they dance from house to house. Want to go see them?"

"Why not? I don't have any other plans."

"It's a boat ride and then a bus ride, but it's worth it." The girl grinned. "They only have this in Dangriga, but I know you'll like it."

Carole studied her. "You seem to know a lot of things."

Estrella shrugged. "C'mon, we have to get going. The boat leaves in a few minutes."

"What about Belle?" Carole looked at her dog. "We can't leave her here all day."

"Bring her along. The water taxi allows dogs. No problem."

The boat allowed dogs, but not the bus. Carole stood outside the depot, arms crossed. *Now what?*

"Rent a car." Estrella pointed to a rental agency across the street and said again, "No problem."

Carole stared at the girl. "Are you psychic or something?" Shaking her head, she said, "I'd swear you can read my thoughts."

Estrella just smiled.

The attendant gave them directions to Dangriga, and within minutes they were driving along the muddy, bumpy Western Highway. They took a shortcut on the Coastal Highway to the Hummingbird Highway. The route was a two-lane, sometimes paved, but more often graded dirt road that connected small, untidy towns. It wound around the lush, green mountains and crossed over shallow streams on rough, plank bridges.

As she maneuvered between the wooden bridge's irregular boards, Carole shook her head. *It's like driving up a narrow ramp to get an oil change. Only no one's directing me which way to turn the wheel.*

"All I can say is I'm glad we rented a four-wheeler."

Estrella pursed her lips and then grinned. "But it sure is a pretty drive."

At the girl's gentle prompt, Carole turned to look at her. *She has a way of putting things into their right perspective.*

"You're right. Though the roads leave something to be desired, the views are spectacular."

Green vistas unrolled at each curve in the road. Palm trees shot up alongside banana, mango, and mahogany trees. They passed acre after acre of aromatic orange groves, leaving their windows open to inhale the citrusy-sweet fragrance.

Finally, Carole's stomach growled, reminding her she had not eaten. When she spotted a horse-drawn wagon ahead with what appeared to be watermelons inside, she pulled over.

"Isn't this charming?" She turned toward Estrella.

The girl wore a gentle, proprietary smile, as if she owned the land and all on it and was welcoming her. "Glad you like it."

Carole studied her. *What an odd little girl. Sometimes she seems more like an old woman than a girl, yet she's a wild child, alone and unsupervised.* With a firm nod, Carole made a decision. *I'm going to look into the adoption laws in this country. See if I can't give Estrella the home she deserves.*

They stopped at the roadside wagon where a Mennonite man in overalls sold fresh fruit from the back of his wagon. Carol bought a bag of green oranges and a small bunch of short bananas for breakfast.

"That watermelon looks good. Would you like a slice?"

Estrella shook her head. "I'm not hungry."

Carole rolled her eyes. "You're never hungry. Don't you ever eat?"

"I ate before I stopped at your place." The girl looked down, her expression hidden in shadows.

"Half the time, I catch you feeding your food to Belle." Carole sighed. "The other half, I see you leave it on your plate." Chuckling, Carole shook her head as she gave Belle a drink of water from her cupped hands.

Two hours after they left Belize City, they entered Dangriga. Crowds of spectators were eating, talking, and watching the entertainers. Carole parked, and they joined the throng. Men and women shook maracas and danced, using oversized bandanas and hand towels as props to help their shimmies and wiggles.

A man wearing an African-print shirt and Rastafarian-knit hat played a large drum with his bare hands. An elderly man, nearly toothless, entertained the crowd, singing and strumming his worn guitar. Though his voice cracked, and his bent, arthritic knuckles played stiffly, the people applauded him enthusiastically.

Carole noticed a gray-haired, white woman holding a native child. *Could that child have been adopted?* She tried to make her way toward the woman, but keeping Belle and Estrella close by while crossing the street wasn't feasible. Instead, she smiled at the woman, telegraphing her support.

Then they spotted the line of people wearing pink mesh masks with colorful hats and multi-patterned costumes. The masqueraders chatted with the crowd as they danced. Some wore shell bands on their knees or calves, rattling with each movement.

A tall man wearing a cardboard mask with red-tipped cow horns danced as he brandished a large stick in his white-gloved hands. Carole and Estrella exchanged a puzzled look.

A girl in tightly braided cornrows leaned over. "That's the two-footed, Charikanari cow."

Young boys seemed to enjoy teasing the dancers, paying particular attention to the white-gloved ones handing out candy.

Several groups followed, each one wearing different costumes, but all wearing the pink mesh masks. Then the entertainers began dancing from house to house as people followed. Their feet and bodies moved to each beat of the pulsating drums as people chanted and cheered them on. Each household watched and then paid the dancers as they moved on to the next.

At the third house, Carole saw Nick. Her jaw dropped in surprise, and she turned, grabbing Estrella by the hand.

"We've got to leave."

"But we just got here." The girl wore a puzzled frown. "There's so much more to see. We can't leave yet."

Carole tried walking against the tide of people, but, with a leashed dog on one hand and Estrella on the other, the going was slow.

"Nick!" called Estrella, motioning for him to join them with her free hand. "Nick, over here!"

Carole rolled her eyes, pretending she had not heard. *I can't escape this guy.* She picked up Belle and carried her in her arms. "C'mon," she said, walking faster.

"Carole, it's Nick," said Estrella. "Wait a minute."

"Hi, Estrella," he said, catching up, a beat later adding, "Carole."

Her lips tight, Carole gave a brief nod without looking at him.

"What are you doing here?"

When Carole didn't answer, Estrella said, "I'm showing Carole the *Joncunu* and *Charikanari* dances. What are you doing here?"

"I was . . . uh . . . I wanted some company, so I met up with a few friends of mine. Would you . . . ."

Carole heard him pause, sensing what he was going to say. "We'd better be going, Estrella."

"Wait a minute, Carole. Nick was just about to ask us to spend Christmas with him."

"Actually—"

"I'm sure he has better things to do," said Carole, tugging at Estrella's hand. "C'mon."

"Actually, I was going to invite you to Christmas dinner. Have you ever had cassava bread and bundiga with green bananas?"

"No, what is it?" asked Estrella.

"It's a special bread made from cassava and snapper cooked Garifuna-style in coconut milk. Hungry?"

"Starved," said Estrella, beaming at him, her dark eyes snapping.

Carole felt betrayed. Annoyed and speechless with suppressed anger, she scowled at the girl.

Estrella slumped, chastised. "What?"

"You're never hungry. Now suddenly you decide you're 'starved'?"

"Sorry . . . I just feel hungry, that's all."

Carole took a deep breath, realizing how petty her words sounded. "I'm the one who's sorry, I . . . ." Her words fading, she looked to Nick for support. "I'm sure Nick is busy with his friends. He doesn't want us—"

"Oh, yes, I do," he said. "I definitely want you to come to dinner."

His haunting, blue eyes were bluer than she recalled. She stared at him, mesmerized. Just then, she remembered what she had been planning to say and turned toward Estrella.

"If you're hungry, we'll find a restaurant." Then turning to Nick, she narrowed her eyes and glared at him. "I wouldn't want to impose, wouldn't want to be accused of barging in or taking advantage of your hospitality.

You know how people gossip." Her sarcasm hung in the air like the dancers' half-raised arms.

He acted as if she had slapped him. Then he nodded slowly. "I had that coming."

You bet you did, buddy. Carole bit back an angry retort as she counted to five, breathing deeply. "C'mon," she said finally to Estrella, grabbing her hand.

"Wait a minute. Nick has something he'd like to say." Pulling back on Carole's hand, the girl turned to him. "Don't you, Nick."

"Carole, you were telling me the truth. I realize that now."

She turned, hoping she had understood correctly, but needing reassurance. "A little more detail please," Carole said in as professionally deep a voice as she could muster. *No feminine, high-pitched tone now.*

Despite the *Charikanari* drumbeat, the lyrics from 'You Gotta Be' swept through her head . . . . *"You gotta be hard, you gotta be tough, you gotta be stronger . . . . "*

"I took the thumb drive to a friend of mine, a studio engineer in Belize City. He actually laughed at the remixing quality, or lack thereof." Nick moved closer to Carole. "I am so sorry I doubted you. If there's any way—"

"Oh, so you think by saying you're sorry that all's just hunky-dory?" Carole sneered. "In your dreams. You put me through h—" she glanced at Estrella, "heck. Now, with a few, simple words, you assume all's forgiven, forgotten?" She snorted. "Think again!"

With Estrella in tow and Belle pressed against her chest, Carole turned and began pushing through the crowds.

"Carole, wait," said Nick.

"Carole," said Estrella, pulling her back, "Nick's trying to tell you something."

Both the crowd's push and the girl's pull stymied her progress. She felt trapped—unable to move, let alone escape. Despite counting to five, she exploded.

"Estrella, stop tugging on me! Now, come on!"

Nick drew alongside. "Don't yell at her. I'm the one you're angry with—take your frustrations out on me."

She looked at his furrowed brow and bloodshot eyes. Taking a deep breath, she knelt on one knee to match Estrella's height. "I'm sorry. Nick's right. I'm angry with him, and I'm taking it out on you."

The girl smiled. "It's all right, Carole. You and Nick just need to talk," she looked at the chaos around them, "not shout over the crowd. Let's go to the beach. It'll be quiet there."

Nick's eyes met Carole's. "She has a good point." Holding out his hand, he helped her up. "I'll carry Belle. Let's go find a quiet stretch of beach and follow Estrella's advice."

"Follow your star," said the girl, holding up her wrist to jingle her star charm.

Carole gave her a smile. "I thought you were starved."

She grinned and shrugged. "Not anymore."

Minutes away from the crowds, they found a deserted beach. Except for the occasional drumbeat that wafted on the breeze, only seagulls and sandpipers interrupted the soothing sound of waves washing against the sand.

Estrella let go of Carole's hand and held her arms out to Nick. "Why don't I take Belle for a walk, so you two can talk?"

Nick did a double-take. "How old are you?"

"Old enough," she said with her characteristic, pointed-chin grin. She took the dog from him and placed her on the sand. "C'mon, girl, let's treasure hunt."

Carole chuckled as they ran off. "They're going to beachcomb for shells," she told Nick. "Stay in sight," she called to Estrella, waving.

"I will." The girl waved back.

Carole took a deep breath, smelling the fresh sea air. After the noise of the raucous crowd, her ears still rang in the stillness of the beach. She took a moment to gather her thoughts.

I'll never forget how Nick distrusted me, broke up with me. Yet despite his nearness—or maybe because of it—I feel more . . . at peace . . . than I have in days. Arms crossed, she sighed.

"Carole, I don't know where to begin . . . ."

Her back to him, she tightened her mouth. *Don't think for a minute that I'm going to help you on this one. You got yourself into it. You get yourself out.*

"Carole, please at least look at me." He gently touched her shoulder.

It was as if an electric current coursed through her body. Despite her misgivings, she couldn't help but turn toward him.

But when she faced him, he again touched her shoulder. *Too close, too soon.* This time, she shrugged him off and took a step back.

His hand dropped to his side as his shoulders sagged. "Okay, I get the hint." He nodded. "Let's take this slow."

Her breathing shallow and fast, she pressed her lips tightly together. Silent, scowling, she watched his Adam's apple bob as he swallowed hard.

"Carole, I acted like a jerk. I know that now." His eyes searched her face, pleading. "I don't know what to say, just that I had temporary insanity when I listened to that recording." He rolled his eyes. "No matter how poorly made it was, it did what Damon intended—made me jealous, nearly unhinged to think . . . . " He took a deep breath.

She glared, recalling the humiliation, the mortification. She thought of the emails and letters she had been forced to write, telling the guests the wedding had been cancelled. Then there were the phone calls, answering their questions, explaining why it had been called off.

"What about the shame you caused me? You added insult to injury. You made a fool of me in front of my friends and family. Even if *I* could forget that, do you think they ever will?" Her anger was fueled by her raw memories.

He started to speak but ended up only making an ineffective gesture with his hands. "What can I say?"

"Your distrusting me and calling off our wedding not only changed our relationship, it altered the way everyone else responds to me. You disgraced me. What do you have to say to that?"

He shook his head. "Nothing, except that I truly am sorry. My only defense is to plead temporary insanity—"

"And the timing . . . ." Her blood pressure rose as the memories ripped through her mind. "Cancelling our wedding just days before Christmas— your expiry date couldn't have been worse."

He hung his head, biting his lip.

"Well, what do you have to say for yourself?"

He lifted his eyes to her. "Don't you think these holidays have been miserable for me, too? Why do you think I came here today?" He answered his own question. "I had to get away from Ambergris, from the dread of running into you, from the fear of seeing that hurt look in your eyes." He swallowed. "Carole, I'm so lonely without you."

"You got along just fine without me for two years—"

"But that was before we got engaged, before we started spending time together every day." He groaned. "You've become a part of me—a leg, a lung. I think of you with every step, every breath I take. What I'm trying to say is I need you."

She studied his face, watching his bloodshot eyes. Her chest heaving, she was torn between telling him she loved him and telling him to shove off, that he was only getting as good as he gave. Finally, she sighed.

"I don't know." She raised her eyes to his and slowly shook her head. "I just don't know if I can risk going through this with you again."

"I promise you, I'll never doubt you again." His blue eyes pleaded. "Can't we try once more?"

Her mouth hard, she thought of the tears, the lonely nights, and the broken promises.

Taking a deep breath, she shook her head. "I just can't trust you."

"Carole," said Estrella, coming up the beach. "When are we having lunch?"

"You're hungry?" She rolled her eyes. "C'mon, we're done here. Let's leave."

Estrella's eyes opened wide as she shook her head. "Oh, no, I don't want to leave. I just want to take Nick up on his invitation to dinner."

"No, we'll find a restaurant." Carole saw Estrella exchange a look with Nick.

A glint in his eye, Nick nodded. "I invited you," he said, picking up her line of reasoning, "and . . . ."

"You insist," whispered Estrella, filling in for him.

"That's right. I *insist* you both stay as my guests."

Carole looked from one to the other. Throwing up her hands, she gave in. "Okay, I can see I'm outnumbered." She turned to Nick. "Lead on."

An hour later, Carole and Nick had found two chairs beneath a tree. Carole could keep her eye on Estrella and Belle, playing with a group of children, while she and Nick finished their meal.

"Estrella sure likes you," said Nick.

Carole laughed out loud. "You mean, she likes *you*. I saw how you two connived to have us stay for dinner."

Grinning, he shook his head. "She's only doing what she thinks is best for you. It's obvious how much she cares for you."

Carole looked at her. "And I care for her. In fact, I . . . ." She turned to him, excited, ready to share her plans when she stopped, remembering their rift.

He bit his bottom lip. "Don't stop. Tell me what you're thinking."

"I'm going to try to adopt her."

Nick's eyes opened wide. "Doesn't she live with her mother?"

Carole's lips pursed. "Estrella says she does, but there's no phone number, no address. She also says she stays with an aunt some nights, but she never introduces us." She sighed. "I'm beginning to think she's a wild child, left on her own to fend for herself."

"Wow." He shook his head. "She seems like a nice enough kid."

"Oh, she's wonderful, bright, sweet." Carole looked at her. "I'd just like to give her a chance at life, give her a good home, an education."

"So you're staying on at Ambergris Caye?"

"You needn't look so surprised." Carole sighed.

"What?"

"That was going to be my Christmas gift to you." She looked at him. "I thought you knew."

"Knew what?"

"That I was staying on Ambergris Caye so you could build your Dive Shop, build up your business." She sighed again. "But that reasoning's flawed now."

"Are you telling me, you were going to stay on Ambergris and give up your career in New York for me?" He began chuckling.

Answering with a grin, she nodded. 'Sounds a little silly now, doesn't it?"

His chuckling turned into laughter. Holding his stomach, he laughed until tears ran down his cheeks.

"It isn't that funny." She scowled at him, annoyed he took her gift so lightly.

"No," he said, the laughter subsiding. He took a deep breath. "Talk about irony."

"How do you mean?"

"That was going to be my Christmas present to you."

She raised an eyebrow. "What was? Staying on Ambergris?"

"No, selling my business on Ambergris and moving to New York so you could build your PR career."

"No." Her jaw dropped. "No!" She shook her head, trying to clear it. "You mean, I was going to give up my career and move here *for you*, while you were going to give up your business and move to New York *for me?*"

Nodding, he gave her a crooked smile. "It seems we've been at crossed purposes."

"You mean, we've been star-crossed lovers." Her laugh was dry, mirthless. Then a thought occurred. "This reminds me of O. Henry's story, *The Gift of the Magi*."

He shook his head. "I'm not familiar with it."

She flashed a crooked smile, recalling the plot. "It's about a young, married couple with only two important possessions between them—his grandfather's gold watch and her golden, knee-length hair. He wanted a watch fob for his watch. She wanted an ornate comb for her hair. Christmas was only a few days away, and neither had any money, so—"

"He sold his watch for her hair comb—"

"And she sold her hair for his watch fob."

Their eyes met, and they both broke out laughing.

"What's so funny?" asked Estrella, grinning, eyes sparkling. Belle was at her side, woofing, wanting to be part of the fun.

"We are," said Carole, indicating with her thumb. "Nick and I."

"You know what they say. Laughter's the best medicine for whatever ails you." She beamed, looking from one to the other.

"It's not so much funny as it is odd," said Carole. "We cancel each other out."

"You don't cancel each other out.'" Estrella shook her head. Then she used her hands as if she was weighing something on a scale. "You counterbalance each other. You make up for each other's shortcomings."

"How old are you?" asked Nick, cocking his head.

"Old enough to see when two people are in love." She flashed an impish grin.

Nick exchanged a look with Carole over Estrella's head.

"Carole, shouldn't we be getting back?" the girl asked.

Carole looked at the time. "Ohmigosh, I lost track." She stood up, gathering her paper plate and plastic utensils. "We'd better get going. It took us over two hours to drive here." Then she stopped and turned to Nick. "When does the last water taxi leave for Ambergris?"

Nick checked his watch and shook his head. "You'll never make it on time, not on those roads, not in the dark."

"Now what?" she asked, annoyed with herself. *What are Estrella's mother and aunt going to think?*

"No problem, I can take you back in my boat."

"I wish," Carole mused. "What do I do with the rental car?"

Nick scratched his head and then got up. "Just a minute. Be right back." A moment later, he had a man with him. "Carole, this is my good friend, Felipe."

"Just call me Pepi," said the man, reaching out to shake her hand.

"Hi, Pepi."

"Nick tells me you need to get a rental car back to Belize City."

She nodded.

"I'd be happy to drive it back for you tomorrow. I need to go into town anyway."

"Pepi, thank you so much!" Carole hugged him. "I really appreciate your help. I'm afraid Estrella's mother and aunt are going to worry if I don't get her back soon."

"Who?" asked Pepi.

"Her mother and aunt," said Carole, pointing to Estrella, standing near the group of children.

"Oh." Pepi nodded, but he looked puzzled as his eyes searched.

"That girl in the red shirt and denim shorts," said Nick, pointing.

Pepi looked, scratched his ear, and shrugged.

Carole chewed her lip, wondering why the man seemed so confused. "Oh, you need the car keys, don't you?" She dug into her purse. "Here they are," she said, handing them to him. "And thank you again, Pepi. You're a real lifesaver."

"No problem, miss. Glad to help you and Nick. Just let the rental company know I'm taking the car in tomorrow." He handed her a piece of paper." This is my driver's license number. Merry Christmas to you both."

"Merry Christmas," said Carole.

They no sooner boarded Nick's boat than Estrella pointed to the twilight sky and said, "Look, it's the Christmas Star."

"Sure enough," said Nick, winking. "Some people call it Venus, but tonight it's the Christmas Star."

Watching the stars overhead, she stretched out on the bench seats with Belle and fell fast asleep.

"Long day for her," said Nick, throwing his jacket over her shoulders.

"So much has happened." Tilting her head, Carole met his eyes. Feeling the heat rise to her cheeks, she blinked and then looked away, uncomfortable with her thoughts.

"She's quite the little matchmaker," he said, standing at the wheel, setting their course.

"You can say that again," said Carole, thinking of her antics.

Nick turned to face her. "There's one thing she said that keeps repeating in my head."

"What's that?"

"She said she's old enough to see when two people are in love." He caught her eye. "Think there's any truth to that?"

"Truth to what? That she's old enough or that she sees we're in love?"

He caught his breath. "You said it, not me."

"What?"

"That we're still in love."

She opened her mouth, but no words came out. She tried again. "I said no such thing."

"You did so. You said, 'she sees we're in love.'"

"It's . . . it's just a figure of speech. That's all."

He left the wheel and took her hands in his. "It's no figure of speech in my vocabulary." He put his arms around her, and, when she did not pull away, brought her to him in a kiss.

Her eyes open, she watched the stars. They seemed to stop in the heavens, twinkling, but not moving. Time seemed to stop. Pulling back from him, she caught her breath and stared at him. "What are you doing?"

"Proposing . . . again. Carole, can you love an idiot who couldn't see what was right in front of him?"

A star shot across the sky, arcing, leaving a reflected trail in the water.

A sign if I ever saw one. She looked at Estrella, sleeping, yet she heard her words reverberating in her mind. *Follow your star.*

In his arms, holding onto his shoulders, she gently swayed right, and then left. She pressed her lips together. "Maybe . . . ."

"Maybe?"

She lifted her eyebrow, never taking her eyes from his. She pouted, teasing, encouraging.

Catching her mid-sway he kissed her, grounding her. He instantly became her hub, her heart, the nucleus of her world. Suddenly, her world stopped spinning. She felt safe, centered.

And she breathed. *How long since I've filled my lungs with fresh air instead of stale memories? This last week I've been panting, gasping for air, but this is the breath of life*—love.

Carole and Nick talked quietly during the four-hour boat ride, not wanting to wake Estrella. She told him about what had happened with Eastwood Enterprises, Damon, and Dante. "Oh, and Gabby has a boyfriend, Angel—pronounced *On-hel*—Ramirez."

Nick shared his ideas of developing a series of marine environmental classes for children and young adults. "Now that I've sold my diving business, I need something to do." He turned toward her. "What are your plans now that you're with Eastwood Enterprises?"

She told him about the contract. "I'll get paid no matter what happens, but, if I don't work in PR . . . ." lifting her head, she pursed her lips, thinking. *Maybe I'll write that novel I've always talked about.*

"What about Estrella?"

"Like I said, I want to adopt her."

Taking her hand, he asked, "Think she could adjust to you, Belle . . . and me?"

Though she did not answer, Carole peered at him through smiling, crinkling eyes. By the time they docked in San Pedro, their called-off wedding was a distant memory, and she had begun thinking of a future with Nick.

Chapter Twenty-one

Carole answered the phone before she tasted her morning coffee.

"Have you seen the headlines?" asked Jeff.

"No, what do they say?"

"'*Signatures for Sale: Director Indicted Fraud*,' and there's more," said the board director.

"What!" Carole had heard him, but she found the news difficult to believe.

"DOI Director Rodriguez turned state evidence on Damon."

She gave a low whistle. "Has the DOI contacted you since the news hit the stands?"

"Yeah, they're as anxious to complete negotiations as we are. They want the land, and we want to wash our hands of it."

"Good, we're all on the same page. How can I help?" She sipped her coffee.

"Send a report to our legal department with your recommendations on negotiations—and copy me. We want to wrap up this tax-deductible gift ASAP."

"Will do, anything else?"

"Carole . . . ." He took a long breath.

"Yes . . . .?"

"You've already more than earned your salary in helping us avoid this environmental debacle."

She sensed what was coming. "But . . . ."

"When Rodriguez turned state evidence on Damon, Damon named you as an accessory to the crime after the fact."

"Not this photocopied-signature hoax again?" She shook her head.

"Uh-huh. You know he's grasping at straws, and I know it. The legal department knows it. But the general public doesn't. Perception's everything. Any connection between Damon and Eastwood Enterprises, no matter how ludicrous, is a liability."

"So now I'm perceived as a liability?" She rolled her eyes. *When am I going to get off this PR rollercoaster?*

"Not to me. I think you've done a bang-up job, and I'll write you a glowing recommendation . . . ."

"But . . . ."

"After you submit this report, your services are no longer required."

"Ah-hah." Smirking, she sighed.

"No sighing necessary. You've got a two-year, ironclad contract which means you'll be paid for the whole two years. Not bad wages for a few weeks' work."

"But I'm a public relations person. What'll I do with my time?"

"Consider it a paid vacation," said Jeff.

She thought of Nick, of staying on Ambergris, of adopting Estrella. She thought of Estrella's cove, of Nick's sold business, of his ideas for marine environmental classes, of the marine-based environmental outreach center—and she got an idea.

"Jeff, I remember Lee Iacocca saying you should never end a conversation or a contract without asking for something."

He chuckled. "What is it you want, Carole?"

"Isn't the DOI going to build the Starsnail Center for Environmental Outreach?"

"Yes."

"I have a friend, an ex-SEAL dive master, who loves working with kids. Think one of the negotiation concessions with the DOI could be to hire just such a person to help with outreach?"

New Year's Eve was a clear and balmy seventy-six degrees. Carole put on a strapless, winter-white sheath and sandals as she dressed for Gabby's party. Looking at her reflection in the mirror, she put her hand to her bare throat and frowned. *It needs something.*

Belle's woof alerted her first, and then she heard the knock. After checking the peephole, she opened the door.

"Estrella, what are you doing here at this hour?"

"I wanted to wish you a happy New Year." She bent down to rub Belle's tummy, and then peered up at Carole. "You look beautiful, like a bride."

Giving a self-conscious chortle, she looked in the mirror. "You're partly right. Maybe not beautiful, but all this needs to double as a wedding dress is a veil."

"Soon enough, Carole, you're going to make Nick a lovely bride."

She studied the girl. "You say the oddest things, yet you say them with authority, as if you already know they're going to happen." Raising her eyebrow, she asked, "Do you know something I don't?"

Estrella gave her a knowing smile then narrowed her eyes, analyzing the outfit. "Your dress is very pretty, but it's so," she clicked her teeth, "plain."

"That's what I thought." Carole's hand went to her bare throat. "It needs a scarf or a piece of jewelry."

"Yes, a necklace." Estrella nodded.

Carole pulled out her nightstand drawer, and, tucked in the back, she spotted the gold starfish necklace Nick had given her. "I'd put that away and forgotten all about it."

Estrella gasped. "Look! A star within a heart! It's a sign."

"What?" Her eyes followed Estrella's pointing finger.

There the necklace lay, its chain folded over on itself, creating a heart shape with the starfish in the center.

"A star within a heart, don't you see, Carole?" Estrella looked up at her. "Follow your heart. Follow your star."

Carole studied the shape, then picked up the necklace and fastened it around her neck.

"Perfect." Estrella gave an approving nod and then paused, as if listening. "Got to go."

"Can't you wait until Nick gets here? We want to tell . . . ask you something."

"There'll be time enough for that later." Estrella giggled. "This is your night." Before Carole could stop her, the girl dashed out the door, calling, "See you!"

As Carole closed the door, Nick knocked. "Okay to come in?" He looked around. "The door's open."

"Estrella just ran out." Carole thought for a moment. "It's uncanny—as if she heard you or sensed you were coming. I swear that girl has a sixth sense."

Taking her in his arms, Nick said, "She's a thoughtful little psychic, leaving you here all to me." He nuzzled her neck, tickling her with his breath. When he felt the chain, he pulled back his head to look. "You're wearing the starfish necklace I gave you."

Her fingers went to her throat. "Estrella and I found it at the back of my drawer tonight."

He smiled. "It's the first time I've seen you wear that since . . . . " His smile drooped. "I thought you'd tossed it."

She shook her head. "Nope, just forgot how much it means to me, how much you—"

He bent his head and kissed her, taking her breath away. When she came up for air, she gently extricated herself from his arms and took a deep breath.

"Maybe it's time we left for Gabby's party." Feeling the heat rise in her cheeks, she found it difficult to meet his eyes.

He cleared his throat. "Maybe it is, at that . . . Oh, don't forget to bring a swimsuit."

"A swimsuit? Why?" She searched her memory, but could not recall Gabby mentioning anything about swimming.

"I thought she'd said something about a midnight dip." He patted his hips. "Got mine on under my clothes."

"Thanks, I'll just put mine in my purse."

At midnight, Nick kissed Carole amid party horns and paper streamers. Looking up at the sky, they saw fireworks bursting over the water.

"Happy New Year," he said.

"What?" She held up her hands. "I can't hear a thing over the car horns, party horns, fireworks, and," she looked around at the other guests, "chatter."

"Let's find someplace quiet."

"What?"

"Let's go to a quieter place," he shouted.

She nodded, and he took her hand in his.

"Where are we going?"

He grinned. "Someplace that has quiet fireworks."

She held back, tugging at his hand. "You don't mean—"

Reading her body language, he quickly said, "No, I'm not being euphemistic. Seriously, I want to show you something very special." When she still held back, he added, "On my boat . . . wearing your bathing suit."

She studied him in the moonlight, trying to read his thoughts. Then she took a deep breath, her instincts telling her to trust him.

A half hour later, Nick cut the engines and turned off the boat's lights. On the way, she had changed into her swimsuit, and Nick had pared down to his.

As the engine whine stopped, Nick put his arm around her waist and said, "Listen to the sea."

She grinned. "I don't hear anything."

"Exactly." He gave her a friendly squeeze. "That's the first half of my promise."

"Huh?"

"Quiet fireworks," he said. "Now look down into the water."

She peered into the black sea, expecting to see nothing but inky darkness. Then, as her eyes adjusted, she began seeing a faint glow. "What is that?"

"Keep looking."

After a few minutes, she said, "I see constellations." She looked up at the stars, then down again at the water. "Not reflections of the stars above, but—"

"It's indescribable, isn't it?"

She nodded. "What's that light in the water?"

"That's bioluminescence."

"Bioluminescence," she repeated, rolling the sound over her tongue. "What causes that?"

"Marine bacteria and plankton releasing a chemical called luciferin."

"Wow!" She hugged him. "This is spectacular. What a wonderful way to spend New Year's Eve, watching nature's fireworks."

Grinning, he hugged her back. "You ain't seen nothing yet. To really appreciate it, you have to swim in it."

She looked from his face to the water and back. She groaned uneasily. "It's one thing to see it when I'm high and dry on the deck, but—"

"Don't worry, it's safe." He took her hands in his and looked into her eyes. "Trust me. Here, watch." Letting go of her hands, he kicked off his deck shoes and jumped into the eerie light.

Immediately, the water exploded in streams and globules of sparkling green-blue light.

"It's phosphorescent," she said, delighting in the light show. She wanted to jump in and join in the fun, but fear held her back. She recalled a high-dive years before in high school. 'Jump,' her classmates had called, but the idea had terrified her so much, she had climbed back down the stairs.

"Jump," Nick said.

His voice recalled her to the present. She looked into the dark water lit up with its eerie light. Panic seized her, making her stomach queasy and her palms sweaty.

She shook her head. "This is close enough."

"That's what you said about diving, too. You only want to skim the surface—snorkel but not dive, look but not leap." His tone became serious. "You need to dive deeper to fully appreciate life."

She looked above her. A shooting star arced across the sky and seemed to plummet into the waves. *A sign.* She looked into the dark water. The plankton created what looked like constellations. *Follow your star.* She heard it in her mind. *Follow your star.*

"Jump," coaxed Nick. "Take a chance on life."

Squealing, she kicked off her shoes and dove in feet first. The water erupted in a phosphorescent splash. Effervescent light exploded from her arms, her legs, her fingertips. Coming up for air, she caught her breath and laughed, reaching out for Nick.

"This is wonderful. I love it." Her eyes locked with his.

"I love you, Carole Kennedy." He kissed her in the moonlight and bioluminescence. "You trusted me enough to jump in. Now, can you take another leap of faith?"

"What's that?"

He reached for the chain around his neck. It was only then she noticed. Her starfish engagement ring hung from it. Her eyes widened in the pale light.

"Carole Kennedy, will you do me the honor of becoming my wife?"

She started to cry, tasting the salt of her tears mingled with the seawater on her lips. She nodded, but was too overwhelmed to speak.

He took the chain off his neck and placed it over her head. "Under the circumstances, it's safer than putting the ring on your finger."

Her tears turned to laughter. All she could do was put her arms around his neck and cling to him, waiting until her outburst subsided into sobs.

"Oh, Nick, I love you." She fingered both necklaces, holding them out from her chest to look at the starfish charm and starfish engagement ring.

Follow your star. Again, Estrella's words echoed in her mind.

"Nick proposed!"

"Again?" Gabby exclaimed over the phone.

Carole laughed. "Again, and I hope you'll be my maid of honor."

Gabby hesitated with an uncomfortable sigh.

"Nothing's wrong, is it?"

"Whether or not I can be your maid of honor," Gabby sighed, "depends on when you have your wedding."

"What? Why?" *Have I done something?*

"If you wait too long . . . . "

Get to the point. "Yes . . . . "

"I'll have to be your *matron* of honor."

Carole squealed. "You're kidding! Angel proposed? Congratulations, Gabby! When's the big day?"

"Valentine's Day, so hurry up and get married . . . soon!"

"Trust me, it's soon," said Carole. "We're getting married January sixth, only four days away."

"Epiphany," said Gabby. "The night the Christmas star led the wise men to their journey's end."

"That's right. I'd forgotten." Carole smiled to herself as she thought of Estrella's phrase. *Follow your star.*

"It's high time you married Nick. You two were made for each other. Even if neither of you could see it, it was written in the stars."

No longer star-crossed, our path is written in the stars. Carole smiled to herself and then remembered why she had called. "I hate to ask you, but would you consider—"

"Being your wedding planner?" Gabby chuckled. "Of course, I would."

"Whew, I was afraid you'd bow out after all we've put you through, what with the wedding on, the wedding off, and now the wedding back on. Want to meet for lunch and talk over both our wedding plans?"

"How 'bout the Black Cat Bar?" asked Gabby. "They've got a great salad bar."

"Only if your cousin's there. I'd like to convince him to play at our wedding."

"Then it'll have to be dinner. He doesn't start until six."

"Meet you there at six."

"Coming," said Carole, responding to the knock at the door. "Estrella, I'm so glad to see you. Come on in. Where were you this morning?"

Belle woofed until Estrella knelt and petted her. "Sorry," she said, looking up.

"No problem. It's just so unlike you. You've never missed waking us up before."

Looking down, Estrella shrugged.

"Is anything wrong?"

The little girl took a deep breath. In a solemn voice, she said, "Carole, I have to go away soon."

"Go away? Why?" *Is her mother taking her somewhere? Is she moving in with her aunt?*

"No, neither of those."

Carole's mouth gaped. "You read my mind, didn't you?"

"Not exactly." She fidgeted, picking at her fingernails.

"No matter." Carole shook her head, trying to clear her thoughts. "Where are you going?"

"Away."

"Yes, but where?"

"Just . . . away."

"Estrella," she sighed, "you're beginning to worry me." She took the girl's hands in hers. "Come over here. Sit on the sofa with me." When the girl got settled, Carole said, "Nick and I are getting married."

She gave a wan smile and nodded. "Yes, I know. Congratulations."

Again Carole shook her head, worried but trying to stay focused on the task at hand. "Nick and I want you to live with us. We want to give you a home—adopt you." She picked up Estrella's limp hand. "Would you like to live with Belle and Nick and me?"

Estrella peered up into her face. "Yes, I'd like that very much."

"Then it's settled. Today, I'm going to the court house to find out what we need to do to adopt you."

The girl's eyes clouded over, and she turned away.

"Estrella, what's wrong?"

"Nothing." A smile flickered at her lips. "Everything's working out as it should, Carole. You're following your star."

"Estrella, you're really worrying me. I'm not kidding." Carole stood up. "C'mon, you're going to the court house with me. I want to keep my eye on you. Okay?"

"Okay." The girl nodded and stood up, obediently going through the motions. Carole shook her head. *She's obviously somewhere else.*

"I'm right here." The girl looked at her—and then through her. Her dark eyes were blank, lifeless.

Carole shuddered. "C'mon, let's get Belle's leash."

Five silent minutes later, they stood at the courthouse door. "I don't think they'll let Belle in there." Estrella gestured toward the door. "I'll wait outside with her until you're sure it's all right."

Against her better judgment, Carole agreed. "It'll just be a few minutes."

Inside, the assistant at the front desk called her supervisor about the dog. Covering the receiver, the woman turned to her with a smile. "She'll be right here."

Carole went to the door, waved, and called, "Just another minute. They're checking."

Estrella waved back as she sat on the bottom step with Belle.

"While you're waiting, can I help you with anything?" asked the assistant.

"Actually, I'm looking into adopting a Belizean child, and I'd like to know what paperwork needs to be filled out, what forms need to be signed."

The assistant nodded politely. "Sure, I'd be happy to give you an overview"

"That'd be wonderful, thanks." Carole gave her a grateful smile.

"You're American?"

"Yes." Carole nodded.

"The Hague Adoption Convention governs Belize, which means to adopt from Belize, the U.S. Government must first find you eligible to adopt."

"Okay." Carole nodded.

"Then, you have to reside in Belize with the child for a minimum of twelve months."

"No problem. Anything else?"

"Yes, the Belize Human Services Department requires that you choose an accredited adoption service. Regarding adoption forms and procedures, they recommend you contact a Belizean attorney." The woman handed her a photocopied paper. "Here's a list of lawyers."

"Thank you." Carole scratched her ear. "This is a special situation." She sighed, again not sure how to begin. "I'm concerned that the child isn't being supervised or given proper care."

"If there's any history of abuse or neglect," said the assistant, "maybe I can find it in the records."

Carole gave a sigh of relief. "That's a great place to start. Thank you."

"What's the child's name?"

"Estrella . . . . " Carole hesitated, embarrassed to admit she did not know the last name. "Just need to confirm the spelling," she said, crossing her fingers.

Again she went to the door and called, "How do you spell your last name?"

"M-o-r-a-l-e-s," Estrella called back.

"Thanks." She closed the door and told the assistant, "Estrella Morales."

The assistant went to the computer and pulled up a list of names. "Morales, Alma; Morales, Carmen; Morales, Dora E.; Morales, Filipa; the only name that's a possibility is Morales, Dora E. Could the E stand for Estrella?" She clicked the name to open the file.

Just then, a familiar-looking woman approached.

"Hello," said Carole, reaching out for her hand. "I'm so glad we're finally meeting. You're Estrella Morales' aunt, aren't you?"

Instead of accepting her hand, the woman scrutinized Carole. "What is it you want?"

Carole took a deep breath, not sure where to begin after the woman's frosty tone. *The best defense is an offense.* She decided to face the challenge head on. "I'm looking into adopting Estrella Morales, and I'd like to find out what's involved."

The woman exchanged a dark look with the assistant. She glanced at the monitor and then turned toward Carole. "What did you say your name was?"

"I . . . I didn't, but it's Carole Kennedy." Carole instinctively took a step back.

"Miss Kennedy, is this some kind of joke?" The woman's eyes were dark and hard as coal as she studied her.

"What do you mean?" She swallowed nervously. "Is anything wrong?"

"Estrella Morales died last October twelfth."

Carole felt the same queasy sensation in the pit of her stomach as she had when she peered into the dark water. Suddenly her palms began perspiring. She felt herself weaving, and she steadied herself on the desk before speaking.

"I'm sorry. I . . . I must have misunderstood you." She blinked and swallowed.

"I said, my niece passed away last October."

"Then there must be two children named Estrella Morales."

"Is this the girl?" asked the assistant, turning the monitor toward Carole.

"Yes . . . but . . . . " Carole's knees felt weak. She leaned against the desk and turned toward Estrella's aunt. "Is this . . . ."

The woman nodded. "That's my niece."

"No, there's got to be a mistake. She's sitting outside on the steps." Carol turned and stumbled to the door as the woman followed her. "Estrella," she called.

The girl was nowhere in sight, and Belle's leash was tied to the railing.

Carole's knees buckled. She felt herself toppling forward, down the steps, when the woman caught her arm.

Carole sat in the woman's office, sipping ice water, petting Belle. Feeling the dog's solid presence was reassuring. *At least Belle's tangible—fur and bone. Everything else is surreal.*

A gentle knock at the door announced the woman. "Feeling better?" She closed the door and sat across from Carole.

Carole nodded. "Sorry for making a nuisance of myself—"

The woman waved off her apology with a wan smile. "Hearing your story was just a shock. That's all."

Carole lifted her lip in a half smile. "I can imagine, Mrs . . . . "

"Call me Alicia." She smiled. "Alicia Morales. This can't be easy for you, either."

Carole shook her head. "It's like a bad dream."

"It's a shock. And I won't lie—it was difficult to believe your story."

"But you believe it now?" Carole searched her face. "Why? What convinced you?"

"You called her Estrella. Only her family called her that. To everyone else, she was Dora."

Carole absorbed that knowledge. "What happened to her?"

Alicia drew a deep breath. "She had an anaphylactic reaction."

"To what?"

"A lionfish stung her."

"Is that what . . . . " Carole swallowed and started again. "Could you tell me about it?"

"She was wading in shallow water near the cove."

"Which cove?" Carole leaned forward.

Alicia smiled at the memory. "She had a favorite beach, where she liked to find—"

"Starsnail shells." Carole nodded. "She showed me."

"She stepped on a lionfish, pulled out the spine herself, and then limped home. Her parents applied the usual home remedies—vinegar and urine."

Carole raised her eyebrows. "Urine?"

Alicia nodded. "It works. Living on the island, you learn to rely on home remedies except in emergencies. The nearest hospital's in Belize City."

"Wasn't this an emergency?"

"Normally, no. Lionfish stings hurt, but they heal. Her parents didn't think it necessary get the wound x-rayed, but apparently a small piece of the spine remained in her foot. It festered, and she went into anaphylactic shock. By the time they rushed her to the hospital in Belize City, she was gone."

Tears stung her eyes. Carole looked down, willing the tears to stop. *At least this explains why I never saw Estrella eat, and why Gabby and Pepi couldn't see her. But why did Nick, Belle, and I see her? What was her reason? Did she have some message?*

As clearly as if she were standing beside her, Carole heard Estrella say, "Follow your star."

Her lashes wet, Carole lifted her eyes and looked around the room. *Estrella?*

Watching her closely, Alicia asked, "Did you say something?"

Carole shook her head. "Is she . . . uhm . . . ," she swallowed hard, "is she buried on the island?"

"She's in a raised grave in the cemetery."

Carole's shoulders slumped. She looked down then cleared her throat.

"Thank you for sharing her story, Alicia. I don't know how to explain what happened. I don't understand it myself. All I can say is Estrella was a wonderful little girl. Whatever her reason for coming to me, I'm just glad I got to know her."

"Nick," she spoke into the phone, "can you meet me at the cemetery?"

"The cemetery?" He laughed. "What have you been drinking?" Then he said, "Okay, I get it. This is some kind of joke."

"Something—"

"Speaking of drinking, have you heard where gravediggers get their coffee? In the burial grounds."

"Will you—"

"Or have you heard about the overweight gravedigger? It was due to his cemetery lifestyle."

"Will you listen to me?" She gave an exasperated sigh. "Something important's come up."

He dropped his act. "You're serious, aren't you?"

"That's what I've been trying to tell you."

"What?"

She sighed. "Not over the phone—I'll tell you when I meet you."

Fifteen minutes later, she arrived at the cemetery. No grass to be seen—all she saw were raised tombs partially submerged in sand.

Belle spotted Nick first, woofing and rolling on her back until he bent down and began rubbing her belly. As he absently petted the dog, Carole described her experience at the courthouse.

"What do you think?"

He stood up and shrugged. "It's difficult to believe we've been living with . . . . " He rolled his eyes. "Interacting with a spirit . . . It's—"

"Unbelievable." She nodded. "Yes, I agree."

"Sorry, but," he shook his head, "I need something more tangible before I can buy into this ghost story."

"That's why I thought the cemetery might be a good place to start. If we see her grave . . . . " Her voice trailed off, and she swallowed.

Nick put his arm around her shoulders. "Come on, we'll look at each headstone until we find hers."

She nodded solemnly as she tugged at the leash. "Come on, Belle, this way."

The dog sniffed the air, perked her ears, and started pulling in the opposite direction. Panting, the dog pulled harder until Carole turned and followed her lead.

"What is it, girl?"

All of a sudden, the dog stopped in her tracks. Whining and woofing, she rolled over on her back, asking to be rubbed. Then she wriggled and panted as if someone was rubbing her belly.

Kneading her brow, Carole looked to Nick for an answer. Beneath his tan, his face paled. He shook his head. She looked above Belle at the raised tomb topped with a cement angel. Estrella's starfish bracelet dangled from the statue's hand. *Dora Estrella Morales,* the tombstone read.

Again her knees felt weak, and she grabbed onto Nick's shoulder. He caught her, his arm supporting her waist.

"Estrella," she whispered.

She listened, half expecting to hear the girl's voice. All they heard was Belle, wriggling on the sand, grunting. Carol glanced at Nick and tried again.

"Estrella," she swallowed, "why did you come to me?"

Again she listened, but all she heard was Belle. Suddenly, the dog's grunting stopped. She righted herself, shook off the sand, and then began to whine.

"What's wrong, Belle?" The hairs on Carole's neck prickled. A breeze blew across her back, tickling, tingling her spine. She looked around, but saw only the sand drifting like fine snow around the cemetery's tombstones.

Chapter Twenty-two

January sixth dawned bright and beautiful, not a cloud in the sky. The wedding day started with a champagne brunch for two in a secluded palapa at the pier's end. Sheer, privacy curtains billowed in the sea breeze, playing peek-a-boo with the ocean view.

Despite the vista, Carole had eyes only for Nick. She sipped her mimosa and nibbled at the croissant, but she was too excited to eat. Then she uncovered the fruit platter heaped with fresh papaya, mango, cantaloupe, honeydew, and starfruit.

She gasped. *Gabby's thought of everything.* "Nick, look! The star fruit's been sliced crosswise into all these stars."

Picking one up, she turned it slowly in her fingers and thought of Estrella.

At eleven o'clock, Nick and Angel, his best man, waited at the altar wearing off-white chinos and Mexican wedding shirts. Carole felt butterflies as Rafael started strumming Schubert's *Ave Maria* on his acoustic guitar. She exchanged a panicked smile with Gabby as her maid of honor turned and began walking down the aisle.

Dressed in her sleeveless, full-length, bisque wedding gown—a slim-fitting sheath with a graceful back cowl—Carole listened to the music, waiting for her cue.

Belize Navidad

This is when Estrella would have started walking in front of me as the flower girl. She looked down at her bouquet and inhaled its fragrance. There, woven among the black orchids, heliconia, and red ginger, was Estrella's bracelet, entwined among the flowers.

"Something borrowed," Nick had said.

Swallowing her sorrow at the girl's absence, Carole raised her eyes and looked at her fiancé. Suddenly, she felt centered, focused. No more questions—she knew marrying Nick was her destiny, her destination. This was where her star had led.

"And on Epiphany," Gabby had said as she arranged the flowers in Carole's trailing tulle veil. "What a perfect day to end your search for love."

Carole heard her cue. To the sounds of *Ave Maria,* she stepped boldly down the aisle into her new life with Nick.

After the readings, Father Francis gave a homily. "How appropriate that today's wedding takes place on Epiphany. Both the Magi and this couple took a journey of faith. The Magi followed a distant star. Carole and Nick followed a glimmer of light in a dark world—for that's what love is, my friends, a glimmer of light in a dark world." He smiled at the couple. "As with the Magi, Carole and Nick were called to follow their star."

Carole blinked as his words penetrated her mind, reminding her of Estrella. *Follow your star.*

"Whether to Bethlehem or matrimony, the three Wise Men, Carole, and Nick were all summoned to their vocations. Keep in mind, God called them all through something in the natural world. For the Magi, God used a star. For Carole and Nick, perhaps it was a person who starred in their lives—a relative or a devoted friend.

"Or an angel," Carole whispered to Nick.

They exchanged a look as Father Francis addressed the congregation.

"Who are the stars in your life? Who does God use to call you to the light? By light, I mean Jesus, who is the ever glorious Light from Light. In our journey of faith, we need to manifest that light, integrate our hopes with our prayer life. Manifest, my friends. Don't hide your light under a bushel—let it shine. As in the axiom, actions speak louder than words. Speak so loudly through who you are, through what you do, that I won't be able to hear what you say."

Amen. Carole squeezed Nick's hand.

After the wedding, the group walked to the beach. There, beneath an arch of palm fronds, Nick and Angel once more took their places for the civil ceremony.

This time, Rafael and his band played *Caribbean Blue*.

Again, Gabby began walking down the aisle created between the separated rows of guests.

Watching her in her tea-length, aqua dress, Carole was suddenly reminded of the sea. *How appropriate for a beach wedding. The hemline of her dress sways as gently as waves and sea froth.*

Then she saw Belle, wearing a garland of flowers for a collar and carrying a floral basket in her mouth. Carole began to cry as she thought of her original flower girl, but Belle's antics turned her tears into laughter. The dog was so pleased with the attention she was getting, she wagged her tail and wiggled down the aisle, responding to Nick's call.

At Rafael's nod, Carole realized it was her cue. Again, she marched toward her future with Nick.

As she exchanged rings with him a second time, she gazed into his blue eyes, the same deep blue as the waters of the sea.

After they sealed their second wedding with a kiss, Nick cued Rafael. "*Belize Navidad,*" he called.

Rafael segued his band from *La Isla Benita* to *Feliz Navidad* as Belle led Carole and Nick toward the wedding tent. Halfway back through the aisle, Belle dropped her basket of flowers. Whining and woofing, she rolled over on her back, asking to be rubbed.

Carole gasped. There stood Estrella next to her aunt. The girl grinned. Never taking her eyes from Carole, she reached down to rub Belle's belly.

Not taking her eyes off Estrella, Carole whispered to Nick. "Do you see—?"

"Yes," he whispered in her ear, nodding, staring at Estrella.

Carole glanced at the girl's aunt, wondering if she could see.

Alicia's narrowed eyes looked puzzled, but then they opened wide. "Is—"

At Carole's nod, the woman bent down and began rubbing the dog. Estrella kissed the woman's cheek and wisped away with the drifting sand.

A breeze blew across Carole's back, prickling the hairs on the back of her neck. Her tulle veil fluttered as the wind sighed through the palms. Unsure if she heard the words with her ears or her mind, the message was clear.

Follow your star, Carole. Follow your star.

Suddenly, the dog's grunting stopped. Belle stood up, shook herself off, and began to whine.

Weak-kneed, Carole grabbed onto Nick's arm. She swallowed and attempted a joke as she became aware of her surroundings.

"C'mon, Belle, you're holding up the wedding party."

The guests chuckled as Estrella's aunt stood up, tears in her eyes.

Hugging Carole, she whispered, "Thank you."

"It's time."

After a silent beat, Nick swallowed. "I'll be there in ten minutes." He hung up and turned to his assistant. "Can you take over the class? My wife's gone into labor."

"Sure. Congratulations! Is it going to be a boy or a girl?"

"Don't know." Nick grinned. "We want it to be a surprise." He turned toward his class. "That was Nature calling." He waved and called, "See you tomorrow."

Nick ran to his converted golf cart and sped out of the Starsnail Center's parking lot at top speed—twenty-five miles per hour. Despite his concern for Carole, he could not help but notice how much had changed in the nine months since they had married. The Center had been built. He was the Marine Environmental Outreach Administrator, teaching students about marine life. Carole had finished the first draft of her novel, and now they were going to become parents. He took a deep breath.

Carole was waiting at the driveway, her packed bag in hand. She carefully hoisted herself onto the golf cart's seat, took a deep breath, and looked at him.

"This is it."

His eyes large, he looked as frightened as she felt. "Are you all right?" he asked.

She nodded.

"How far apart are contractions?"

"Ten minutes, give or take."

His jaw opened and then snapped shut. "Why didn't you call me sooner?"

"The doctor said not to come in until contractions were ten minutes apart."

He rolled his eyes. "But does she realize we're forty-five minutes away?"

With a smile, Carole reached for his hand. "It'll be all right." Then, as a contraction took her breath away, she looked at Estrella's bracelet on her wrist. "What's today's date?"

"October twelfth, why?" He turned toward her.

She groaned as she felt the baby kick.

"Are you going into labor?"

"Yes," she said, chuckling but panting. "That's exactly what I'm doing, but I just realized something." She turned toward him. "Today's the anniversary of Estrella's passing." In answer to his raised eyebrows, she said, "Her aunt told me."

"Not to be insensitive, but what does that have to do with the price of fish?"

"Something tells me, you and I are going to be the proud parents of a baby girl." She grinned. "What should we name her?"

Belizean Recipes

PORK PIBIL

2 pounds pork butt roast
2 tablespoons achiote paste
½ cup orange juice
½ cup fresh-squeezed lemon juice
1-2 habanero peppers, seeded and chopped, or to taste
1 teaspoon ground cumin
1 teaspoon paprika
1 teaspoon chili powder, or to taste
1 teaspoon ground coriander
Salt and pepper, to taste
½ cup red wine vinegar
2 red onions, sliced into rings

Directions

Prick the pork roast all over with a fork. Rub the roast with achiote paste and set aside. In a large bowl, combine the orange juice, lemon juice, and habanero peppers. Blend in the cumin, paprika, chili powder, coriander, salt, and pepper. Marinate the pork in the mixture, rolling several times to coat all. Cover and refrigerate overnight, turning two to three times.

Preheat the oven to 325 degrees F. Place the pork and marinade in a casserole dish and cover with aluminum foil.

Bake for 1 hour or until the meat pulls apart easily. The more slowly it bakes, the better. Be sure the meat thermometer reaches an internal temperature of 170 degrees F.

Alternative Methods

Bake at 200 degrees F. for 2-3 hours. Be sure the meat thermometer reaches an internal temperature of 170 degrees F.

Roast in a slow cooker on low (without foil) for 3-4 hours or until the meat pulls apart easily. Be sure the meat thermometer reaches an internal temperature of 170 degrees F.

While the pork is roasting, make the sauce. Bring the red wine vinegar to a boil in a small saucepan. Add the onion rings. Reduce the heat to medium-low, and simmer 10 minutes, or until the onion rings are tender. Drizzle the sauce over the pork. If desired, serve with white rice and tortillas to create tacos. Serves six.

DARASA (TRADITIONAL GARIFUNA DISH)

6 green bananas
¼ cup coconut milk
1 teaspoon salt, or to taste
½ teaspoon black pepper, or to taste

Directions
Peel and grate the bananas. Mix the grated bananas with the coconut milk. Season the mixture with salt and black pepper.

Drop about ½ cup of the banana mixture onto clean banana leaves. *Tightly* fold and tie the leaves into rectangular shapes.

Place the Darasas in a large skillet and add enough water to cover. Bring to a boil and continue boiling for one hour or until jelled. Makes twelve Darasas or serves six.

BELIZEAN COCONUT PRAWNS
1 large egg
½ cup all-purpose flour
¾ cup Belikin (Belizean) or other beer
1 tablespoon baking powder
2 tablespoons all-purpose flour
2 cups flaked coconut
6 prawns
3 cups coconut or vegetable oil

Directions

In a medium bowl, beat the egg with ½ cup flour, beer, and baking powder. Place the remaining 2 tablespoons flour in a bowl and the coconut in another bowl.

Holding the prawns by the tails, dredge them in the flour. Shake off any excess flour.

Dip in the egg/beer batter, and shake off any excess.

Roll the prawns in the coconut and place on a foil-lined baking sheet. Refrigerate for 1/2 hour.

Heat the oil to 350° F in a deep-fryer.

Deep-fry the prawns in batches of two. Turning once, deep-fry for 3 to 4 minutes or until golden brown. Use tongs to remove the prawns and drain on paper towels.

Serve steaming hot with your favorite dipping sauce. Serves six.

RUM POPO

2 large eggs
1 12-oz can evaporated milk
1 14-oz can condensed milk
1 tbsp grated nutmeg
1 tsp cinnamon
½ tsp vanilla
2 tablespoons rum (optional)

Directions

Beat eggs well (10-12 minutes) with a fork or egg beater.
Slowly add the evaporated milk while continuing to beat.
Slowly add the condensed milk while continuing to beat.
Stir in the nutmeg, cinnamon, vanilla, and rum, if desired.
Refrigerate and stir well before serving. Serves four.

About Karen Hulene Bartell

Author of *Sacred Choices, Sovereignty of the Dragons, Untimely Partners,* and *Belize Navidad,* Karen is a best-selling author, motivational keynote speaker, IT technical editor, wife, and all-around pilgrim of life. She writes multicultural, offbeat love stories steeped in the supernatural that lift the spirit.

Born to rolling-stone parents who moved annually, Bartell found her earliest playmates as fictional friends in books. Paperbacks became her portable pals. Ghost stories kept her up at night—reading feverishly. The paranormal was her passion. Wanderlust inherent, she enjoyed traveling, although loathed changing schools. Novels offered an imaginative escape. An only child, she began writing her first novel at the age of nine, learning the joy of creating her own happy endings.

Professor emeritus of the University of Texas at Austin, Dr. Bartell resides in the Hill Country with her husband Peter and her *mews*—five rescued cats.

VISIT HER AT:

Web site: KarenHuleneBartell.com

Facebook: KarenHuleneBartell

Twitter: KarenHuleneBart

Amazon Author's Page: Karen Hulene Bartell

Goodreads Author Page: Karen Hulene Bartell

My Goodreads Blog: Karen Hulene Bartell

Why is the title, *Belize Navidad*, significant? Why do/don't you like it? What would you have named *Belize Navidad*? Is the title a clue to the theme(s)?

Did you enjoy *Belize Navidad*? Why/why not?

What do you think *Belize Navidad* is essentially about? What's the main idea/theme?

What other themes or subplots did *Belize Navidad* explore? Were they effectively explored? Were they plausible? Were the plot/subplots animated by using clichés or were they lifelike?

Were any symbols used to reinforce the main ideas?

Did the main plot pull you in, engage you immediately, or did it take a chapter or two for you to 'get into it'?

Was *Belize Navidad* a 'page-turner,' where you couldn't put it down, or did you take your time as you read it?

What emotions did *Belize Navidad* elicit as you read it? Did you feel engrossed, distracted, entertained, disturbed, or a combination of emotions?

What did you think of the structure and style of the writing? Was it one continuous story or was it a series of vignettes within a story's framework?

What about the timeline? Was it chronological, or did flashbacks move from the present to the past and back again? Did that choice of timeline help/hinder the storyline?

Was there a single point of view or did it shift between several characters? Why would Bartell have chosen this structure?

Did the plot's complications surprise you? Or could you predict the twists/turns?

What scene was the most pivotal for *Belize Navidad*? How do you think *Belize Navidad* would have changed had that scene not taken place?

What scene resounded most with you personally . . . either positively or negatively? Why?

Did any passage(s) seem insightful, even powerful?

Did you find the dialog humorous...did it make you laugh? Was the dialog thought-provoking or poignant . . . did it make you cry? Was there a particular passage that stated *Belize Navidad'* theme?

Did any of the characters' dialog 'speak' to you or provide any insight?

Did the quotes at the beginning of the chapters 'set the tone' for the subsequent action? Which ones? How so?

Have you ever experienced anything that was comparable to what occurred in *Belize Navidad*? How did you respond to it? How were you changed by it? Did you grow from the experience? Since it didn't kill you, how did it make you stronger?

What caught you off-guard? What shocked, surprised, or startled you about *Belize Navidad*?

Did you notice any cultural, traditional, gender, sexual, ethnic, or socioeconomic factors at play in *Belize Navidad*? If you did, how did it/they affect the characters?

How realistic were the characterizations?

Did any of the characters remind you of yourself or someone you know? How so?

Did the characters' actions seem plausible? Why/why not?

What motivated the characters' actions in *Belize Navidad*? What did the sub-characters want from the main character and what did the main character want with them?

What were the dynamics between the characters? How did that affect their interactions?

How did the way the characters envisioned themselves differ from the way others saw them? How did you see the various characters?

How did the 'roles' of the various characters influence their interactions?

Who was your favorite character? Why? Would you want to meet any of the characters? Which one(s)?

If you had a least-favorite character you loved to hate, who was it and why?

Was there a scene(s) or moment(s) where you disagreed with the choice(s) of any of the characters? What would you have done differently?

If one of the characters made a decision with moral connotations, would you have made the same choice? Why/why not?

Were the characters' actions justified? Did you admire or disapprove of their actions? Why?

Carole had moments where she struggled with her faith. When was the last time your faith faltered? What helped you get through that time?

What previous influence(s) in the characters' lives triggered their actions/reactions in *Belize Navidad*?

Did *Belize Navidad* end the way you had anticipated? Was the ending appropriate? Was it satisfying? If so, why? If not, why and what would you change?

Did the ending tie up any loose threads? If so, how?

Did the characters develop or mature by the end of the book? If so, how? If not, what would have helped them grow? Did you relate to any one (or more) of the characters?

Have you changed/reconsidered any views or broadened your perspective after reading *Belize Navidad*?

What do you think will happen next to the main characters? If you had a crystal ball, would you foresee a sequel to *Belize Navidad*?

Have you read any books that share similarities with this one? How does *Belize Navidad* hold up to them?

What did you take away from *Belize Navidad*? Have you learned anything new or been exposed to different ideas about people or a certain part of the world?

Did your opinion of *Belize Navidad* change as you read it? How? If you could ask Bartell a question, what would you ask?

Would you recommend *Belize Navidad* to a friend?

www.ingramcontent.com/pod-product-compliance
Lightning Source LLC
Chambersburg PA
CBHW071234250626
47163CB00001B/179